Ar gyfer Jean, a gwrando ar ein stori. Gyda diolch.

For Jean, who listened to our story. With thanks.

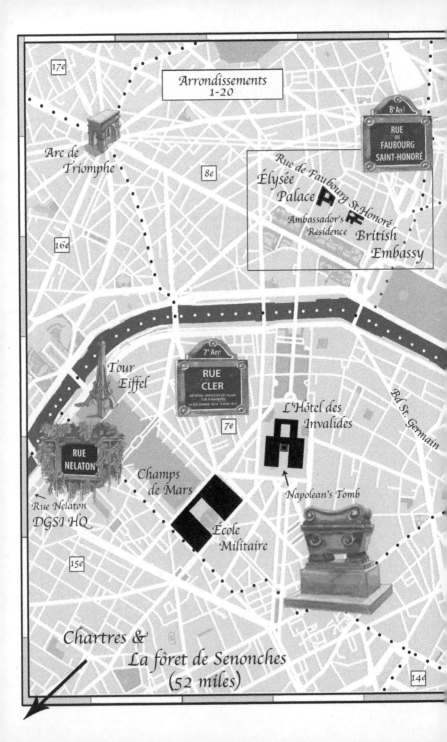

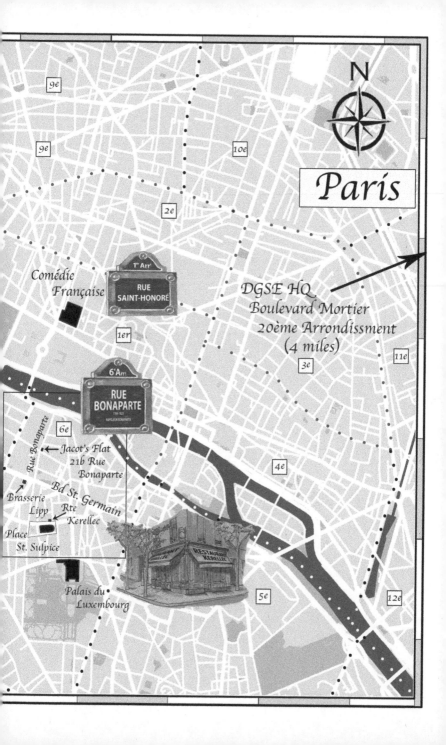

I

Colonel Daniel Jacot's flat,
Montagu Square, Marylebone, London W1

They had been dead for nearly thirty-five years, but he could still hear them. Sometimes, usually in the early hours, as Jacot drifted in and out of sleep, he would begin to hear men screaming – faint at first, then growing louder like a crowd of off-stage theatrical extras pretending to be a procession moving closer. Sometimes, he would wake up quickly. Sometimes not – when the mental video would play itself through – every detail in real time: the ship riding gently at anchor off East Falkland; the Argentine missile hitting them full on; the explosion; the screaming; the burning, third degree, full thickness burns to his hands and back, with less serious burns elsewhere on his body. During the worst episodes he would wake up – his hands hurting as they had thirty-five years before, and the room filled, by a cruel trick of the memory, with the smell of his own burning flesh.

He woke with a start. The flat was comfortably heated, but the inside of his duvet was damp, icy damp. Colonel Daniel Jacot got out of bed and made his way to the bathroom. He shaved without looking into the mirror. He didn't want to look at himself that morning. He emerged twenty minutes later – showered, scented with Trumper's Essence of West Indian Limes and immaculately encased in a dark-blue, Savile Row suit with a cream silk shirt and a maroon, knitted silk tie. As he was leaving the flat, he hesitated and walked into his sitting room past two packed suitcases – he was expecting to be despatched abroad at short notice by his boss, Lady Nevinson, the UK's National Security Adviser. France was the rumour. The good lady would confirm the details officially that morning. Picking up a bottle of Calvados – the black silk gloves he wore to hide his scarred hands slipped a little as he twisted the cap – he poured himself a large measure, added a little apple juice and drained the glass in one go. He added a further, smaller measure and drank it neat. After brushing his teeth again, he set off for Lady Nevinson's office in Downing Street.

II
Castelnaudary, South of France

Whoever was shooting at him was uncannily accurate, thank God. Three bullets in quick succession hit the same prominent rock less than ten feet above his head, accompanied by a burst of noise and a sprinkling of sharp, shrapnel-like pebbles that bounced off his combat jacket. Jacot hit the ground and crawled down the hill. *They must be using a sniper rifle with an infrared sight.* The inky darkness that seemed to coat every bush and stone in the valley was suddenly no protection at all. *But they wouldn't expect him to go down the hill placing himself closer to his pursuers – sideways would be the natural instinct.* Crawling and scrambling into better cover, he lay absolutely still, face down.

And then a fourth shot – its nearby sharp crack masking for just a second the barking and slavering of tracker dogs in the valley. Followed half a second later by a more distant thump.

Bullets travel faster than the speed of sound. As he had been taught in basic training, the *crack* is the sound a bullet makes as it passes close by. The catch-up *thump* is the noise made by the gun that fired the bullet. The time lapse between the crack and the thump enables a trained ear to gauge the range and direction of the shot.

Fired from half a mile or so back down the valley – nearly maximum range – he was still in with a chance. He half slithered, half rolled further downwards into a small fold in the hill.

The long burst of automatic fire, maybe fifty rounds, took him by surprise; same 7.62mm calibre, but this time a machine-gun – firing tracer. As they arced in the air uncomfortably close, every third or fourth bullet carrying an incendiary coating, they looked like a string of underpowered Christmas lights against the blanketing darkness of the valley. They all had the same trajectory – the machine gun was firing on a fixed line. No drooping of shot meant that a sandbag was propping up the barrel. Alarmingly, the bullets were chewing up the hillside where he had just been. He hoped they could see him.

Hell's teeth it was dark in this part of France. No ambient light at all. And the going was rough – olive trees and spiky bushes set amongst rocks. Not just ordinary rocks, but sharp rocks that cut the knees and twisted the ankles. He was tired. No sleep for the last thirty-six hours and only a single water bottle, though he had managed a refill from a sluggish, hillside stream. No food, except for some unripe olives straight from a tree, and a Mars Bar he had hidden in his webbing pouches.

The dogs were getting closer, yelping with excitement as they closed in on their prey. They had been within earshot for more than an hour. They sounded hungry.

He had to make sure his weapon would work. He was going to need it very soon. Stopping briefly for a glug of water, he quickly blew sand and dust off the working parts and wiped them with an oily rag. He checked the muzzle of his rifle. He had fallen over so many times in the last few hours that the knotted condom that kept the muzzle free of debris had torn, and it was clogged with sand and small leaves, *probably thyme from the smell.* Jacot cleared the obstruction and added a further squirt of oil to the working parts for good measure. *Keep calm. Maintain discipline. Think.*

His pursuers were closing fast, not far away now, moving easily and confidently through a terrain that was rapidly bringing him to a stand-still. *Maybe, following behind dogs meant that you never fell into a hole or grazed your leg, or tripped over a stone. Maybe, everyone in the group had night vision goggles. They certainly knew the valley better than he did.*

Only a matter of time now. They were close enough for him to hear the half-savage, half-soothing words of control and encouragement from the dog-handlers.

He decided he would go up the other side of the small re-entrant at an angle, get some height, find a decent spot to meet them, with good fields of fire. The gorse bushes were tearing at his thin, French military-issue trousers. *Great for a parade in the sun, they took an ironed crease well, but not so good in this rocky, unforgiving landscape.*

Too dark for the basic iron sights on his rifle to be of any use, the central part of the human eye doesn't work in complete darkness, he would have to fire by instinct.

A small dry-stone wall appeared in the corner of his eye. Although partly crumbling, it would provide some all-round defence. *What the hell, why not here?* With luck he could get a few shots away before the whole thing came to an end. The dogs were very close. Jacot clambered painfully over the wall. Making his FAMAS rifle ready, round in the chamber, he jammed himself into a decent firing position, placed two spare magazines of twenty-five on a rock close to his right hand,

and slipped the safety catch off.

It went quiet. All he could hear was the sound of a gentle night breeze and his own breathing – no dogs, no men, no shooting.

Jacot heard a dull click just a few feet away and a soft voice. One of the dogs was being unleashed. He fired in the general direction on automatic. He kept pressing the trigger. Twenty-two, twenty-three, twenty-four, change magazine. He heard something in the air: a dog leaping up on the wall, a large dog. Twisting away from his firing position and with one hand on the wall – he stood up to face the creature directly. It was big, about half the size of a grown man, and panting fast. He could just make out that it had long white fur. The green, wolf-like eyes were plain enough to see even in the blackness of the night.

'I think we have captured you, mon colonel.' It was the voice of Sergent-chef Paradis who removed his night vision goggles and turned on a powerful torch. Standing on the wall was a Pyrenean Mountain dog wagging its tail. Behind, stood Paradis with three tough looking Legionnaires in attendance and another dog of the same type, but still on a lead. Jacot recognised them: recruits who had recently passed out, but who were awaiting assignment to the 3rd Foreign Legion infantry regiment garrisoned in French Guyana. They were Paradis' temporary private army and went everywhere with him. They all looked pleased to see Jacot, including, thankfully, the dogs.

'Better give them a petit morceau, *treat*, I think you say in English,' said Paradis, handing Jacot two heavy-duty dog biscuits. The dog on the wall jumped down and sat obediently in front of Jacot who handed over a biscuit. The crunching sound as it was despatched made him feel a little queasy. The second dog was released by its handler and came to sit by the first. They were almost identical. It made short, crunching work of the second biscuit.

'Thirty-one hours it has taken us to track you down,' said Paradis. 'Pas mal. Not bad, for a man of your age, Colonel Jacot. Not bad at all. Your weapon please.'

Jacot made the weapon safe and gave it to Paradis who peered at it with his torch. 'Good. Good.' Paradis re-cocked the weapon, fired the remaining blank cartridges into the air and handed it over to one of the Legionnaires. As he approached Jacot to physically check his pouches – standard procedure where live and blank ammunition have been used on the same exercise – Jacot guiltily remembered the Mars Bar he had managed to conceal from the rigorous pre-exercise search. One of the points of escape and evasion training was to live entirely off the land. He removed the empty wrapper from his left pouch and dropped it discreetly on the ground. Paradis thrust his hands into the pouches. Jacot made the customary declaration that he had no live or blank rounds or empty cases in his possession.

Paradis then began to shout in incomprehensible Legion French. *Merde* was the only word Jacot recognised, frequently. It sounded bad-tempered, but the young Legionnaires were unperturbed. There was some toing and froing, more shouting from Paradis, and then a small, paper-covered package was shoved into Jacot's hand, followed by a French Army mug filled with what smelled like red wine. Jacot took a long gulp. It was rough stuff, the *Pinard* of lore and legend that had kept the French Army on its feet for more than two centuries. 'Pas de Pinard, pas de Poilu,' as he had often heard in the last couple of months. But it was good. They refilled his mug and pointed to the package, a slightly stale and flattened baguette filled with the pungent garlic sausage favoured by the rank and file. Paradis was shouting again, this time into the radio. The three Legionnaires grinned. The dogs were given more biscuits. Paradis unfolded a map and took a compass bearing.

One of the young Legionnaires came up close to Jacot, offering him a large tub of the thick antiseptic ointment favoured by the Legion for minor injuries of every type. Jacot gently peeled off the thick leather gloves he had been wearing to protect his hands. The gloves had protected them well – there were no cuts or abrasions from the harsh countryside, but they hurt, a deep aching in the bones. The ointment quickly soothed them. The Legionnaire drew a pair of black silk gloves from his pouches and handed them to Jacot with a mock gallant bow, causing huge merriment among his companions, especially Paradis.

'Ça va bien, mon colonel?'

'Well, yes, thank you, chef Paradis.'

Paradis grinned menacingly. 'You were not expecting live ammunition, I think?'

Jacot smiled. He had been surprised and at one point even a little nervous, but would not give Paradis the satisfaction. In any case, senior non-commissioned officers of the Foreign Legion knew what they were doing. Paradis' bronze-coloured sniper's badge, the highest of three grades of *tireur d'élite* in the French armed forces was always prominent on his uniform. The young Legionnaire with the ointment also sported the more junior, silver version. Jacot had never been in any danger.

'Huite kilometres, just about. Transport will meet us there. Allons,' barked Paradis.

They marched slowly at first over rough ground. Once they reached a good path Jacot expected the pace to quicken. But this was the Legion – they kept the pace slow, 88 paces per minute. Both dogs were clearly used to it, but Jacot struggled to keep in step. As a Guardsman, he usually marched at 116. Paradis put his compass and map away and they loped along. After a few minutes, Paradis began to sing softly. The tune was taken up, one by one, by the young Legionnaires: *Le Boudin*, the most famous of the Legion's marching songs:

Nous sommes des degourdis,
Nous sommes des lascars,
Des types pas ordinaires,
Nous avons souvent le cafard,
Nous sommes des Legionnaires.

Then the chorus, almost growled out:

Tiens, voila du boudin, voila du boudin, voila du boudin.

Boudin meant black pudding and was the nickname in the 19th Century Legion for the sleeping blanket rolled on top of the backpack – so Paradis had explained. It looked like a black pudding. A peculiar song to English ears, mournful and monotonous, it was strangely stirring, and good for marching at night. Jacot knew the words, but it was a song for Legionnaires only and sacred to them, so he merely hummed along.

Another Legion song followed, this time with a bawdy flavour. Paradis sang lustily in a light baritone – his newly-minted Legionnaire trio accompanying him with enthusiasm. Then, for a few minutes they marched in silence, enjoying the night. As the Legionnaires in front of him scuffed the sides of the rocky path, pushing past bushes and small trees, Jacot was surrounded by the smell of lemon and thyme, the smell of the Mediterranean, not far away. It made him a little wistful – Monica Zaden, his friend in the French security service, wore a scent with strong lemon and thyme topnotes. When Lady Nevinson had despatched him to France he had hoped to see more of her. *No such luck so far.* Once he took up his posting in Paris it should be fine, he re-assured himself.

After the period of silence Jacot sensed what was coming next. He had spent nearly two months being trained by Paradis, coming to know and relish the man's foibles; the peculiar habits and dry humour of non-commissioned officers were always good for morale. Paradis was a man of many parts, but appeared to have four passions: the Legion, women, alcohol, and the songs of Dean Martin. He hummed, whistled and strummed his fingers all day to a Dean Martin soundtrack in his head. He just couldn't help himself. In the darkness he began to sing *Volare*, solo, with gusto.

Paradis was pitch perfect and clearly proud of his beautiful voice. As he finished the first verse, the three Legionnaires repeated it. They weren't bad singers, but what Jacot found extraordinary was that Paradis had drilled and practised them to sound exactly like Dean Martin himself. While Paradis enunciated the words clearly, the backing Legionnaires mimicked Dean's slurred, slightly drunken style. It was enchanting.

After nearly an hour, they made the rendezvous with the lorry and its driver, who hurriedly extinguished a cigarette as they approached. Paradis opened the cab door for Jacot, but he shook his head and clambered into the back with the troops. The lorry hurtled along the rough country roads, all three young Legionnaires busy smoking and exchanging erotic details of the girls they hoped to meet on pre-embarkation leave.

The *Quartier Capitaine Danjou* in Castelnaudary wasn't far away. Named after the Legion's greatest hero and home to the 4th Regiment of the French Foreign Legion – responsible for training all new recruits and providing professional courses to Legionnaires and non-commissioned officers as they progressed up the ranks.

'You need bed, mon colonel. It's nearly midnight now, but we have asked for food to be put in your room. No PT tomorrow you will be pleased to hear. But, please, I will debrief you at 10 sharp in my room in the training block.'

'Goodnight, chef Paradis, and thank you for organising an unusual and challenging exercise,' said Jacot with a straight face.

'I think you left this behind, mon colonel,' said Paradis, saluting smartly and pressing something into Jacot's hand. He then swung himself back into the cab of the lorry. As it pulled away the young Legionnaires waved.

Jacot waved back and then looked at what Paradis had put in his hand. It looked like a small black envelope. He laughed – it was the wrapper from his contraband Mars Bar, flattened out and then neatly folded.

He was tired and weary, completely *cream-crackered* in British Army slang, thought Jacot, as he climbed the stairs to his room slowly and a little stiffly. The troops had pretty much had to lower him over the side of the lorry. The baguette and the *Pinard* at the end of the exercise had kept hunger at bay for an hour or so, but he was ravenous now. He wondered what Paradis meant by food.

Even when they had shared a few drinks together, and Paradis had ranged far and wide in conversation, he never referred to his background. In the Legion most sous-officiers were not French. From the accent and the occasional remark, Jacot came to the conclusion that he was originally from somewhere in the West Indies, but not the English or French speaking islands. Possibly, he was of Dutch extraction.

Paradis had impressed Jacot with his high military standards and his drive to impose them on everybody around him, including himself. The standards applied, luckily, to food. On a plain, zinc cookhouse tray had been laid out a lobster salad, a small baguette, cheese, fruit and a half bottle of the dry, but peppery Corsican white wine currently favoured by Paradis. It had an Italian name, *Patrimonio*, and Jacot assumed Paradis had acquired a taste for it while serving with 2ème REP, the parachute regiment of the Legion, headquartered at Calvi on Corsica.

Jacot ate hungrily, took a quick shower and then fell into a deep sleep on the plain soldier's bed.

She came out of the door of a white, stuccoed house and walked towards Kensington High Street. It was a nice neighbourhood. The American word *toney* – always a favourite of his, summed up the area well. Even from fifty metres away he could see she was an attractive woman in her late forties, maybe a bit older, well-turned out in a green cotton dress, cardigan of more or less the same shade, and black, calf-length boots. She was carrying a black, patent leather Gucci handbag, and talking as she walked into a white iPhone. Animated and laughing, she shook and re-arranged her long auburn hair after a gust of wind hit her just before she crossed to the south side of the street. She walked towards the Waterstone's bookshop on Kensington High Street. He followed at a distance. At the door she stopped and looked around briefly before going inside.

Amanda Brookwood experienced the sense of well-being and pleasure she always found in bookshops and put out of her mind the strange feeling she had had a couple of times in the previous twenty-four hours that someone was watching her. 'Amanda, sweetheart, it's just middle-aged paranoia while your husband and children are away,' was how her closest girlfriend had described her worries during a telephone call. With a number of long plane journeys ahead, she decided to treat herself to a new biography, preferably of a major historical figure – she wasn't at all interested in modern celebrities. A couple of thrillers would also be fun – just the ticket for the Business Class Lounge at Heathrow and a long flight, accompanied by a couple of soothing glasses of champagne. She preferred more traditional thrillers and detective novels; much of the modern stuff was too dark for her taste. She liked plenty of excitement, enjoying shoot-outs, car chases, clever poisonings and even street fisticuffs. She liked other things too in her thrillers: handsome heroes, at ease with the world of action and decision – not necessarily matinée-idol good looks, but nice to look at all the same; and confident.

But ultimately for her there had to be a puzzle to solve. 'Who did it?' was central to the fun. Occasionally, she spotted the villain, villains, or even guilty organisation, early on. But what she really liked was being taken by surprise at the end of a book and then looking back over the pages to see where the clues had been cleverly hidden.

In the end, she read them for re-assurance, even though most thrillers and detective novels involved murder most foul. In works by her favourite authors, the good guys always won – order was restored. She stuck rigidly to them these days as a result of an experience the year before. On a long trip to Africa, she had taken with her three of the most up to date, cutting edge detective novels, and nothing else. Up till then she had felt it important to read the latest stuff. The first of her choices began with the severed arms of a dozen teenage girls found buried in a remote forest. She should have checked before buying it; too macabre and depressing to provide any enjoyment. Turning to the next one, she discovered it was set in a bleak, inner-city council estate, beset with casual violence and Islamist extremism. Quite how the author could arrange an ordinary, decent, rational murder against such a background she couldn't imagine. Finally, almost in despair and stuck in the British Embassy of some West African hellhole, she started the third volume, only to discover it involved a deranged, homicidal stalker pursuing young women in a distinctly unattractive American city.

Peering into the front window of Waterstone's, he could see her towards the back of the shop, browsing. He liked looking at women, gauging the heaviness of their breasts, the smoothness of their thighs, imagining what it would be like to have sex with them. But he mustn't daydream – this was professional, not pleasure.

He didn't need much, just to be able to gauge her height and weight, and what she was like on her feet – light or heavy, or springy. The black leather boots suited her, and she moved gracefully between bookshelves with a light step. About sixty kilos, he calculated, and 1.7 metres in height.

Her hair was going to be important. It was always much more difficult if they had a bun at the back. In this case, *no bun, no problem*. He squinted through the plate glass window. He had seen enough.

Like a hangman peeping through a cell door the night before an execution, he had carefully worked out the drop and the forces required to break her neck.

Jacot spotted the *Restaurant Salammbô* further down the street – the bright red awning was hard to miss. But he walked straight past it, feeling a little silly as he did so, even though that was where he was heading for lunch. Intense counter-surveillance training was all very well, certainly adding a new layer of awareness to his life, but it also brought with it a streak of paranoia.

Anyone looking at him would see a smartly dressed, middle-aged man walking slowly down a hot, sunny street in southern France, without a care in the world, looking languidly in the windows of the smart shops in this part of Aix. Actually, in surveillance terms Jacot had just conducted a *walk-past*. 'Take in the whole street, not just ground level. Look up discreetly, mon colonel,' was how Sergent-chef Paradis had put it in his heavily accented-English. 'Check everything, but only once.'

Jacot had got to the end of the street. 'Don't go back on yourself, mon colonel. Non, non, non, non,' said Paradis after Jacot's first surveillance exercise. Four 'nons' was severe for the Sergent-chef. There was only one further level of disapproval on the Paradis scale – the curious and idiosyncratic 'maximum mistake'. Jacot had taken the point. It is rare for people in real life to perform a U-turn on foot. He would take a round-about route back to the top of the street, and, if the coast looked clear, enter the restaurant.

It was Aix's smartest establishment, serving a hybrid cuisine: partly derived from the sheep-based farming of the nearby Luberon, with its earthy and spiced flavours, but near enough to the Mediterranean to be laced with tomatoes and olives.

Jacot went in. It was cool inside, but still bright because of mirrored walls – pleasingly with not a smear or speck of dust on them. He quickly logged the other diners and made a mental note of where the door to the Gents was, and a fire escape door to the side.

'You need to know the exits. You may need them. Your target or your attacker may use them. Toujours the exits,' as Paradis put it. After eight weeks in his constant company, Jacot was beginning to think half in

English and half in French.

A grey-haired man in a pale beige jacket, sitting at a corner table, raised his hand. Lady Nevinson had said that her messenger was ex-military. A Highland regiment, thought Jacot. Something about the freckled skin and the blue eyes suggested Scotland. As he got closer Jacot recognised him. The Army was less than half the size it had been when he joined. Everybody knew everybody these days.

'Gregory Norton.' He stood to introduce himself. He didn't put out his hand, instead tapping Jacot gently on the shoulder and waving him into a chair. They sat down. 'I am sure we met in Sarajevo. We crossed over in the same Headquarters for a bit. The mysterious Guardsman in the gloves in the intelligence cell.'

Jacot laughed. 'Frightful place, mostly underground because of the shelling. I remember you well. On the rare occasions the bombardment went quiet you dashed into the open air to play your bagpipes.'

'That's me – I was banned from playing them inside by the general.' A waiter arrived and poured rosé from a vase-shaped bottle with curious indentations, into two pleasingly large glasses filled with ice cubes. 'It's from the Var, hence the odd shape of the bottle. About forty miles from here, I should think,' said Norton. 'It's good stuff. The locals drink it with ice. Curious habit. Having fun with our Foreign Legion friends?'

After eight dry weeks, except for a couple of expeditions to Legion bars with the ever-thirsty Sergent-chef Paradis, Jacot took a large sip of rosé and laughed. 'Well, it's been interesting, and I've made some new friends, mainly rather fierce non-commissioned officers. It was nice to live again for two months with good order and military discipline. I am grateful to Lady Nevinson for organising it.'

'I bring a message and a parcel from the good lady which she said also contains your orders. The message first.' Norton geared himself up to deliver it from memory. '"I am enjoying looking after your collection of Japanese poetry." Very cryptic. Very cloak and dagger. The good lady said I had to say it exactly as she gave it to me. Some sort of code?' Norton smiled.

Jacot looked surprised.

'Anything wrong, old boy?'

'Shall we say Lady Nevinson has been going through my confidential personal files? I keep a record of some of her more outrageous private pronouncements on a certain top politician. They have the succinctness and clarity of those short Japanese poems.'

'*Haiku?*'

'Absolutely. I labelled the file with something misleading, and stuck a

TOP SECRET UK EYES ONLY on the outside. But the inside label says *Lady Nevinson's Haiku*. Each one has a kind of footnote, a date and some background. Something amusing and insubordinate to do in my lunch hour.' They both laughed. 'I noticed your tie,' said Jacot. 'Greyhounds?'

'Very observant. Since leaving the Argylls I have been a Queen's Messenger.'

'Of course, and the greyhound represents speed.'

'In a way. The full story is more interesting. Charles II, in exile after his father's execution, was about to despatch four loyal apparatchiks back to Blighty with messages for his supporters. Keeping the Royalist flag flying when things were looking grim. They suddenly realised that they had no proof of identity, and it was too dodgy to carry letters of introduction. Cromwell's secret police ran a pretty tight ship. So the king broke off four small silver greyhounds that adorned his favourite silver wine cooler, and gave one to each messenger as a token of identity. We wear them now on a tie, and in full rig we still have a silver greyhound dangling beneath the royal arms on a blue-red-blue ribbon. Looks great in a kilt. Not on the sporran you understand, but on the mess jacket.'

Jacot laughed. 'So, you are now Lady Nevinson's messengers as well.'

Norton smiled. 'You know her concerns about security.' They reminisced about military life as soldiers do. Norton had served for five years in the Balkans, in various capacities, and was full of alarming tales of the Balkan underworld and how its tentacles reached into the heart of Western European life. 'Arkan wasn't the worst of them, by any means; probably, the most flamboyant – with his pet tigers and tarty girlfriends, but not the worst. Some of them are still around.' At one point, Norton grew melancholy. 'I have to say I enjoyed every minute of it. Not so much fun for my wife and children though, and just as soon as she had finally got me out of the army,' his eyes clouded, 'she was laid low…'

Jacot's natural sympathy was quickly displaced by a powerful urge to see Monica Zaden that came out of nowhere. For a moment, he thought he might share his worries about her with Norton. Perhaps another time. He gripped the table with his hands to bring himself under control, and drank a glass of rosé.

Norton recovered quickly, also draining a glass of rosé, and went on to talk about his four children: his hopes for them and his plans for the future. Despite the death of his wife, Jacot could tell that Norton had built for himself a life that he found passable. Being a Queen's Messenger gave him both a purpose and status, and it kept him on the road, without too much time to dwell on the past. When back in the UK he had plenty of children to visit.

At the end of lunch they both had something stronger for the road. Norton muttered darkly as Scotsmen do about the selection of Scotch whisky in foreign countries, settling, in the end, for a peaty *Laphroaig*.

Jacot asked for his habitual Calvados. As he gave the waiter his order, Norton's face registered a mix of mock disbelief and disappointment. 'For God's sake man, change to whisky. I'll send you a bottle of the regimental brew to lure you over.'

Jacot felt he got on well with Norton – there was something solid and trustworthy about him. In any case, Highlanders and Guardsmen were very much alike under the skin. Norton had drawn back from discussing his wife and Jacot had suppressed his desire to talk about Zaden. Perhaps when they knew each other a little better…

Norton was spending a few days in France on leave, 'Vineyards, cathedrals, restaurants, that sort of thing.' They agreed to meet in Paris ten days later – 'Chew the fat, put the world to rights, have a few beers. You must tell me about your experiences in the Falklands. Yes, we were all sorry to miss that one. You didn't say anything in Sarajevo and, of course, none of us mentioned it. I can tell you a few more yarns about my time in Belgrade in exchange.'

At the end, Norton handed over a small parcel sealed with wax. Jacot signed a receipt, bid farewell to his new friend with whom he had shared a good deal of excellent rosé, and left. He slipped the envelope into his pocket. He would open it later. He knew what was inside – a formal letter of appointment to the staff of the British Embassy in Paris, and perhaps some bon mots from Lady Nevinson.

It was mid-afternoon and the taxi back to Aubagne would take forty minutes. He was meant to be back in camp by six. Just time for a quick wander around the local museum reputed to be choc full of Cézannes – it was after all pretty much his hometown.

V

French Foreign Legion Headquarters, Quartier Viénot, Aubagne

His eight-week training period was nearly at an end. The emphasis had been split between the military skills of fitness, weapon handling and unarmed combat; and intelligence related skills such as observation, awareness and counter-surveillance. Sergent-chef Paradis had supervised everything, although much of the time was spent with the Legion's formidable fitness instructors. It was all highly reminiscent of the Brigade Squad – the eight weeks being beasted in the ranks that the Guards regiments in the old days had required for potential officers before going to Sandhurst.

The last few days of his training were to be spent at the headquarters of the Foreign Legion in Aubagne, a small and undistinguished town near Marseilles, where the Legion had established itself after leaving its ancestral hometown of Sidi Bel Abbès on Algerian independence.

Thankfully, the art and science of fitness had moved on. The idea was no longer to make you suffer, but to make you better. By the end of each day he was exhausted, but he felt much stronger. Even his burned hands ached less. Nevertheless, it had been hard going, especially not drinking very much for so long – his efforts to reduce his alcohol intake in Lent always having ended in disappointment.

Other than a weekend dinner party with the Commandant of the regiment at Aubagne, Jacot hardly ever set eyes on an officer.

Once his basic fitness and strength had been improved, the instructors moved him on to fighting techniques, how to handle himself in a fist or knife fight. The Legion seemed to have plenty of experience of both. As he was being put through his paces in the gym Paradis would sometimes appear briefly to watch – like a football manager or a racehorse trainer.

Paradis had always promised a final test of some sort at the end of his training. It seemed natural that the end of such an intense eight weeks should be marked by a challenging ritual.

Instructed to turn up at the gym in tee shirt, boots, lightweight trousers and leather gloves, Jacot had hoped it might be something like climbing ropes against the clock, or doing as many press-ups as he could. The Legion was obsessed with press-ups. Although Jacot had been excused most of the traditional humiliations of military training handed out to the *hommes du rang*, the lower ranks, Paradis had forced him to do punishment press-ups on a number of occasions after some especially egregious weapon handling mistakes. 'Maximum mistake,' he would bark. Followed by, 'En position' – the traditional two word overture to a session of rapid press-ups. At least, if it was in the gym, it couldn't be a parachute jump, the possibility of which he had been dreading.

Entering the building, he could see Paradis standing in the boxing ring with the chief fitness instructor of the 4th regiment – a tough-looking individual with a shaven head, *boule a zéro* in Legion slang – whose main interest and pleasure in life seemed to be shouting at recruits. Both men were in the same order of dress as Jacot, minus the gloves.

'Bonjour, mon colonel. I trust you have recovered from the exertions of the last few days,' said Paradis, grinning. The chief fitness instructor didn't smile, but that wasn't unusual.

Jacot wondered how his burned hands were going to perform in a boxing match, but decided to put a brave face on it. 'Bonjour, chef Paradis. A little boxing match is just what I was looking forward to.'

'Non, non. Not with your hands,' replied Paradis. 'Something with a genuine flavour of the Legion, and something that will stand you in good stead – a knife fight. I have instructed you in these techniques and will act as umpire. Your opponent will be my colleague.' He pointed to the chief fitness instructor who this time allowed himself just a flicker of a smile.

Jacot smiled back with feigned enthusiasm. *Fair enough*: knife fighting was central to the Legion's self defence techniques, and his instructors had put a lot of effort into his training.

Paradis took the cloth off a small tray revealing two Legion bayonets, the blades covered in masking tape – just a single thickness, Jacot noticed.

Paradis took him outside for a brief warm-up, followed by a quick massage of his hands, and a generous application of the Legion's all-purpose cream. 'I have taught you the knife personally, mon colonel. OK? And I am the best in the Legion. C'est *mon numéro*, party trick, I think you say. Listen, my colleague is a good fighter, but he has one weakness. Understand this please – his eyes always move a millisecond before he strikes to the point of attack. The eyes. Toujours the eyes, mon colonel. He will move fast but it should be just enough – you are faster than you were two months ago. And don't worry, I will make sure you don't get hurt.'

They went back inside. Jacot noticed that a number of other sous-officiers were in attendance to watch the event including, ominously, the NCO in charge of the medical centre with his bag of bandages and ointments.

Paradis called them both into the ring, gave each of them a bayonet, and explained the rules of the engagement. Jacot and his opponent shook hands. Jacot had a plan – go for his opponent as aggressively and as quickly as he could. Put him off his guard, and then defend, staying away from the ropes to the ring. He didn't want to get cornered.

Paradis stood out of the way and said in English, mimicking Jacot's voice, 'Gentlemen, you may attack.'

Jacot lunged, a wide, sweeping, backhand slash, but from a position too far from his opponent for it to be effective. It certainly surprised the chief fitness instructor who circled him warily waiting to strike, beads of sweat appearing on his shaven head. Jacot watched the eyes, 'toujours the eyes.' They seemed impassive, blank like a poker player's, but the weakness identified by Paradis was there. Just a fraction of a second before he struck, the eyes would signal what was to come. He lunged; Jacot sidestepped. He attacked from above in a stabbing movement; Jacot twisted his body out of the way at the last minute. The fitness instructor wasn't as good with a knife as Paradis, for sure, but he was significantly better, faster and younger than Jacot. Jacot was still on his feet, but it wasn't going well. The sous-officiers watched in silence.

Jacot felt he should attack again, lifting his right arm aiming at his opponent's neck that looked undefended. He slightly changed the grip on his blade, preparing to strike.

For a brief second, he looked at his opponent's neck rather than his eyes, stupidly – and in that moment the chief fitness instructor attacked with great energy. Jacot diverted his right arm from its own lunge, just managing to parry a blow aimed at his chest. But he lost his balance, and before he knew it he was on the ground with his opponent's bayonet at his throat – he could smell the polished steel through the masking tape.

Paradis shook his head but said nothing. The sous-officiers left the scene looking disgruntled and disappointed. Jacot felt a little embarrassed; perhaps they had expected more of a display from the 'colonel de la garde royale Celtique' – who, for reasons few of them could fathom, was being trained at the heart of the Legion establishment.

He had that unpleasant feeling of somehow having let the side down. After picking up his stuff from the changing rooms, Jacot left the gym. It was a beautifully sunny day – hot, southern French sun. As he crossed the vast parade ground, with its great monument to the Legion's dead brought with them from their old depot in Algeria, he could see why the

Legion had settled on this spot. It reminded them of their lost spiritual home in North Africa.

At the corner of the parade ground he spotted Paradis in huddled, furtive conversation with the five sous-officers who had provided the ringside audience for the fight. They were a few yards away and hadn't seen him. There was lots of Gallic shrugging and what looked like shaking hands. On closer inspection, Jacot realised it was money changing hands. *Trust Paradis to run a book on the fight* – he crossed his fingers that he wasn't paying out.

Paradis was chuckling and counting a wad of Euro notes in his wallet as he came towards Jacot. 'You were looking at his neck as you attacked. Maximum mistake! But I will buy you the biggest glass of Kronenbourg I can find – beer of the Legion. They said the Celtic colonel would last maximum 90 seconds. You made 92!'

After pouring a glass of wine, Amanda Brookwood checked her packing, making sure that the two diplomatic passports and the official credit card provided by the foreign office were securely in her handbag. It was time to set the house alarm and watch a little television before going to sleep. The house was warm but well ventilated. As she was on her own, it was best not to leave an open window anywhere.

She slept heavily for a few hours, waking just after four in the morning. The car would come for her at six, *time for another hour in bed.* It was dark, but a faint glow from the west London street lights crept in from behind the bedroom curtains, ruffling gently in the night breeze.

How odd. She thought she had closed all the windows. Switching on the bedside light and grabbing her dressing gown, she stepped onto the first floor landing. Leaning forward, she peered down the staircase – the alarm seemed to be off. *Oh, dear!* She must be really losing it.

The gloved hand pushed her powerfully in the small of the back, slipping slightly on the silk of the dressing gown. As the top part of her body tumbled forward – with a slow, almost balletic sweep, he kicked her legs from under her. She somersaulted into the air, head down and soundless, the air trapped in her throat by horror and surprise.

If he had got it right, and her head hit the stairs at the correct angle and speed, he should be able to hear the snap. If not, he could finish her off quickly and simply enough at close quarters, without leaving a trace. But it sounded good – the snap of her vertebrae breaking was there. It was the same noise as breaking a wishbone – just a little less of a crack. He walked down the stairs. She lay with her neck at an odd angle. *Always a good sign.* Her eyes were open. *Best to check.* Picking up her left wrist he searched for a pulse. He liked to be sure.

Slipping quietly out of the front door, he closed it very gently almost with tenderness – like a father leaving for work early and trying not to wake his sleeping wife and children. Without looking round, he set off at normal walking pace to the end of the street. He would walk all the way to St Pancras. A taxi or bus would be too dangerous, with just an outside chance that the police might interrogate as many late night drivers as they could find.

He was a small man with a light, almost feminine walking style, and encased in a thick overcoat. From behind a casual passer-by could easily mistake him for a woman.

He walked quickly and confidently, without hurrying, as if on a routine walk to an office that opened very early. He felt good. He enjoyed killing, not sexually, even when extinguishing an attractive female target as he had just done. But he got a kick out of what he felt was his perfect professionalism. And the feeling of power, ultimate power, that invariably caused an intense thrill and rush in the hours after a successful assignment. Although it was four twenty in the morning, he felt no need at all for coffee or nicotine.

In a street to the north of Kensington Gardens he stopped at a red pillar-box, appearing to check the times for postage. This time he did look round. The street was empty. He leaned past the pillar-box and pulled a padded envelope he had concealed there the day before from behind some iron railings. It contained his passport, one of his numerous passports, extra cash, a ticket on the Eurostar train leaving for Paris at 05.40, and a disposable mobile phone.

He never liked using mobile phones. The rigours of his professional life meant that he preferred to receive his instructions in writing, left quietly for him in some discreet spot, a safe deposit box or a dead letter drop. But they said the target was on the move.

Usually, after completing a task, he enjoyed sightseeing, drinking in the culture and civilisation of the city, and it was normally a city, before returning home. But he had a second, urgent task to perform. Sure enough, as he switched the mobile on a text message appeared:

Proceed Gare Montparnasse. Most urgent. Target info to follow.

Jacot got down from the train after it came to halt in the Gare de Lyon. He had little baggage, just washing and shaving kit, a couple of books, and, nestling on the top of his small back-pack, a white Legionnaire's képi placed on his head by the Commandant at Aubagne when they had said their goodbyes. Jacot was genuinely touched. It was quite something to survive eight weeks of training at the tender hands of the Legion.

Paradis' parting gift had been more practical – a half bottle of Calvados. Paradis grinned hugely on handing it over. The cap was professionally sealed, but the bottle did not appear to have a label. Probably a brand only available to the Foreign Legion Sergeants' Mess. Jacot shuddered – it was probably lethal. *Might come in handy on a very cold night.*

According to the instructions received from Lady Nevinson, he was to be picked up at the station by someone from the Direction générale de la sécurité intérieure, DGSI, – the new name given to France's Security Service by President Hollande in 2014; and taken to an apartment that had been rented for him. He would have the weekend to rest and sort himself out, reporting to the Embassy first thing Monday morning to be briefed about his new job. It was Friday afternoon.

Coming out of the station, he immediately spotted the DGSI man waiting in a dark blue Peugeot, engine running. What Paradis had said a couple of months before was true – once you have undergone intensive counter-surveillance training the world never looks the same again. The man spotted Jacot too. Guards officers were easy enough to pick out and Jacot was wearing the suit in which he had arrived at Aubagne, with a blue-red-blue Brigade tie knotted around his neck – the collar and suit were very much looser come to think of it.

The DGSI man did not say much, but drove at breakneck speed in a westerly direction. Jacot was intrigued where he was going to stay in Paris – at least it did not appear he was being exiled to the dingy eastern suburbs. As Notre Dame appeared on the left he thought for a moment he might be lucky enough to be allocated something on the swish Île de la Cité…, but no: DGSI man was still hammering along as the Pont Neuf disappeared behind them. And then half way along the great bulk of the Louvre, the car swung left across the Pont du Carrousel and onto to the Left Bank. A bit more kamikaze driving, and they pulled up in the rue Bonaparte, reversing accurately into a tiny parking space.

They got out, and the young man led him to a dark blue door beside a traditional looking patisserie. He unlocked the door and they climbed to the second floor. Jacot wasn't even breathing hard when they entered the flat.

'Here you are Monsieur Jacot,' said the DGSI man in the tiny hallway. 'This is your apartment. Here are the keys. I wish you a pleasant stay, as they say. Perhaps I will see you at the Rue Nélaton.' He was about to stick out his hand when he noticed Jacot's black silk gloves and reddened slightly. Gilles Navarre, DGSI's director and a very old friend of Lady Nevinson's, had probably warned him. He nodded and left, closing the door behind him.

Jacot turned from the hall and went into the main body of the flat, a small sitting room with two half-height windows overlooking the street. It was plainly furnished in the modern style, the colour scheme yellow and white. He turned on the lights and was astonished. Above the fireplace was CRW Nevinson's portrait of a staff officer in a Great War dugout – just as he had it at home in London. *A melancholy fellow whose mood never improved.* Some of his books had also been sent over. P.G. Wodehouse, and his shelves on the history of the French Army. He wondered who had put it all together, possibly Lady Nevinson herself.

Checking the cupboards in the only bedroom, he found most of the stuff he would need: suits, socks, shirts and his collection of gloves for concealing and soothing his disfigured hands. For the past thirty-five years he had usually worn plain, black, silk gloves when not in uniform, and brown leather when in khaki. But after their recent adventures together, Monica Zaden had suggested a modification: black silk still, but faced on the palm side with strips of chamois leather to allow a better grip. She had sent a couple of pairs to Aubagne for him with a short note wishing him well. He had sent a long and light hearted thank you letter back straight away, hoping to establish a regular correspondence… to no avail. Paradis had further refined the design – on each right hand glove the trigger finger was all chamois, courtesy of the Foreign Legion's tailors.

Another cupboard contained his uniforms: the khaki service dress, unchanged in design since the First World War, gleaming Sam Browne belt, plus various other accoutrements – all hanging neatly and in the correct groupings. He would wear this uniform on Monday morning for his first day at the embassy. Best to get off on the right foot.

Also his formal mess dress, a short scarlet jacket, blue waistcoat and tight trousers or 'overalls' as they were more properly called, worn with jackboots and spurs. Like many Guards Officers Jacot found wearing uniform in the evening rather tedious, and so usually wore a more or less formal concoction of his own, a cream silk shirt with black bow tie, dark green velvet smoking jacket, faced in even darker green silk, loose dark blue uniform trousers with a thick red stripe down the side, and patent leather shoes.

NSAREP was the title of his job, National Security Adviser's Representative – the official in the embassy responsible for sharing with the French intelligence services, both civilian and military, the various written products of the Joint Intelligence Committee. And, perhaps more importantly, given the new intelligence entente cordiale, liaison with the French president's intelligence officials at the Elysée Palace. In effect, he was going to be Lady Nevinson's man in Paris.

Scouting round the rest of the small flat he was touched and grateful. Someone had made a huge effort to make sure that he was comfortable. Everything was in good order, almost new. Plenty of wine in a rack in the kitchen with a couple of bottles of white Burgundy cooling in the fridge: *St Romain*, a not particularly well-known or expensive appellation which had gallantly refused to go along with the oaky style of its more illustrious neighbours. Alongside the bottles were various patés and salads that would keep him going over the weekend. While holed up with the DGSI in their UK safe house some months before, it had become clear to him that French spies enjoyed their comforts; they had made sure Jacot would feel at home in Paris.

He would order some more wine, the best he could afford, in case of a special guest or an emergency. He was strongly hoping to entertain Monica Zaden soon – so better get hold of some good champagne: *Roederer Cristal* was his favourite for special occasions. And he would need some whisky for Norton – that peaty stuff he was drinking in Aix. They were due to meet a week on Monday. He felt slightly lonely in Paris and was looking forward to it.

Going into the bathroom to lay out his washing and shaving kit, he was delighted to see above the hand basin a large spray bottle of Trumpers Extract of Limes, and there were two spares in the cupboard as well. When sprayed on after shaving it gave a bracing, stinging effect to the skin. Afterwards, all that was left was a faint smell of limes, but it lasted through the day, and the limes smelt freshly squeezed. Jacot thought the spray bottle a little unmilitary, but he couldn't splash after-shave on with his hands in the usual way as the liquid stung the scar tissue painfully – so spray bottles it had to be. Nevinson could not have known it was his favourite – unless she recognised the smell, but that was unlikely. With any luck, it was Zaden who had organised the flat. He hoped it was Zaden. *Yes, it must have been Zaden*, but the sinking feeling in his stomach that he had missed his opportunity with her wouldn't go away.

Before he got too comfortable with his congenial new quarters, he felt he should check the security of the place. The inner front door was solid, to say the least. Giving it a closer look, Jacot realised it was thick reinforced steel, painted in wood effect, and with some fake beading that made it look at first sight like a real wooden door. It was probably bullet proof. The locks were impressive – double bolts that entered grooves on all four sides of the door when the key was turned. The flat was certainly secure from intruders, unless he forgot to lock the door. But escape would be difficult in a crisis. At a pinch, he could scramble out of the kitchen window, but it was a twenty-foot drop to the terrace below – probably doable in an emergency. After all, a rooftop escape across Cambridge had been no problem a couple of months before; and that was without the benefit of eight weeks under Sergent-chef Paradis.

Perhaps he should have a large glass of the white Burgundy from the fridge, and then listen to some music. Annoyingly, early afternoon was both too late and too early to have a drink. Waiting until seven o'clock, however, was going to be a bore.

Better to occupy his mind with a plan for his new job. He wondered who in the British Embassy in Paris would be on side and who wouldn't. The ambassador probably would be OK – he had one further job in him and was known to be angling for Washington. He would be keen to butter up Lady N. The intelligence people and the military he would have to gauge on a case-by-case basis. A round of familiarisation meetings that would last much of the week would kick off on Monday morning. H Paris, the Head of the Intelligence Station, was away but Jacot would make an appointment to see him on his return. Lady N was not an admirer of their organisation. 'Often impressive people – easily impressed by the quality of the intelligence they gather,' was her harsh formula. But she had her allies and admirers in the system. *It would be interesting...*

Whether Nevinson had posted him there to keep him out of trouble, especially after his brush with the CIA, or whether she wanted him to have a more active role wasn't clear. No doubt she would make contact at some point, in her own time.

Remembering his gun was still in the small backpack, he took it out and placed it in the drawer of the bedside table with four spare and charged magazines. With any luck it would stay there for months.

Gregory Norton lay down on the bed, tired after his four-mile run around the outskirts of Chartres, but pleased, reckoning he was in good shape for a sixty-three year old. The hotel room was lovely – tall windows with a grand view of the north side of the cathedral, and decorated in a French country house style: handsome, Louis Quinze, gilt mirrors sprinkled about the place, and the wall opposite his bed dominated by a faded old master painting with a religious theme, hanging serenely over the mini-bar. *The Supper at Emmaus* by the look of it.

Definitely one of the oddest and most unsettling stories in the Bible – the Gospel according to Luke, if his memory served correctly. Most of the big artistic names had given it a go but most had failed. Only the slightly mad Caravaggio, in his view, got anywhere close. Yes, he and Catriona had gone quite cultural after the children had left home: galleries, concerts, cathedrals, opera. They had visited the National Gallery several times together. Caravaggio's masterpiece had become a favourite. She knew a good deal about paintings and was able to explain the clever techniques behind them clearly – how exactly Caravaggio persuaded or tricked the viewer into believing that he was actually sitting at the supper table as well. *Funny painting* – he had never worked up the courage to tell Catriona that to him Jesus looked as though he had just thrown some dice rather than broken bread.

But the most extraordinary thing about the Caravaggio version was the look of astonishment on the faces of the Apostles – as they realised the man they had invited to supper was in fact the Resurrected Jesus. Their expression had remained impressed on his memory. *Gobsmacked!* would make a good secular title for the painting. None of the extraordinary drama had been captured in the French provincial version on the wall that depicted a very jolly looking Jesus, with a halo like a golden frisbee, presiding over a lavish supper in the company of two silk clad gentlemen, who looked half-cut rather than moved or astounded. But it was attractive enough, and Catriona would have been amused.

It was his first visit to the town – he had been charmed by its medieval alleys; and moved by its stunning cathedral, comforted a little too, particularly by the cool blue interior. It hadn't been a good day – there were no good days since Catriona had died, but it had been an OK day; although even OK days tended to sour towards the end. For nearly forty years of marriage, an essential part of any positive or joyful reaction to anything had been his desire to share it as quickly as possible with his wife.

He was tempted to stay in Chartres for three nights – really get to grips with the place. Do a proper, detailed reconnaissance of the cathedral and go for another run along one of the straight and level roads leading out of the town, into the beautiful countryside of the Beauce, to get an impression of what it must have been like for a pilgrim to approach the place on foot.

He checked the Rolex on his wrist, and realised that dinner, always good for morale, was at least a couple of hours away. Still, he might slip in a quick half bottle of something before having a bath. The Loire being the closest wine-growing region to Chartres, and famous for its white wines, he hoped there might be something cool and refreshing inside the mini-bar. Feeling curiously embarrassed about wanting a drink so early, he was relieved to be just out of Jesus' eye line as he bent down to open the door of the little fridge. Amongst the jumble of peanuts, miniatures of gin, vodka, whisky and outrageously overpriced champagne, there was an ice-cold bottle of something called *Montlouis*.

Pouring the wine into a glass, he sat back in a leather armchair close to the window and looked out at the north side of the cathedral. The wine was good, light with a lemony aftertaste. He drank the first glass in one go and then poured the rest of the small bottle.

He loved cathedrals and cathedral cities. The last one he had looked around had been Strasbourg, a couple of months before, while on a Queen's Messenger run. It had been a cold October. A couple of old chums had been in town on business at the same time so too much rich Alsatian food and glorious Alsatian wine had been put away. The memory brought a smile to his solemn face. Then he frowned. While walking from the cathedral to rendezvous with his chums in a restaurant, he had noticed a very tall man walking in the street. Very tall. Older than when his mug shot had hung in UN Headquarters in Sarajevo. Slimmer. But it was him for sure. Out of prison. Fifteen years he had been given at The Hague. The man stopped in front of a shop window. Another man, dressed in a beige overcoat and wearing a hat and a scarf walked towards him, stopped at the same window and passed a package over – quickly, surreptitiously. Done like a magician's trick. A 'Brush Contact' was the technical term. Frankly, none of his business; the man had served his sentence. But then once they were in the restaurant a bit later… He had nearly mentioned it to Dan Jacot during their long, boozy lunch in Aix. But it seemed so unlikely that he had left it. In any case, he didn't want to rock the boat and possibly lose his job. One of the problems of moving on the fringes of the intelligence world was that he risked making himself ridiculous by indulging in conspiracy theories. Out on his run he could have sworn a dark blue car passed him twice, slowing down a little each time. Absurd.

From time to time his gaze would move from the window to the bedside table. Throughout his married life, when away from home, he had kept a photograph of Catriona at his bedside. He didn't anymore, although he still carried a photograph of her in his suitcase – to have no reminder of her with him would be unthinkable, but it was safer to keep her in his suitcase. He could look at her when he had to, when he couldn't stop himself, when the desire to remember her, connect with her in some way, became overwhelming. He was determined to impose discipline against what the military part of him saw as pointless sentimentality. She was gone: that was it. Perhaps one day they would be re-united. Perhaps.

But wherever he found himself, his eyes still moved involuntarily, by long established and cherished instinct, to seek out her image. Each time he realised the photo wasn't in its usual place and that she herself was dead, he was overcome with a breathless, panicky sadness.

In order to drive out these thoughts, he focussed on the painting again.

Looking at it carefully, and with Caravaggio's version also in his mind's eye, he was struck forcefully by how odd and unsettling the incident in Strasbourg had been. It was probably nothing, but he decided he would tell Jacot when they met up in Paris. He would know what to do.

Why not text him now? Just a quick message with the barebones to get him started. *No, how silly!* He was starting to behave like an old woman. No one in his right mind would want to be pestered by work stuff on a Friday evening. Anyway, they were due to meet up on Monday week. *It had kept for a couple of months. Why couldn't it keep for another few days?*

'How dare you! This is the Ladies changing room. Get out, or I'll call security,' Lady Nevinson snarled at the figure standing just outside her wood-panelled booth.

'Yes, Lady Nevinson, deliberately so. Do you mind if I close the door and perch on the bed for a bit?'

'Ingoldsby, for God's sake, you gave me a fright.' She was embarrassed. Richard Ingoldsby was the head of counter-espionage at MI5 and one of her closest allies. But his features were so bland and his style of dress so plain that he could be difficult to recognise. He blended into the background wherever he was. Even the sound of his voice could be someone else. 'What on earth are you doing here? There had better be a bloody good reason why you have barged in on my private morning swim. Make it quick and convincing, or I'll have you posted as liaison to some Third World Toilet.'

Ingoldsby was unruffled. She knew perfectly well he wouldn't dream of disturbing her unless it was a vital matter of state. 'Lady Nevinson, we have a problem. You know you weren't entirely happy about the Queen's Messenger who fell down the stairs, Amanda Brookwood was her name, even though the official world and his wife was insisting it was just an unfortunate accident. Been doing some ferreting around and some thinking. I have had a chat to a friend from the Middle East. As you know they are in an uneasy mood these days.'

'Not Mossad. Not before breakfast. Anyway, wasn't Mrs Brookwood on the Hong Kong run? What on earth would Mossad know about the Chinese that we don't – given we've got a huge station out there?' She flung her towel in irritation to the floor. She took a deep breath. 'Sorry to be short-tempered, but I'm tired, and this cloak and dagger stuff is such a bore.'

Ingoldsby let her irritation bounce off him, 'But necessary. Let me explain: my friend is sure, "*AFI* is sure" was the exact phrase, that there is something odd about the death of Amanda Brookwood –something we haven't seen, and they only suspect. It's nothing to do with the

Chinese, but he wouldn't say any more when pressed. I was lucky to get even that much, but he owed me a big favour. From the way he spoke, the tone and the body language, it looks as though they are worried too. They don't like the way things are going.'

'*AFI*, forgive me?'

'Sorry. AFI is Israeli Air Force Intelligence. The Israeli Air Force is their lead organisation on signals intelligence which gives us a clue on the provenance.'

'You still haven't explained why we are behaving like we're in the middle of East Germany during the Cold War.'

Ingoldsby leaned towards her, 'Because my friend suggests that Brookwood's death may be a symptom of a wider conspiracy with fellow travellers everywhere. Literally, everywhere: Number 10, your office, Albert Embankment, Vauxhall Cross, the GCHQ Doughnut, the Bundeskanzleramt, the Elysée – things are badly out of kilter in France apparently. And so on, and so on. Even the military and the judiciary here might be infected. Brookwood was a former barrister, after all. We just don't know. You yourself have told me a number of times recently that the world seems to have gone a bit mad.' He smiled, 'At least here at the Berkeley to get into the swimming pool you either have to be a member or staying at the hotel. So I reckoned we would be able to talk privately.'

'Navarre in Paris?'

'Navarre is one of us.'

'Thank God for small mercies, Ingoldsby.' *Something odd about the man though, a face difficult to describe and even more difficult to hold in the mind for any length of time.* 'I'm going to need a little more than the vague disquiet of a chum of yours.'

'There is more, Lady Nevinson. Er, if I might suggest, keep your dressing gown done up. My "chum", as you call him, won't tell me everything, but is happy to talk to you personally. I'll wait outside.'

'Keep your eyes open, Ingoldsby, in case anyone comes.'

'They won't, Lady Nevinson. No lift can stop at this floor – not for the next twenty minutes anyway. If anyone walks up the stairs there's a sign saying *Closed for chlorination until seven*. But please be quick.'

A short figure slipped in to the booth, shutting the door behind him. 'Lady Nevinson, my name is Oscar Samuel. Technically, I suppose I am a "blue and white illegal". You could have me arrested and deported. And if my bosses in Tel Aviv knew I was here I'd end up in a military prison in the Negev Desert.'

'I don't for a moment suppose that's your real name. But go ahead.' Lady Nevinson was at her haughtiest.

'No, it is. That was a condition Ingoldsby laid down. But it's just between us. I was originally in the Israeli Air Force but now do other things.'

'All right, all right. Just get on with it. I am, of course, grateful.'

'As you know, we Israelis, have a difficult relationship with Europe. Things have turned sour for you recently, and at first we thought it would be OK – we didn't care that much. If Jews no longer felt comfortable in Europe they could go to America or come to us. Make *Aliyah*, settle in Israel. To be honest, the English have never been that popular with us – because of history. I am sure you understand.' He paused and swallowed hard, clearly nervous in her presence. 'But now we are worried. We always kept tabs on the main European countries – outbreaks of anti-Semitism and that sort of thing. We had an agent on the inside of the Austrian People's Party, if you remember.'

'Yes, I do remember and its leader and his leather shorts came to a mysterious end…'

'He *caught the measles*, as we say, Lady Nevinson. It was a bonus that his last port of call was a gay bar in his hometown. A nice flourish. Great art, almost, though sadly impermanent. And in contrast to the current practice across Europe, the Austrian police were hugely and rapidly indiscreet.' He smiled. 'Don't look so shocked.'

'I'm not.' She smiled back. 'It's just taking me a little time to get used to having a strange man in my changing room.'

'I'm sorry, Lady Nevinson, there was no other way. Perhaps we Israelis have become too cautious over the years. The prospect not just of losing but of ceasing to exist creates a pessimistic mindset.'

Outside by the pool, Ingoldsby could hear the murmur of their voices but not what they were saying. They seemed to be taking a long time. He was getting nervous: trade-craft like reprogramming the lifts was amusing, and, despite her protestations, he knew Lady Nevinson was secretly excited by the tricks of the trade, but he didn't want a row with the management. Security services needed to have warm working relationships with famous hotels that attracted rich and influential foreign visitors.

'If it's any comfort, Lady Nevinson, we believe the same kind of process is going on in France.'

'Coming here for a general chat with me, Mr Samuel, may have discharged your obligation to Ingoldsby – whatever that was. We had formed some of the same hunches or intuitions. But if I am to take forward this matter, something also clearly in the interests of the State of Israel, I am going to need chapter and verse. Go away, Mr Samuel, and think about it. I swim here Mondays and Wednesdays when I am in

London. Good day.'

She grabbed a towel and went out to the pool. One of the most relaxing locations in London with a grand view over Chelsea and the West End – it was one of the few places she could truly unwind. She needed the exercise as well. Given the current security situation, she couldn't do much walking, not while she was in London. Swimming was good for her and she enjoyed the breakfast afterwards. Ingoldsby, thank God, had gone, presumably in the wake of that Mossad fellow, Samuel. She had been play-acting – a little. In reality, she was desperately interested in what he could offer her and knew the risk he was taking in coming forward. Amanda Brookwood's death had been pronounced a tragic accident by the authorities. If it was being hushed up...

She took her dressing gown off and looked round. The pool was empty. Standing in front of a poolside mirror, she took a long hard look at herself. Not bad. Not bad at all, for sixty plus. She didn't mention her true age to anyone – not even herself.

She missed being young, or younger. She hadn't noticed at first – there were no boys at school or home. But once up at Cambridge, she started to realise. Heads turned as she rode into town on her bicycle from Newnham, not just undergraduates – visitors, tourists, men of all kinds would turn to look at her. It didn't matter whether she was lightly clothed in the summer or wrapped up like Captain Scott in the cold Cambridge winters – the heads turned. Dawn, dusk or darkness – if they saw her face, even briefly glimpsed under a street light or in the flash of a car's headlights – the heads turned.

It was the same at parties, and the same for many years in the Foreign Office. She was an extremely good-looking girl. Wherever she went, whatever she said or did, as long as there were men present, she was welcome and made a fuss of. At the dullest dinner party or the most excruciatingly boring meeting, she could feel the admiring male glances. She was still attractive. Gilles Navarre tried to re-seduce her every time they met, sweetly. It was a relief to know that he could still be trusted in these turbulent times. Jacot invariably carried out a not so cold-blooded inspection of her turn out when he was in attendance. She laughed to herself, he always looked if she straightened and smoothed her dress – but at the hands, not the legs.

Dear, oh dear, she missed the heads turning – so much. Better pull herself together and get on with 50 lengths. There was breakfast to look forward to as well. She dived in and struck out in a vigorous crawl.

She liked doing proper, racing turns at the end of each length.

X

Restaurant Kerellec, Place Saint Sulpice, Paris, 6ème

It was a small, run-of-the-mill restaurant in a quiet corner of the Place St Sulpice, with a grand view of the eponymous church dominating the square. The splashing of the huge fountain in front of the church muffled the sound of traffic. Although in the fashionable Luxembourg area of the Left Bank, few tourists ventured that far. They usually penetrated half way down the rue Bonaparte and then turned right towards the famous cafés of Boulevard St Germain – *Les Deux Magots, Café Flore* and the *Brasserie Lipp*. As a result, le patron had immediately noticed the quiet Englishman when he had first come in for a meal the previous week.

The menu was provincial food from the various regions of France, with an occasional emphasis on the cooking of Brittany, le patron's home province.

Le patron, who had dutifully performed his national service in an infantry regiment of the line as a young man, could see immediately that his new customer was a soldier. Quiet, polite, smartly dressed, but oddly, always wearing gloves, usually of black silk. Restaurant owners observe these details. One afternoon as the man read *Le Monde* he noticed the burns on his wrists, and the mark in livid red scar tissue where his watch must have been when he got burned.

Everyday for nearly a week the man came alone – mainly for supper but on two occasions for lunch. He invariably brought a book or newspaper to read, in French. Whatever the time of day, he ordered a strong gin and tonic to begin with, and then another; followed by a half a bottle of the restaurant's general issue, white Burgundy – in the last couple of days a bottle – followed by Calvados. He drank too much, thought le patron.

Jacot was a little nervous. He was making the final preparations for his first visit to the Conseil National de Renseignements in the Elysée Palace – a small group of experts in various fields – Jacot thought there were about ten, whose job was to keep the president up to speed on developments that might have an effect on France's interests.

His Magenta-enabled mobile, back on after a few weeks silence in Aubagne, rang. Magenta was the codename for an unbreakable code system, both the hardware and the computer programmes and by extension the group of people who used them. It was Lady Nevinson.

'You'll be fine. His opposite number at their embassy in London attended a meeting yesterday in the Cabinet Office – in that conference room overlooking the Number 10 garden, and the prime minister was taking a breath of fresh air before lunch in a new pair of kitten heels. Apparently she used to do that at the Home Office before the Brexit turbulence deposited her into Number 10. I am sure it was all fired back to Paris in a suitably breathless telegram. I could probably wangle a copy from GCHQ, if you want.' She sounded upbeat. Nevertheless, Jacot still felt a little nervous about his imminent appointment at the Elysée.

'No, no please, I am trying to set up a trust relationship with the French.'

'I was only teasing.'

'I know, and I am sure you have gauged the mood correctly, Lady N. I was just checking in with you as it's a big step, certainly never done before.'

'Best of luck. You can tell me all about it – I'll be in Paris in the next few days.'

'Routine liaison?'

The tone of her voice changed. 'No. Sadly, not. Ingoldsby brought someone to see me earlier. We may have a problem. Don't get too comfy behind your desk.' She broke the Magenta connection.

Funny thing to say, thought Jacot as he placed the files for the French into a despatch case he then locked, slipping the key into the top left pocket of his service dress, just below the medal ribbons.

The registry in the embassy had produced special file covers for the purpose to his own design, copying the leather folders used by the Joint Intelligence Committee in London, but with a twist. On one side scarlet leather, embossed with the royal arms and the arms of the French Republic, with the classification in English: *MOST SECRET UK/FRANCE EYES ONLY*. Jacot was proud to have dispensed with the ghastly Americanism – *TOP SECRET*, foisted upon poor Mr Churchill against his will and good taste as the Americans muscled into Bletchley Park in 1942. The reverse side was the same but in blue leather, with the inscription in French: *TRÈS SECRET DEFENSE SPÉCIALE FRANCE / ROYAUME-UNI*.

The British Embassy and the Elysée Palace were neighbours, less than a hundred yards apart on the rue du Faubourg Saint-Honoré, an elegant and upmarket street dotted with boutiques and cafes – very different from the Whitehall Jacot was used to where there were few shops, except the ones that sold sandwiches to the workers in various ministries, and a number of pubs. The same applied in Washington – the government quarter was the government quarter. But in Paris the presidential palace and the ministry of the interior found themselves on the city's smartest shopping street. Jacot decided to avoid such a public route – he was carrying highly classified documents.

Putting on his forage cap, with its badge of a Celtic cross, and picking up his leather swagger stick, he headed downstairs into the embassy gardens and the back way to the Elysée. Technically, the avenue Gabriel running behind the embassy was a public right of way, but few people used it as it was so heavily policed. He took care to avoid any puddles so that his highly polished brown shoes remained gleaming for his appointment.

He turned right into the Avenue de Marigny, running alongside the palace and pressed the bell on an imposing armoured door, opened in quick time by a pair of armed gendarmes nationales. They checked his papers thoroughly but courteously, asking him to remove his hat as their eyes flickered between face and passport photograph. Then he was escorted into an inner courtyard and handed over to one of the palace ushers in black tailcoat, white bow tie and silver chain of office. Jacot had expected to be escorted in through a side door, but they suddenly emerged into the main courtyard of the palace and climbed the steps together at a brisk pace, proceeding at speed through the main door past a uniformed officer of the Garde Republicaine, resplendent in red and blue, and up a grand staircase to the left.

'The famous *Escalier Murat* constructed here when Marshal Murat, Napoleon's brother-in-law, lived in the palace. He had a liking for gold,' the usher smiled, proudly pointing at the exquisite balusters in the form of gilded, giant palm leaves that seemed almost to be floating free, unattached to the staircase itself. Despite being constructed in the First Empire Jacot felt it had a curiously art deco feel.

'Lovely, lovely,' Jacot tried not to gush or gawp, but couldn't help it. He felt he shouldn't put even his gloved hands on the shining, gilded handrail. As a Guardsman he was used to going in and out of Buckingham Palace and Windsor Castle, but neither was the seat of political power. The Elysée Palace was, and he could sense it – the pomp, pageantry and gorgeous decoration were there to proclaim and dignify power, not history or heritage.

The single staircase became a double staircase at the first landing. Murat and his architects understood how to make a spectacle. At the top they entered a small room, dominated by a portrait of François Mitterrand, under which stood a French officer in uniform. The usher introduced them, 'Colonel Carolet de Liron – Colonel Jacot for your appointment,' and then silently withdrew.

De Liron shook hands, gently, hardly gripping Jacot's hand at all, then pointed to the open door of the next room, 'The ante-chamber to the president's office.' Through the door, Jacot could see another usher and a naval aide de camp – he was rather hoping for a glimpse of the nuclear briefcase, but good manners and military discipline prevailed, and he quickly looked back at his host who smiled and said, 'Sadly, my quarters are not so well appointed.' Turning around, he opened a small door and beckoning Jacot, began to climb a steep and cramped, wooden spiral staircase. Jacot followed, holding tightly to the plain wooden handrail. At the top was a tiny office, just room for a desk and a couple of chairs, though this being the Elysée the furniture was Louis Quatorze. A small round window overlooked the lead palace roof.

Jacot noticed the anchor on his képi, Troupes des Marines, the descendants of France's colonial infantry, with traditions as proud and strong as the Legion's and songs just as haunting. They were still responsible for garrisoning France's confetti of Empire, scattered across the globe. On the bookshelf against the back wall was a large silver framed photograph of a young, strikingly attractive woman sitting with six children on a beach in one of France's départements outre-mer.

'My wife and our dear children in Nouvelle Caledonie last year, my previous posting. All French, all Catholic,' he grinned.

He had planned calling formally on John Barkstead, Head of the MI6 Station, *H* Paris for short, and had booked an appointment with his secretary.

But instead, Barkstead dropped by Jacot's austere office on the top floor of the embassy. Jacot winced at his over-firm handshake, unusual in the UK except among a few old-fashioned military and business types who persisted in the belief that not trying to crush someone's hand in greeting was usually a sign of effeminacy, or worse. The Americans were the ones most to be feared in the firm handshake stakes, particularly graduates of the US military academies who usually wore large rings on the third finger of their right hands. They were invariably beautifully designed and very much part of a long élite military tradition. Those in the services who had not graduated from these institutions sometimes regarded class rings with resentment.

Ring knocking was their envious term for the influence and status that came from having attended West Point, Annapolis or the air force academy at Colorado Springs. It was said that if a graduate of any of these academies ran into opposition at a meeting or orders group from an outsider, fellow graduates would knock their rings on the table to remind others of their status.

'You have a very plain office Colonel Jacot – just a picture of the Queen on the wall, but not, I see, one of the official ones.'

'Well, winning the Gold Cup at Ascot would be wonderful for anyone. It's the sheer joy on the face and an improvement on all those rather bad official portraits, all orders and decorations, not much of the real person. Do sit down. Would you like some sherry?'

'Yes, please. Rumours about ice-cold sherry are already circulating in the embassy.'

Jacot took a bottle of his favoured Manzanilla out of the tiny fridge below his desk and poured two glasses.'

'Santé,' said Barkstead.

'Iechyd Da. It's good to be in Paris,' replied Jacot. Barkstead was staring at his gloved hands. 'The Falklands… I was blown up on that troopship – Exocet strike.'

'Yes, yes. I am so sorry, I hadn't realised. Well, it could have been worse. The operation to prevent the Argies getting more Exocets was run out of this station.'

'I know. Nicely done. As we both know the French have never been given the full credit for all their co-operation. Even now in the British press you see criticism, from time to time, that they should not have allowed their Exocet maintenance team to remain in Argentina.'

'Yes. Quite. Always a difficult one that. Do you withdraw the team, making a grand gesture of solidarity and please the press and the historians? Or do you leave it there, hoping to make a difference? One of the team was, if I remember correctly, not just an employee of Aérospatiale. Strange, wasn't it? A number of the missiles seemed to miss for inexplicable technical reasons.' Barkstead smiled, knowingly. 'The last one to be fired, unusually from the land, did the opposite of what it was meant to. When the operator moved the gizmo left – the missile went right. Very clever.'

'It still managed to hit one of our ships just before the end. But in the end neither of our carriers were lost.' Jacot smiled back.

They talked about French and British politicians and their prospects. Barkstead wore the weary cynicism of his trade lightly – leavened by an unsparing wit. He had a professional spy's ability to sum up human personalities in a few words, one of which invariably began with the third letter of the alphabet. Like a Bach fugue he seemed able to dream up endless variations. Jacot was highly amused. In London, he had kept a secret file recording Lady Nevinson's acerbic exasperations. As he knew from his encounter with Gregory Norton in Aix, the good lady had retrieved the file and read it. He decided to keep a similar file in Paris, transferring into it immediately some of Sergent – chef Paradis' glorious pronouncements on the human condition. He felt that Barkstead's pithy judgments were also worthy of record.

Barkstead was clearly after personal information, but other than a brief description of how he came to be wounded thirty-five years before, Jacot gave nothing away, keeping the conversation rigidly to the manifest glories of Manzanilla and life in Paris. Barkstead probed. Jacot parried, as politely as he could.

'Where are you living?'

'The rue Bonaparte. A rather civilised spot. I was a bit worried that Lady N might exile me to some outer suburb,' replied Jacot.

'The Left Bank is always nicer. Which end are you – Seine or Saint

Sulpice?'

'Closer to the Seine, but I do go to a little restaurant in the Place Saint Sulpice from time to time.' Jacot had had enough of being questioned – time to turn it round. 'Listen, can I give you another glass of sherry and ask you for some advice?'

'Of course, of course. Anything I can do to help.'

Jacot poured them each another glass and pulled out a file from his desk drawer. 'Thing is, Barkstead, my job is to sanitise our stuff for the French. Fairly routine, but the French intelligence they give to us seems to use a different grading system from us and the Americans.'

'Yes, I know, it can be a bit tricky. They are less comfortable with ambiguity than we are. Out of character for a civilisation that still uses the subjunctive a good deal.'

'Yes, well, to be honest I am not too sure I am that comfortable with ambiguity either.'

'I should hope not. You are a Guards Officer not a foreign office official like me.' Barkstead grinned in a friendly fashion and then rolled some of the Manzanilla round his mouth. 'Top sherry, by the way. But back to Source and Information Rating. What I tend to do is simplify things for the French reader by using only half of the usual system. We usually grade sources, as you know, from A meaning *Reliable* – to E meaning *Unreliable*, with various shades in between. Trouble is the shades like *Usually* or *Fairly Reliable*, are not in themselves reliable. And we are never allowed to use that useful, all-purpose suffix, *ish*, or the CIA's favourite qualifier, *Ballpark.*'

Jacot laughed, 'This is starting to sound like a script from *Yes Minister.*'

Barkstead continued, 'So what I do is just use *A: Reliable* and *B: Usually Reliable*, and grade anyone we are not at all sure about *F: No basis exists for a reliable judgement on the individual concerned.* Same detail for the Information Content Rating, with its numbers from 1 to 6. For MI6's counterparts at the Boulevard Mortier I tend to use only, *1: Confirmed*; *2: Not Confirmed but Probably True*; and *6: No basis exists…* Obviously, where we might be dealing with actionable intelligence on terrorist whereabouts and so on we just pass the information along as quickly as we can.'

'Thank you, Barkstead. My guess is I'll get the hang of what they want in the president's office pretty quickly.'

Barkstead got up to go. He felt the need to shake Jacot's hand again, even more firmly this time. Jacot returned quickly to his Apple Computer to make some notes on how he would design his intelligence product for his French contacts and worked for some time on a spread-sheet. As he finished on the keyboard he winced and rubbed his right hand, noticing a slight indentation on the palm of his soft silk gloves.

He had another glass of sherry, it was nearly lunch time, and looked out of his window onto the rue du Faubourg Saint-Honoré below.

Dealing with professional spies could be difficult. Because of their training they were always after something, a piece of information that could be useful to them. Or seeking to create an impression. At the end of every conversation you had a feeling of slight violation, as if your pockets had been picked. He hadn't told Barkstead anything he couldn't find out from standard embassy information. He would, of course, be hugely suspicious of Lady Nevinson and her intentions. But he seemed friendly enough – maybe he was just trying to be nice.

Monica Zaden sounded hurried and tense, saying she couldn't speak at length just then, but would be back in Paris the following week.

'Let's go out. What about the theatre – my French is certainly up to it these days?' said Jacot trying to keep his tone as casual as possible.

'Yes, yes. Sounds great. See you Friday. Let me know the plan. I look forward to seeing you – very much.' She rang off.

Jacot thought long and hard about where they should go together. He hadn't seen her since their hair-raising experiences in Cambridge and London. He understood, given the circumstances, that it was best for him to get out of London for a while, and lie low abroad. At his farewell interview with the great lady, she had told him about his posting to the Paris Embassy which he welcomed. She then mentioned 'a short period of training with the French military – somewhere nice in the South of France' – which he also welcomed. It was only when he got to Aubagne that he realised the 'short period of training with the French military' actually meant eight weeks with the Foreign Legion. No possibility of seeing Zaden. Just Paradis, his sous-officiers mates and the ever-loyal Legionnaire trio awaiting a foreign assignment, with Dean Martin providing the soundtrack.

In the end, he didn't really mind – an eight-week refresher with the Legion was just what he needed. Good for his fitness, mental alertness and, come to think of it, for morale. If, as seemed to be the plan, Lady Nevinson intended to get him away from *flying a mahogany bomber* and use him in a troubleshooting capacity in the field, then eight weeks with Paradis was time well spent. He had enjoyed the effort required, the results achieved, and had also come to like Paradis – a peculiar individual in some ways, but with a comforting, rock-solid reliability about him, rather like the best NCOs in his own regiment.

The only snag was that he had found it difficult to keep in touch with Zaden. He had been hugely relieved at her call.

Like most Englishmen of his type he had learned French throughout his childhood, holidayed in France frequently, but ended up not being able to speak very much of the language. He was fluent enough now. The seeds planted all those years ago, first at a Dickensian, Surrey preparatory school, and afterwards in the historical and breezy splendours of Harrow on the Hill, had come good in late middle age, sprouting in the austere countryside of south western France. He could follow a conversation and understand French television and radio perfectly well, thanks to many hours with Paradis. But there was a catch.

Paradis had sprinkled his instructions with plenty of 'Mon colonel, this and mon colonel that' – but other than an examination by the medical officer, Jacot had been entirely in the hands of the sous-officiers. They never swore at him, but he had heard them swearing a good deal at the long-suffering *hommes du rang*. Like British non-commissioned officers, they used a vivid and biting vocabulary, derived largely from descriptions of the sexual act. But French being the language it was, much of the swearing had a certain economy and elegance. 'Get yourselves out of the shit', for instance, used as a kind of all-purpose encouragement, a bit like 'sort yourselves out' – was simply 'demerdez-vous.' *Wonderful.*

As a result, Jacot's head was full of barrack-room phrases of limited use on the Parisian diplomatic circuit. More worryingly, he wondered about the quality of his spoken French. Paradis was no Professor Higgins and wasn't even originally French. His total immersion language training meant that he spoke a curious hybrid of English public school French, leavened and salted with the vivid imagery of the Foreign Legion – flavoured with a slightly Caribbean accent.

If he could manage television, he could certainly manage a play. Why not the Comédie Française, just half an hour's walk away? He didn't know much about French drama and wasn't sure he would be able to take four hours of Racine with his interminable rhymes, but there might be something lighter on the calendar.

Luckily, the following week, they were giving daily performances of *Le Bourgeois Gentilhomme – The Would-Be or Wannabe Gentleman*, Molière's great prose comedy about social climbing in 17th Century Paris, with the original music by Lully, court composer to Louis XIV. It was about the only French play Jacot knew well – always a favourite of both school and university productions and always very, very funny.

Lully was rather dull in Jacot's view and being court composer to Louis XIV hardly a recommendation. Versailles in the 17th century must have been a stultifying place for everyone except the king himself. Even getting Louis XIV out of bed required more than a hundred courtiers – all vying for favour, climbing over one another to ingratiate themselves with the monarch.

As a Guards Officer Jacot had been exposed to court ceremonial of a more gentle style. It was the custom before state dinners at Buckingham Palace to present the Captain of the Guard to the Queen in the Music Room, as she passed through on her way to meet the guests. God knows when the practice originated, but it was charming and added colour to the occasion. The Captain of the Guard was ushered into the room by a footman in full livery, directed to stand on a particular piece of patterned carpet, and told to wait. The view over the gardens on a summer's evening was fabulous and the room impressive.

His ceremonial uniform, always immaculate, would be given extra care and attention before appearing in person in front of the Queen. More polishing, pressing and brushing than usual – if that were possible, but with one procedure quietly abandoned. Before parades bearskins were often brushed and groomed with hair spray. Entirely against regulations, but it gave the bearskin an attractive sheen. Her Majesty was said to have a sharp nose for dubious hairsprays.

An amusing play would be just the thing to break the ice. Laughter was, after all, the best aphrodisiac. Followed by dinner, nothing over the top. Definitely not too much garlic. And then dancing. He rather liked the sound of an establishment on the Left Bank recommended to him by Paradis: *Chez Rolfe's*, with apparently a souped-up sound system that played 'songs from the great singers', as Paradis put it, and not too loud.

Le patron nodded as the English officer came in just before Christmas and showed him to his usual table. He preferred to sit with his back to the wall.

They exchanged the usual pleasantries, but this time the Englishman added a Christmas salutation in Welsh, 'Naddolig llawen.'

Le patron beamed and returned the compliment in his native Breton, 'Nadolih llauen.' It's more or less the same in the language of my forebears. I thought you were English.'

'I am; but most of the soldiers in my regiment were Welsh and it rubbed off onto me. Over the years, I have become a little Welsh by absorption rather than birth. I speak a little of the language and support the national rugby team.'

'I knew you were a soldier the moment you came in.'

'Still am, for a few more years. Colonel Daniel Jacot, les gardes royale Celtique, currently attached to the British Embassy.' He stood up and offered his hand.

'Caporal Jean Kerellec, cinquième d'infanterie de ligne. Well, I was a briefly a corporal at the end of my national service, currently patron of the restaurant named after my family.' Breton men were firm handshakers, but as he gripped Jacot's gloved hand, he remembered the burn marks and could sense the brittleness of the skin underneath. He quickly released the pressure.

It was a Sunday and the Welsh colonel, the label le patron now gave him, was eating a three-course lunch. Le patron was proud of his table d'hôte menus, feeling that they represented good value for money and true French provincial cooking, in contrast to the over-priced, Americanised food his less scrupulous colleagues churned out to eager tourists less than half a mile away. He would rather die than serve a frozen croque-monsieur. The colonel had begun with a salad, followed by guinea fowl casserole and was now, under the affectionate eye of le patron, working his way through the restaurant's selection of cheeses, accompanied by a large Calvados.

As his new favourite customer left that day, le patron was impressed by his dark-blue suit: beautifully cut, single-breasted, with two vents at the back and five buttons on the cuff. When he had stood up to go, the bottom left side of the jacket caught briefly on the back of the chair, pulling it open to reveal a brightly coloured silk lining – *prune de Damas* was the correct description of the colour, thought le patron, approvingly. Yes, the Welsh colonel was definitely something of a dandy. He was so absorbed in admiring Jacot's suit that it took his eyes a few moments to register and then recognise something else revealed for just a moment, a dark blue leather shoulder holster with a pistol secured in it by a short strap, fixed in place by a highly polished brass button.

He watched him walk out of the restaurant into the square – it might have been a trick of the wind or a natural stumble, but after half a lifetime in the restaurant business le patron suspected only too well what was going on – the Welsh colonel was drunk, or very nearly so.

XV
21b rue Bonaparte, Paris, 6ème

The buzzer went. Jacot looked into the video entry-phone and pressed the button to let Lady Nevinson in. Never having been visited by her at home before, he was slightly ill at ease.

She came through the door in a swish of turquoise silk and ensconced herself on a sofa by the window. As ever, she smelled marvellous, *rather minty tonight*, thought Jacot, probably a present from Gilles Navarre, her friend of forty years and current Head of the DGSI, France's equivalent of MI5.

She did not pause to take his hand, as she sometimes did, or exchange any other sort of greeting. Jacot was relieved as it avoided a double awkwardness – he wasn't wearing gloves and didn't like his hands being touched without them on. And, in the normal course of events, he would exchange kisses on the cheek with a woman he knew well who was visiting him in his own home. He wasn't sure how she would react to being kissed.

'Good tan,' was the first thing she said. Quickly followed by, 'Gin and tonic please, Colonel.' It was the first time they had met since Jacot had begun his eight-week adventure with the Foreign Legion – a tough couple of months, and Jacot rather resented the high-handed way she had organised it without any input from him. But he was used to her ways. The fact that she noticed his tan before asking for a drink was a sign that she was concerned about his welfare.

'Lady Nevinson, you are too kind. I am rather suntanned, as it happens.'

'Look, I'm sorry, I had intended to ring you up and do all those polite things, enquire how you are and so on. I have been keeping a close eye on your training, as you know. One day soon I'd like to hear all about it. But for now I've only got a few minutes, and there is a more pressing matter I need to warn you about.' She didn't draw breath. Jacot had managed to say nothing at all so far. 'In Paris for a couple of days, supposedly liaising with the French on counter-terrorism which I am, but I'm also here on a hunch. A Queen's Messenger, an ex-barrister by the name of Amanda Brookwood had a fatal accident last week – fell down the stairs at home in London. Everyone tells me it was just a ghastly accident. The statistics for people falling down the stairs are hair-raising, apparently. But Ingoldsby isn't convinced and nor is a friend of his. Neither am I. There's also a strange, garbled report of a plot from outside the UK against prime minister's life from when she was still home secretary. So I've come to seek advice from Gilles. It's more complicated than that but.... For now you don't need to know anymore but I just wanted to warn you to be careful.'

'Don't worry, Lady N, you'll feel better after one of these.' He preferred strong gin. So did Lady Nevinson. It didn't matter what brand, but it had to be over 40 per cent alcohol by volume, at least. Mixed with a small can of tonic water, straight from the fridge. Large bottles of tonic were useless, going flat too quickly. Plus two chunky cubes of ice and a small piece of lime, sliced just before going into a tallish glass. The tonic bubbles danced on the surface as he handed it to her – he could feel the coolness of the iced liquid on his hands. Of all the English drinks, he felt it was the most seductive – refreshing, with a good alcoholic hit at the same time.

She looked round the flat. 'Nice, very nice. Glad to see the portrait arrived in one piece.' She took a long sip at her gin and tonic.

'Thank you for organising the move.'

'Well, it was only partly me. The French took over at this end and set things up for you.'

Jacot wanted to ask if Monica Zaden had been involved. Probably – he would like to be sure though.

But Lady Nevinson moved swiftly on. 'You've met *H* Paris?'

'Yes, of course. He is charming, as you would expect. I'd be surprised if there was much spying going on here, though. It looks like mainly liaison.'

'Nicely put. But I suspect you don't really approve of these people any more than I do. Anyway, they don't like you very much.' She smiled. 'It's nothing personal, don't worry.'

'What do you mean? I'm not keen on our American friends but always punctiliously polite with their wholly owned British subsidiary.'

Lady Nevinson took a slug of her gin and tonic and pulled a piece of paper out of her handbag. 'Do you know what this is?'

'It looks like a standard signal format.'

'Go to the top of the class. It's a signal asking me for details of any intelligence operations I may have authorised in France. Copied to the chairman of the Parliamentary Intelligence and Security Committee, and one of those *Advisers to the Prime Minister on Security and Political Correctness* – I think the one that looks as though he is wearing a wig from Berman and Nathans. It's not only cheeky, but it also suggests that they may have tabs on you that you may be unaware of.' She handed Jacot the signal. 'It's the first skirmish in a new bureaucratic war. I hope it stays bureaucratic.'

Jacot looked at it, and then turned over the page. 'Yes, I see what you mean. Who is it from? Funny signature, *XYZ*.'

'*XYZ* is the formal telegraphic signature of Valentine Walton, *C*, or Chief of the Secret Intelligence Service. From the founding of the service the Chief has always signed letters in green ink. In the same way his telegraphic signature has always been *XYZ*.'

'Why has he copied it to the ISC?'

'Oh I don't mind them. The ISC is a place where the prime minister can safely store assorted duds who still crave status of some sort. Largely ineffectual, anaesthetised by moral relativism. No, it's that terrorism fellow. If you were to engrave the words *deeply moderate* on one of those Buddhist prayer wheels and spin it for a thousand years you still wouldn't be able to do the man justice. The ultimate nightmare – a dim man with a first class honours degree. Now we have lost the deputy prime minister, you might want to start a new file on him.' She laughed.

Jacot tried not to look embarrassed. 'I shall look forward to it.' Lady N was actually rather proud of her own *First* from Cambridge, but Jacot thought it better to let her colourful and inaccurate judgement pass without comment. Plus the fact he was genuinely pleased to see her.

She turned towards his bookshelves. 'Wodehouse, all of them, I see. Lovely bindings. Which one has the story about Spode, the ludicrous fascist in blackshorts, when he is about to tear Bertie Wooster limb from limb; and stops mid-strangle, because Wooster seems to be in on the terrible secret that the awful Spode has an interest in a women's underwear shop? Something that might be fatal to a would-be dictator's reputation as a hard man.'

'It's in *Code of the Woosters.*' Jacot took down the volume in question. 'Hysterical. The large, imposing and bad-tempered Spode is setting about Bertie when he suddenly remembers the get out of jail card that Jeeves has given to him. Spode owns a lingerie shop in the West End called *Eulalie*. He blurts out the word and suddenly Spode becomes friendly, very friendly, even straightening up Bertie's clothes, dishevelled in the struggle.'

'*Eulalie*. Yes I remember. Useful, and just in case you run into problems or backchat from any of our intelligence people here, let me give you a *Eulalie*. Just say *PAR 1*.'

'PAR 1 it is, Lady N.'

'About thirty years ago in this city a senior member of the intelligence set up here was due to be moved to another posting and was asked to hand over his star agent, supposedly a communist trade union official with close ties to the then Socialist government. He managed to get the handover postponed a few times. But, eventually, it became clear that there was no agent and *PAR 1*, as he was designated, admitted that he had invented the whole thing, fabricated the reports, incidentally all lapped up in London, and pocketed the funds involved to finance a high old time in the City of Light.'

She was in full magnificent flow. Mozart's Flute and Harp Concerto provided a suitable accompaniment to her revelations. 'And what do you think they did to PAR 1? Put him on trial?'

'Well, no. I shouldn't think that's how it works at all.'

'No, Jacot, absolutely right. Nothing more was said. A glowing report on the individual concerned was raised and a lucrative job secured for him in a merchant bank.'

She got up to look out of the window. 'It's a good street to live on. Two year posting, probably – unless I need you back in London, or I get sacked, in which case they'll probably despatch you straight back to the Army. I am glad to see you well set up. What's that Celtic Guards phrase you always use when checking on your troops?'

'"Boots fit? Mail getting through?" As far as I am concerned they do fit, and it is getting through. You mentioned something about a friend of Ingoldsby's?'

'I did. Still need to know – for now. But what I can tell you is that you must maintain absolute security.'

'I always do, Lady N. Trust no one. By the book. Enemies all around us.'

She looked directly at him and spoke slowly, 'Not against our enemies, you understand, but against those who might appear friends. The world is a different place these days.'

'I understand perfectly.'

She laughed, 'Now that I have put you in the picture and as your – what is that ghastly term they use these days?'

'Line manager,' I think.

'Yes, now as your "line manager" I have checked up on your welfare and morale and warned you of our little problem, I can tell you all about tonight's adventure. What do you know about the so-called affair in the avenue de l'Observatoire when someone tried to murder then Senator François Mitterrand in the 1950s?' She smiled. 'Sounds a bit like a

Sherlock Holmes story. I seem to remember he had some cases in Paris.'

'Well, actually, Lady Nevinson, no mention is made of Paris; at least not in the Canonical stories. Holmes probably travelled through Paris on his way to and from Switzerland – remember he fights Colonel Moriarty at the Reichenbach Falls, although at that time he could equally have made a crossing via the Hook of Holland. Most authorities would... '

She rolled her eyes, 'I had forgotten, briefly, mercifully, what a know-all you are. Navarre should be here anytime now. We are going to the Brasserie Lipp where Mitterrand had dinner that fateful night. Then he is going to walk me through exactly what happened, the secret version under wraps until now – an intelligence battlefield tour.'

Standing in the window all dressed up to go out and excited by the prospect of her secret tour, Jacot thought she looked fabulous for a woman in her sixties. She had told him after his last adventure that while serving in the embassy in South Vietnam, Navarre had come to her aid during the fall of Saigon, when she had missed the last plane out. He smiled. Rescuing a beautiful woman in distress was a basic and powerful male fantasy – there must have been many young male diplomats keen to help her out – trust Gilles Navarre to elbow, or rather schmooze his way to the front of the queue.

'There's his car and driver. Have a nice weekend. Oh, just one more thing, your French colleague is due back in Paris this week. She helped with the flat. Thought you'd like to know.' She was gone, the rustle of her silk dress growing fainter as she rushed down the stairs.

'Relax now, Celia. Thank you for sharing your concerns with me. I have informed our counter-espionage people and will report back. Let's just enjoy the tour.'

Navarre's armoured Renault gently came to a halt outside the Palais du Luxembourg. 'So, Celia, it's October 1959 and the height of the Algerian War and Senator Mitterrand, as he was then, is driving home to his apartment in his blue Peugeot from the Brasserie Lipp after a night-cap with some friends. A five-minute drive – modern traffic has made it a bit longer for us. Just about here, there's the Palais du Luxembourg in front of us, he suspects he is being followed. So he swings round the other side and tries to shake them off – without success. In a panic he abandons his car pretty much here. You see the gardens of the Paris Observatory just there.'

Navarre's driver stopped the car

'Is this the spot?' Lady Nevinson leaned forward excitedly with a rustle of silk. 'Nowhere to hide, only the odd statue.'

'Absolument. Mitterrand legs it straight down the path and then throws himself into a flowerbed. His pursuers fire a Resistance-era Tommy-gun into his car – seven wonderfully placed, photograph-friend-ly bullet holes. He is the hero of the hour, surviving an assassination attempt by French Algerian extremists the OAS – I think there was a famous English film about them.'

'Yes, *The Day of the Jackal,* a book and a film. Although in that they were after de Gaulle,' said Lady Nevinson.

Navarre continued with a conspiratorial twinkle in his eyes, 'I'll get to de Gaulle in a minute. Except all was not as it seemed. A few days later one of the would-be assassins, a shady, right wing low-life and onetime parliamentary deputy let it be known that the whole thing had been a set up at Mitterrand's instigation – to give his flagging political career a boost, and get him back on the front pages.'

'His word against Mitterrand's?'

'Not quite. A few hours *before* the attack the low-life had handed in a letter to a post restante – franked with the time and date and witnessed by a postman – setting out in excruciating detail what was to happen later. The only possible explanation was that he and Mitterrand had concocted the whole thing together.'

'What we call in England a *False-flag* attack.' She smiled. 'And in the intelligence services, for that matter. But he survived to become President in 1981.'

'He did, he did, Celia. Just. He was able to muddy the waters enough, but it was close. Most of our politicians in the 1950s and many of our people had something to hide – secret sympathies with the OAS, exaggerated records in the Resistance, co-operation with Vichy. In a more confident era he would have been finished. In the end, his opponents made the mistake of allowing the affair to become a joke – when Mitterrand rose to speak in parliament or elsewhere his opponents would make Tommy-gun noises.'

'And de Gaulle?'

'That's the oddest thing, cherie, he was the sitting president and loathed Mitterrand but held his hand "for the good of France", or some such formulation. But now we think we know why.'

'Do go on Gilles, it's lovely to be in on a proper secret instead of all the squalid stuff we deal with these days.'

'De Gaulle admired Mitterrand's sense of theatre.' He took a sitting bow and finished with a wave of his hands and 'Voila!'

'Is that it? "Voila", indeed. I have been tricked into the back of your car under false pretences,' she said with not entirely mock outrage.'

'That's it, but it's not all. De Gaulle admired the theatre element because it's exactly what he himself had done when he arrived in Paris on the day it was liberated. As he walked down the nave of Notre Dame, snipers inside the cathedral fired at him from close range – the bullets ricocheted off the pillars. The people in the pews took cover. But de Gaulle, with his shoulders back, strode down the aisle unperturbed and unharmed – miraculously. No one ever knew who the snipers were and unlike most snipers they couldn't shoot straight or weren't trying to. Some say the noise was made by excited pigeons.'

'I must read a biography of the great general when I get back to London tomorrow. Thank you Gilles, I have enjoyed tonight very much.' She kissed him in the French manner on both cheeks.

He took her hand. 'Remember, Madame la Baronesse, in these turbulent times; nothing is ever quite what it seems. Nothing.'

The telephone rang, his Magenta-enabled mobile. Not many people had the number and Jacot was slightly startled – it was unlikely to be Lady Nevinson after her visit. But it was.

'Lady Nevinson, how was your intelligence battlefield tour?'

'Very interesting, but it will have to wait until I next see you. I've only been back in London a few hours, but it looks as though we have another problem. You met Gregory Norton, didn't you, very recently, when he delivered your orders? He was on his way past you so I thought it would be jolly. He said he knew you. I'm sorry I never got down to see you myself. I should have mentioned it when I dropped by – Gilles had plans for some kind of summit in Nice, but events overtook him.'

Jacot shuddered. Being treated like a schoolboy in front of the Foreign Legion would have been too much. 'We crossed over in Sarajevo in the 90s. Yes, we hit it off. Nice man. He had a couple of weeks leave to take and was off on a tour of French cathedrals and working on his fitness. He's due in Paris soon. We had pencilled in a few beers and a visit to Notre Dame. Monday week, I think.'

Lady Nevinson paused before speaking again. 'I'm afraid he won't be in Paris. There's been a terrible accident, in Chartres, which adds up with what you have just told me. He was run over while jogging last night. Hit and run.'

'Oh, God. How awful. He was such a nice man and deserved a bit of good luck.'

'Yes, quite. I got to know him quite well. He did a number of little tasks for me. I think he enjoyed "cloak and dagger" as he called it.'

'What do you want me to do, Lady N, – identify the body I suppose?' Jacot's spirits sank. He took the conventional religious view that the body was merely a suit or casing for the soul and had identified a number of bodies during his life. But it was still an unnerving and distressing experience – terrible things could happen to the suit or casing.

'No, no. Don't worry about that. There's no body for you this time. The French police already have a DNA match. I understand the injuries

were severe – what our American colleagues call a "closed-casket job."'
Jacot groaned – Lady Nevinson could be depressingly matter of fact. She
went on, 'It's just that I have had a call from Gilles Navarre. They are not
entirely happy, and he suggested you get down there with one of his
people. I'm not entirely happy either with this coming on top of Mrs
Brookwood.'

'Where was Norton found?'

'A couple of miles from Chartres on one of those straight country
roads. The DGSI have the details. Today, please. Gilles has despatched a
driver for you. Let me know when you get back. Oh, and while I have
you, some French technical type has come up with a solution for our
phones. No one can work out your geographical location from the signal
any longer. It's very clever – the signal jumps all over the place. Gilles had
yours sorted out while you were running around the hills of southern
France. Feel free to use it generally again – not just with me. Something
to tease the Americans with. NSA won't like it at all.'

'Thank God for that. More importantly, what do you mean by "not
entirely happy"?'

'Gilles didn't explain. It's not a four-alarm fire, yet, but he thought I
should know. Norton, unlike Brookwood, was a Magenta person.'

'Have they got his phone?'

'Yes, yes. They have. Untouched. It's with the DGSI who are having
a look. Nothing to worry about there.'

Jacot was sad – in the usual way for poor Norton but also for himself.
It had been good to renew their acquaintance from the Balkan years. He
had been looking forward to staying in touch. In fact he had been looking
forward more than he could say to seeing Norton the following week,
relying on it even. He dug out his best Calvados, pouring two fingers into
a glass. *Why not make it four fingers? A toast to the dead.* Jacot drained the glass
in one go and got ready to leave.

Looking out of the window a few minutes later, he saw a car pull up,
and a familiar figure step into the street. Jacot switched on the alarm
system, locked the door, and took the stairs two steps at a time. The tac-
iturn driver smiled, waited for a pedestrian to walk past and then asked
Jacot politely if he was armed. Jacot smiled, shook his head and made for
the car. But the driver was persistent. 'It is an instruction from Monsieur
le Directeur, relayed he says, from Madame la Baronesse.'

He got the message, turned around, re-entered the front door and
dashed back up to his flat. Taking off his jacket he strapped on a shoulder holster. He then retrieved his Glock 17 pistol from the bedside table,
pushed a magazine into the pistol grip, popped a spare magazine into his

coat pocket, and returned to the car that then pulled away at high speed.

Jacot found the intelligence business exhausting from time to time. When working with the Americans they never stopped striding around, making chopping movements with their hands and fixing you with steely glares. With the French, it was cars. Even the most clapped out vehicle from the motor pool, on the most routine mission, was driven as if in a Hollywood car chase. It was unnerving, unnecessary, and risked drawing attention to themselves. Sergent-chef Paradis would not approve. While instructing Jacot on the defensive driving phase of his recent course, he had been adamant that speed should only be used when required. Better not to be noticed at all. Jacot told the driver to slow down.

Jacot patted his shoulder holster. He missed his Browning 9mm pistol, a re-assuring friend over many years, even though he had fired it in anger only once, in Belfast. But it was being phased out from both the British military and intelligence services and replaced with the Austrian made Glock. A few days on his course in the south of France had been given over to bringing him up to speed with the new weapon. Paradis had detected his reluctance to change so explained in patient detail why the Glock was a better weapon; and then with great style demonstrated its capabilities. He insisted Jacot embraced the change fully, forcing him to strip and assemble his own personal weapon fifty times, half with a blind-fold on, and then fire two hundred rounds on the range. In the end Jacot came to agree. The Glock was a better weapon, lighter, more accurate and, crucially, its magazine held seventeen rounds – four more than the Browning; though with luck, he would not get involved in any situations where the difference between a thirteen and seventeen round magazine would be the difference between life and death. The Glock also had a better safety catch, inside the weapon rather than bolted on to the outside, giving a quicker reaction time and making it safer to carry made ready, with a round in the breech.

On the Périphérique, the driver picked up speed again, but it was clear he was well trained and on the ball so Jacot relaxed in the back seat and merely enjoyed the ride. He attempted conversation, but other than ascertaining that his name was Gaston, the young man gave little else away.

Jacot turned his mind to the task ahead. Liaising with the police was always tricky in England. They could be efficient, but were also often chippy. Most of them didn't like public school boys and Guards Officers weren't usually flavour of the month either. He wondered if France was any different. But then he remembered that outside Paris and the great cities, serious crime was the responsibility of the Gendarmerie Nationale – a paramilitary force whose officers were usually graduates of the École

Spéciale Militaire de St Cyr, the French Sandhurst. It was run on military lines answering to the Ministry of Defence rather than the Department of the Interior. When President Mitterrand had wanted all French police forces to switch from the traditional képi to a more American style peaked cap, the Gendarmerie Nationale had simply refused. They remained proud of their dark blue képis to this day.

There would be another advantage – the French Police were not usually resentful of the French Intelligence Services. There was none of the rivalry and failure to co-operate that disfigured so many British operations. As far as he could tell, the intelligence people in France still enjoyed a natural authority and respect.

As Jacot entered the station, he could feel it was different from the English version. It was clean, didn't smell of frying food and the gendarmes inside were immaculately turned out, and slimmer than their English counterparts. Behind the desk was a formidable and attractive female non-commissioned officer, with jet-black hair pulled back in a bun, dressed in a dark blue jersey with her képi on the desk beside her.

'Colonel Jacot?' she smiled, lifted up the counter and beckoned him to follow. 'Colonel Aumonnier is expecting you.' Jacot's mind had been focussed on Norton's tragic death since he got the news from Lady Nevinson and he was happy to be briefly distracted by the smiling lady gendarme. He followed her down the corridor, rather enjoying the highly polished floor, just like Wellington Barracks, and stealing a sly glance at his escort's pleasing figure set off to advantage by her dark blue denim trousers.

Colonel Aumonnier, who looked very old school indeed, commanded the gendarmerie station at Chartres, the seat of the prefecture of Eure-et-Loir, and an important market and ecclesiastical town.

Jacot quickly told Aumonnier all he knew about Norton and what Lady Nevinson had told him on the phone. They then climbed hurriedly into a waiting police car, a midnight blue Renault Mégane. In the front were a driver and a man introduced as the senior forensic examiner for the Beauce, the region around Chartres. The Mégane pulled away at high speed and arrived a few minutes later at the site of Norton's death. The body had been removed, but a small posy of flowers attached to a nearby tree marked the spot.

The forensic examiner took Jacot through the probable sequence of events, in French; showing him the spot where Norton was hit by the car, where he bounced, and where he ended up. In all, poor old Norton had been thrown about thirty feet. It had been dusk although visibility the previous day had been excellent, and Norton had been wearing a Day-

Glo belt round his waist and across the right shoulder, a kind of neon yellow Sam Browne belt. The car had been travelling at about 60 plus kilometres or 40 miles per hour – hitting Norton, who had been running towards it, on the right hand side of his body. A glancing, but massive and catastrophic blow.

As they stood above the ditch at the spot where Norton finally came to a halt, the examiner explained that death had been more or less instantaneous – catastrophic internal injuries from the contact, followed by a crushed skull and broken neck from bouncing along the road. The car had not slowed, and there were no signs of an emergency stop further down the road. The forensic examiner shrugged wearily: hit and run drivers were sadly the norm in some parts of the country. He almost spat out the French word for them: *chauffard*. There was no way the police could tell for sure the circumstances. It was a remote and unbusy road.

Jacot could follow what the forensic examiner said and also Aumonnier's interventions and comments in French. As far as they could tell, this looked like a tragic and typical hit and run, possibly a drunk driver or someone whose attention was not on the road – maybe the driver had been on a mobile phone or changing a CD, or fiddling with an iPod. A moment's inattention was enough in a car travelling at more than 40 mph. He was beginning to wonder why Lady N had despatched him down here – nerves about a possible connection between Norton and Brookwood, or possibly nerves about Norton's Magenta status. Maybe, it was all for good form and diplomatic niceties. And yet Aumonnier was visibly uneasy, and the forensic examiner obviously professionally excited by what he had come up with.

'It's sad, but at first it looked OK,' said Aumonnier. 'Our record here in France is getting better on road safety, but a drunk driver, or some young fool on the phone to his girlfriend… it happens. Even not stopping is not unusual – to run and hope the whole thing will go away, not to check on the victim – all this is normal enough.' He smiled wearily, and the forensic examiner shook his head.

'But it's not that simple is it, mon colonel?' said Jacot.

'No, it's not. Far from it, which is why you are here today. There is one thing we cannot work out. One tiny detail possibly wrong.'

Aumonnier turned to the forensic examiner who produced a colour photograph of Norton's left arm that he began to explain in detail, using a pencil as a pointer. There was some bruising, and the tracksuit top had been shredded at the elbow as Norton bounced along the road. On the wrist, Jacot noticed a watchstrap in the regimental colours of the Argylls: red, navy, yellow and green, attached to a plain steel Rolex – with the glass shattered. Some of the glass remained in the face of the watch. Other fragments were scattered around and beneath the wrist that lay splayed out from the body, each one numbered in red ink and arrowed by the forensic team.

Aumonnier went on, 'The problem is that nearly all the bits of the Rolex glass were found near the wrist – it looks as though the watch face shattered as Colonel Norton finally came to a stop. But one large, and two smaller fragments, were found lying on his thigh. We have tried and tried, talked and talked, but we cannot account for it. We got the people down from our criminal research centre at Rosny-sous-Bois – they cover all of the country outside the big cities and have huge experience in cases like these. They cannot explain using the laws of physics why the glass is like that.'

Jacot was puzzled, 'Is it not possible that in the violence of bouncing along the road somehow pieces of glass ended up in that way? The marked photograph shows the relevant shards only a few inches away from the rest of the glass. The momentum and forces involved in this kind of accident are significant. Or what about an animal nosing about after death?'

Aumonnier nodded, 'Yes, I know, it seems a tiny detail. We are not sure. If it had been a French provincial jogger, I think you would say, then maybe it would not seem so significant. But...'

At this point, the forensic examiner set a lightweight laptop on the bonnet of the police car. He motioned to Jacot and Aumonnier, who both moved behind him and peered intently at the screen. He pressed a button, and the computer began to show exactly what the hit and run would have looked like, in particular, how Norton's body would have bounced and finally come to a halt. It was just a computer programme, without sound, but Jacot winced at the violence of the accident. As the body tumbled, the programme recorded and indicated where the various bits of glass from Norton's Rolex had ended up and matched the bouncing to the multiple wounds and grazes on Norton's body. *Poor man. Thank God, it must have been quick.*

Right at the end of the demonstration, once the body had been still for a moment, the computer programme made Norton's left wrist move as if under its own steam. It seemed to rise from the road of its own accord, move across the body, wave almost, and then return to the road. It was an eerie movement to watch. The programme followed each piece of glass from the watch face. It was clear that only this precise movement could account for the position of the final three pieces of glass.

'Let's get in the car,' said Aumonnier. 'All three of us in the back. And then run it again. Just the last bit.' They got into the car, the forensic examiner in the middle, flanked by Jacot and Aumonnier. The peculiar post mortem wave appeared again on the screen, a farewell almost.

'You're sure it's not some kind of spasm?' said Jacot.

Aumonnier said softly, 'Dead men don't wave.' He leant forward and mimicked Norton's wrist movement. Once, and then again. 'Does it remind you of anything? We have all had it done to us. First, by our mothers and then maybe nurses. Colonel Jacot would have had it done on his first day at Aubagne.'

'Taking a pulse,' said Jacot, as it dawned on him. 'Someone took his pulse to see if he was still alive.' The examiner nodded enthusiastically.

'Or the other way of looking at it – someone took his pulse to check he was dead,' said Aumonnier, who went on to issue a series of staccato instructions into a radio microphone. The forensic examiner got back into the front seat and the car shot away.

'I'd like to see his room in the Hotel Éliane, if I may,' said Jacot.

'Of course, of course. We'll drop you there now. It's still under guard. We have done everything we need to, but use gloves.' Aumonnier glanced at Jacot's hands and smiled. 'No need, then.'

After dropping Jacot, Aumonnier had to attend a meeting with the Mayor, but suggested that he and Jacot meet for a drink an hour and a half later, opposite the cathedral. Jacot agreed. It seemed a shame to come all the way to Chartres and not visit the cathedral that was only five minutes away. But first, he had business to attend to –Aumonnier had agreed that Jacot could carry out a full search of Norton's room in the hotel – still cordoned off and under police guard.

The Hotel Éliane was clearly the smartest hotel in Chartres, dominating the impressive, ordered row of Seventeenth Century houses immediately to the north of the cathedral. Norton had chosen well. Not quite as grand as the Bishop's Palace, nevertheless, it must have belonged to an important ecclesiastic, with a taste for the finer things in life. Jacot was met by a gendarme at the front door, who hurried him through the lobby and up to the second floor where Norton had been staying.

The gendarme tore off two strips of yellow gendarmerie masking tape securing the room as a crime scene, opened the door with a key and motioned for Jacot to go inside, dangling a pair of plastic forensic gloves for him to use. When he noticed Jacot's gloved hands, he smiled and popped them back in his pocket, solemnly announcing, 'Colonel Aumonnier has left instructions that the room has been fully searched by the French Police, but you are welcome to go through it yourself. Except you must sign at the end. I will wait at the door.'

Jacot thanked him. Walking into the room, he went straight towards the full length windows with their magnificent view of the northern aspect of the cathedral – dominated by the north steeple, the taller of Chartres' two steeples but somehow to Jacot's mind the lesser, lacking the drive and yearning for the sky of its southern neighbour.

He looked out of the window for a few minutes, breathing deeply, as if gathering strength for some kind of physical and mental effort. He turned round slowly, but to the surprise of the gendarme at the door kept his eyes shut. Jacot was trying to connect with the atmosphere of the room where Norton had spent his last hours. Perhaps there was something there that would explain what happened to Norton and why. After a few minutes he opened his eyes. The gendarme quickly looked away. Dividing the room into segments Jacot made a visual inspection of each part – top to bottom and then back up again. As he finished each part, his head moved onto the next, jerking slightly – like a drill movement. At the same time his hands flexed and unflexed repeatedly as he concentrated.

His phone vibrated. A message from Aumonnier:

Just heard from the DGSI in Paris – nothing at all unusual on Colonel Norton's mobile phone. All family and friends. Except one thing that is of interest – on Friday night he uploaded your contact details and selected message – nothing typed or sent as far as our people can tell. A bientôt. Aumonnier.

He wasn't going to conduct a fingertip search; the Gendarmerie Nationale and their forensic people knew what they were doing as they had demonstrated earlier in his visit. What he wanted to do, particularly now that he knew Norton may have thought about getting in touch on Friday night, was to imagine what his last hours had been like.

The room was pleasant and well decorated in understated, if somewhat faded luxury. Prints of medieval Chartres provided most of the wall decoration – not that much was needed thanks to the view.

A single oil painting on the wall above the mini-bar provided a country house feel to the room. Aumonnier had told him that Norton seemed to have had a lot to drink on the Friday night, both from the minibar and during dinner in the hotel. *Not much of a painting,* thought Jacot. But a good subject: *The Supper at Emmaus.* Eighteenth Century by the look of it and decadent. He remembered the account from his schooldays. One of the most haunting accounts in the New Testament: two of the Apostles walking to the village of Emmaus on the third day after the Crucifixion – bump into a man on the road whom they don't recognise, '…their eyes were holden…', was the King James text. They persuade him to stay with them for supper as it's evening. When he blesses the bread and breaks it they realise it's the Risen Christ. One detail of the story Jacot had always found charming and puzzling in equal measure: as the trio reach Emmaus the unrecognised Jesus '…made as though he would have gone further…' A key set-piece Resurrection appearance by Jesus, and yet He seemed reluctant to impose Himself on these two erstwhile close companions. Jacot had always assumed it was basic good manners.

Sitting down in an armchair by the window, Jacot remembered that this was where Norton had sat that Friday night. Aumonnier said that the maid had found the silk cushion very compacted and a number of glasses and bottles from the minibar on the small table next to the chair. Jacot checked his phone again. As he looked up from the phone, he was struck by just how dominant the painting on the wall was – unmissable, unavoidable and in direct line of sight.

XIX

Cathedral of the Assumption of Our Lady, Chartres

He wanted to say a prayer and light a candle for Norton but had a little time to spare for a quick inspection of the cathedral's interior before his rendezvous with Aumonnier. A place he had visited many times over the years, it never ceased to both comfort and amaze. As he entered through the great West Door, the luminous blue light that shone into the cathedral through its stained glass windows lifted his spirits. As he walked up the nave, the light rippled, almost caressed his dark blue overcoat. He looked at the light as it moved over his arms, intensifying as it trickled onto his shiny black silk gloves. It was like walking past a brightly lit tank filled with gorgeously coloured tropical fish.

'Not a good place to be an atheist', Jacot remembered Napoleon's reaction to Chartres cathedral on a visit just after his 'coronation'. Even a man whose only religion was himself had felt the power of a thousand years of Christian devotion.

In 876 Charles the Bald, Jacot could never quite remember whether he was Charlemagne's father or grandfather, had presented the cathedral with one of the most important, precious and moving relics of the Middle Ages, the short tunic or *Chemisette* worn by the Virgin as she gave birth to Jesus. From then on, Chartres had been one of the most important places of pilgrimage in Europe. The sick, blind, maimed and disfigured flocked to the cathedral in the hope of a cure. It had been the Lourdes of its day.

The interior always seemed plainer, more austere, more impressive than any other cathedral he had visited either side of the Channel. Particularly striking was the complete absence of tombs that do so much to clutter up many English cathedrals. Jacot smiled to himself as he remembered why this was from some half-forgotten guidebook of his youth. As guardians of the *Chemisette,* the canons of the cathedral assumed for their church the status of the birthing chamber of the Virgin, a place that should be preserved pure and undefiled and not used as a place of burial. Only one tomb had ever been allowed in the cathedral; at the insistence of the King himself, a soldier who had died saving the town from the Huguenots during France's religious wars was accorded this signal honour. But the canons soon found an excuse to re-inter even such an ardent Catholic hero elsewhere.

He made a quick circuit of the interior, taking a few minutes to focus on some of the highlights, promising himself that he would return soon when he had more time to spare. Eventually, almost as if on automatic pilot, he found himself on the south side of the ambulatory where he wanted to say his prayers, beneath the most extraordinary of all Chartres' stained glass windows – the Blue Virgin, Notre-Dame de la Belle Verrière.

He looked up at her. The thick, slightly irregular glass in the Ruby background that framed her produced an oily, shimmering colour like a thin slice of Turkish delight.

She gazed quizzically down at him as she had gazed on every suppli-cant for nearly a millenium, sitting enthroned in Heaven, face on, with the Christ Child on her knee. At first sight in the gloom, it looked as though Jesus was actually sitting at her feet, reminding Jacot of stiffly posed school photographs from centuries later. Wearing a gold and jewelled crown as Queen of Heaven, adorned with French royal fleurs de lys, nat-urally, her head leant slightly to the right as if weighed down by the regalia. Her body was covered in robes of Twelfth Century Chartres Blue, bright, pale, deep and glowing all at the same time.

Six angels, two holding candles and four swinging outsize censers with athletic abandon, supported her throne. Beneath, in a series of smaller panels a depiction of her Son's first miracle, the changing of water to wine for the Wedding at Cana.

The message was spiritual but communicated by plain matter – glass, stained in a way that was only produced for a brief period before the tech-nique was lost. Legend had it that to obtain Chartres Blue the glazier added Sapphire to the mixture.

Putting a 20 Euro note in the box, he lit a candle in memory of Norton and knelt on a small cane kneeler of the uncomfortable type common to French cathedrals. Surprisingly, his knees didn't ache at all – probably the result of all that fitness training with the Legion. Removing his gloves he placed his hands together.

As was his custom, he said the Lord's Prayer first in English and then in Welsh, followed by the Collect for his regiment, the Celtic Guards. Finally, he prayed for Norton reciting in a low whisper the Collect for the Argyll and Sutherland Highlanders downloaded onto his mobile phone – a standard, slightly sentimental military prayer, but with an extraordinary line in the middle '…enable us, while loving our own country best, to enter into the fellowship of the whole human family…'

He got up from the kneeler and turned towards the nave, gazing up at the splendours. The cathedral was quiet, hushed. Then he heard the sound of violins tuning up. In the choir, a string quintet appeared to be rehearsing for a concert later that evening. He moved closer to listen. The lead violinist smiled at him as they paused to prepare the next piece, and Jacot sat down in a side pew to listen to them. The opening bars of the first movement of Mozart's String Quintet Number Three in G Minor soared through the cathedral. A devoted fan of nearly all Mozart's music – this was one piece he did not want to hear. There was a surprised and deep sadness in the music, and a sense of dread and disappointment that made it one of the least re-assuring pieces Jacot had ever heard. He never listened to it at home. Mozart had written the piece soon after the death of his beloved father, Leopold, and in the wake of a quarrel over the will with his adored sister, Nannerl.

For Mozart, G Minor seemed to be the key of despair. It was as if he had peered briefly into the abyss, that terrible sense of the futility of human existence and the vastness of the Universe – that all is not for the best. That death awaits soon, very soon – and it means extinction, total extinction, for ever. And that there is nothing more terrible, nothing more true.

There was probably a good German compound word to describe the feeling. A philosopher or psychiatrist would use words like 'existential unease' – but Jacot knew it for what it was, straightforward fear, a powerful, inescapable, claustrophobic, all-engulfing terror of death. He began to shake and gasp for breath. The flimsy wooden chair he was perched on only added to his sense of fragility. He craved something solid, desperately.

Gradually, he got a grip of himself. It seemed rude to move in the middle of the piece, even in a rehearsal, but he got up and walked quietly a few feet towards a huge column of masonry between the nave and the transept. Pushing his back against it – hard, with all the strength he could muster, there was some comfort in the cool solid stone. At least he could breathe again. He could still watch the quintet and luckily, they were so engrossed in their music that no one had looked up. But the column wasn't enough – the only remedy for these episodes, a partial and temporary remedy only, was human company and alcohol.

The mood became more joyful towards the end of the movement. Jacot applauded quietly at the end, smiling again at the First Violin as she changed the music. Slipping away into the bluish darkness, he tiptoed back towards the Blue Virgin in the south part of the ambulatory – to say good-bye.

Hell's teeth he needed a drink. By the time Aumonnier arrived in the small bar opposite the cathedral twenty minutes later, Jacot had managed two industrial strength gin and tonics. His hands had stopped shaking, and the stark terror that had nearly overwhelmed him inside the cathedral had gone, for now at least.

Ordering brandy for himself and another gin for Jacot, Aumonnier said, 'I understand from Monsieur le Directeur that you were at the same school as Monsieur Churchill? We have two streets in the town named after him. He is greatly respected here in France, still. The Second World War was won on the playing fields of Harrow, n'est-ce-pas?'

Jacot laughed. It was a charming and unexpected way to break the ice. He replied politely and gave Aumonnier a potted history of the school, ending with a short description of its unusual football game which involved both kicking and catching a big round ball – and being able to tackle anyone on the pitch, whether they had the ball or not.

Aumonnier laughed at this, 'A good lesson for life, I think.' He came across as genuinely interested in the game, asking about its rules; so Jacot went into more detail, rather enjoying the process of revisiting his boyhood.

'It was played in the Easter Term in usually foul weather on undrained pitches. At the start of a game we looked like peacocks with shirts in bright house colours. One house wore scarlet, one dark blue hoops, another canary yellow. My own house wore purple and white although the official colours were described as magenta and silver. By the end of a match we were all a uniform, muddy brown. I hate to think of the laundry bills my parents had to pay.'

'Magenta!' Aumonnier laughed, knocked back his brandy and shook Jacot lightly and gently by the hand.

'So you work for Navarre as well as the Gendarmerie Nationale?' said Jacot.

Aumonnier gave one of those peculiarly Gallic shrugs. 'I am a loyal Frenchman, but not everyone agrees on what that means these days, if they ever did.'

They drank steadily on into the evening. It was Aumonnier's turn to give Jacot a potted history – about the glories of the cathedral and especially its stained glass, removed and hidden during the war to protect it from damage and German depredation. The town had been fortunate to survive the war intact, narrowly escaping destruction at the hands of the advancing American Army. Luckily, a young artillery officer had refused to open fire on the cathedral that was being used by the *Boche* as an observation post, and who had left in a hurry soon after.

It was a common complaint that the British dwelt too much on the war, and that the French had suppressed its inconvenient memories, but as Aumonnier spoke Jacot could sense that the war and all it had meant was still very much alive in France. His account had a passion and immediacy that seemed also to underpin his own loyalties in a later age. Aumonnier had a certain idea of France.

As the sun began to go down, Aumonnier summoned Jacot's driver on his mobile and he was driven silently back to Paris. As the car accelerated away from the town, Jacot looked back at the stately silhouette of the cathedral on its modest hill looming across the fertile corn lands of the Beauce – a sign of great hope to generations of pilgrims as they approached.

Hôtel de Charost, rue du Faubourg Saint-Honoré, Paris, 8ème

The British Ambassador's Residence, the hôtel de Charost, was a palace, really, just two buildings away from the Elysée Palace, and on a similar scale. A hangover from the times when Great Britain ruled the world, it had originally belonged to a French nobleman, but had been taken over by Pauline Bonaparte, Napoleon's favourite sister. The Duke of Wellington bought it from her when he became ambassador in Paris after Napoleon's first abdication in 1814.

Jacot had never been in the building before. He had been summoned from the embassy next-door for an 'urgent' interview with the ambassador. He felt a like a young subaltern waiting to see the commanding officer – not quite sure why. But as he waited in the massive hallway, he took the opportunity to have a good close look at the most famous piece in the embassy collection – a reduced, but absolutely faithful copy of Canova's sculpture of Pauline Bonaparte. A great flirt, with raven black hair, deep blue eyes and a luscious figure, Napoleon's brother officers were always trying their luck. Napoleon, when First Consul, once caught her behind a screen in his own office – *in flagrante* with one of his generals.

Jacot found it a powerfully erotic sculpture, completely out of place next to a bust of Winston Churchill, and a huge portrait of Queen Victoria as a slightly grumpy imperial dominatrix. Pauline was shown as the goddess Venus at rest, half reclining on a chaise longue, naked, except for a sheet carefully and tantalizingly placed just a millimeter above the bikini line and covering her thighs.

Jacot noticed the hands. The left – languidly draped along a thigh and holding an apple, her prize in history's first recorded beauty contest. The right – lightly stroking a mass of curls on her head tied in a Psyche knot – usually described by art historians as 'a gesture full of seductive promise'. That was certainly one way of putting it, thought Jacot. *Come and get me now*, or whatever it would have been in her Corsican-accented French might be more accurate and to the point.

Monica Zaden came strongly into his mind. Her extraordinary face and hair dominated so much that he had never looked at her hands. Perhaps subconsciously, he didn't want her to notice his – as if that were possible. He must check them out next time. He had been pleasurably re-assured that it was Zaden who had organised the decoration and equip-ping of his flat.

He looked again at Pauline Bonaparte. Her head was slightly raised as if someone had just walked into the room. The sheet, half-heartedly pre-serving her modesty, looked hurriedly applied. If someone like her walked into the Officers' Mess of the Celtic Guards, there would be a riot. Flirtatious, hungry for luxury, men and pleasure, she nevertheless stuck by her brother, sharing his exile on Elba and funding him during the Hundred Days with the gold Wellington had paid for the house. Much of her exquisite and valuable jewellery was found in Napoleon's carriage after Waterloo. Heartbroken at Napoleon's eventual exile on St Helena, she tried desperately but unsuccessfully to join him there. Jacot approved of her loyalty.

The ambassador strode into the hallway in a battered tweed suit. Jacot shot to his feet.

'Sorry to summon you in that way. We need to have a chat – some-where private. While they are making the tea, why don't I show you the garden, Colonel? One of the glories of the Residence even though it's winter.'

'That would be very nice, sir.' Jacot followed Her Britannic Majesty's Ambassador, Sir William Goffe, through the glassed in gallery and out into the garden. Jacot could hear the sound of traffic from the avenue Gabriel.

'Best when the roses are out. About ten years ago one of my prede-cessors planted hundreds of scented roses strategically around the garden – it smells wonderful in the summer. Everything is at its best by early June when we have a bash for the Queen's Birthday, although it can be a bit hot for you chaps in uniform. I'll take you down to the gate at the bottom – it's the same one Bonaparte used to make nocturnal visits to a lady who lived in the house at the time. As you know nocturnal visits still play a large part in French political life.' The ambassador smiled. 'But I haven't really brought you here to gossip.'

'No, sir. I didn't think you had.'

'I received a diplomatic telegram about half an hour ago. It was for me personally, from the Foreign Secretary, but with an instruction to brief you as soon as possible. Hence, the abrupt summons. It has been copied to Lady Nevinson, of course, but is on close hold otherwise. It's relevant to this dreadful Colonel Norton accident. I understand you are dealing with the case. It's a full report on the other Queen's Messenger who met an accidental death a few days ago, a lady by the name of Amanda Brookwood. I had met her a few times. Ex-barrister. Lovely girl. She fell down the stairs at home just before going on the Hong Kong run. Broken neck. The decision was made to keep it quiet. Things are delicate enough as it is with the Chinese over Hong Kong. Nevertheless, it was immediately and thoroughly investigated by Scotland Yard, the forensic people and, naturally, our agencies. There is absolutely no evidence of foul play! But obviously now with Norton as well someone in the FCO has brought the various strands together in a thorough report. Let's hope Norton too was a tragic accident.'

Jacot decided to lie. 'Thank you for the briefing, sir. I have just returned from Chartres and the Gendarmerie Nationale are thinking possibly a routine hit and run. A drunk driver may have run Norton over while he was jogging and then didn't stop. I walked the route outside Chartres and had a long chat with the local forensic examiner. Poor old Norton bounced along the road for some distance.'

'How awful.' The ambassador looked shocked.

Jacot knew that the best lies always contain an element of truth so he continued, 'Chartres has a very on-the-ball pathologist who is not yet entirely satisfied – a few loose ends to clear up still.' His comment hung in the air for a few seconds. Jacot wondered if the ambassador would ask for further details.

But he avoided Jacot's gaze and changed the subject completely. 'Come in; let's have some tea.'

They returned to the house. A small table had been set up in one of the ground floor rooms. Sir William poured the tea. Looking round warily he said, *'Hédiard,* in the Place Madeleine. It's their Pondicherry Blue – infinitely superior to anything we produce. But say nothing. Drinking French tea grown in India of all places could cost me my job.' He handed Jacot a cup and then with his other hand a small plate covered in thin slices of lemon. Jacot noticed the fingers – long but sturdy, with manicured nails, the perfect half-moon cuticles slightly larger than usual. The small finger of the left-hand was adorned with a large gold signet ring worn next to a further narrow band of gold.'

'I see what you mean, Sir William, about the tea. It's different from the English style.'

'And better?'

'And better.'

'It's not the only thing they do better. Governing, for instance. None of the sort of nonsense we have gone in for recently both at home and on the other side of the Atlantic. They have an elite, well educated, well trained – to undertake the complex business of governing. Entry is open to anyone but, naturally, the spectrum of acceptable opinion among candidates is necessarily limited. Those of us engaged in the great affairs of our countries broadly understand what needs to be done and that is that. As a military man you must sympathise?'

'Of course, of course, Sir William,' said Jacot in the flattest, most non-committal tone he dared muster. He knew better than to argue openly with such a massive sense of superiority.

Sir William, sensing that Jacot wasn't on side grunted and returned to the important business in hand – the deaths of Amanda Brookwood and Gregory Norton. 'Listen, Colonel, the FCO report on Brookwood also has a section where they try to see if there are any possible connections between her and Norton…just in case, I suppose, there are any loose ends as you put it. There isn't much. They probably met at the Queen's Messenger annual summer shindig, unless one of them was on the road. Occasionally, they might have crossed over in the Club Lounge at Heathrow. There's usually an expedition to the 'Varsity Match at Twickenham in December. There are only sixteen full time and a couple of part timers – always on the road so there's not much contact.'

'Did they visit any places just before or just after each other?'

'No. London have gone through the records. Amanda Brookwood had been on the Hong Kong run quite a bit. We have to escort a lot of stuff out there to keep it away from the prying eyes of Chinese Intelligence. But Colonel Norton did mostly Europe and Latin America.'

'No connection then?'

'Look, they have plotted their work trips and there was never any crossover. The nearest they ever got to each other was when Norton did a run to the embassy at Bern, and Brookwood was in Europe at the same time. Back end of October.'

Jacot kept his voice level. 'Where in Europe?'

'Oh, the French consular run, I think. We have a big consulate in Lyon. Nice spot, you should visit.'

'Just Lyon?'

Sir William looked at a piece of paper on the table beside him. 'Actually, no. She was carrying some blank passports, and the DVD of the Queen's Speech, and went on to Strasbourg afterwards to deliver them to the bits of our EU Mission that are there. But that's still more than a hundred miles from Bern.'

'Absolutely right, sir. Sorry to press you but Lady Nevinson was insistent. Thank you so much for tea. I'll dash off a message to her now. I'll keep in touch with Chartres but as you suggest it looks like a pair of ghastly, unconnected accidents. Fate.'

Jacot was ushered out of the residence. As he walked to the gate, he got the distinct feeling that Sir William Goffe was watching him. He turned right into the rue du Faubourg Saint-Honoré walking slowly past the embassy next door. Once again, he felt he was being watched. Deciding to stick to his usual routine, he walked unhurriedly back to his flat in the rue Bonaparte looking into shop windows as he progressed.

Once home he acted quickly, pressing the speed dial for Lady Nevinson on his Magenta phone.

'Jacot, what is it?'

'Lady Nevinson, sorry to worry you, but I have just been briefed by the ambassador on the telegram you also have a copy of. Ghastly accident. No possible connection between Brookwood and Norton – blah, blah, blah. He seemed particularly anxious that I should believe him. I did not let on about the police's suspicions in Chartres – you saw my text to you. As far as Sir William is concerned we believe the two deaths to be ghastly accidents and I won't be doing much more except to ask about a few loose ends. But there is a connection and I know how we can work it out.'

'Go on', said Lady Nevinson, her voice suddenly steely. She listened without interruption. As he finished she said, 'I'll ring the police here in London. If you could do the same at your end. And Jacot, you were right to keep it from the ambassador. Remember my warning – do not, I repeat do not discuss what you have done with anyone in the embassy. Warn the people in Chartres not to say anything.' She broke the connection.

Within thirty minutes, an unmarked Special Branch car containing Richard Ingoldsby and a Metropolitan Police forensic computer analyst was on its way to Amanda Brookwood's family home in Kensington. The duty deputy commissioner at Scotland Yard had initially, and as he subsequently discovered, unwisely, questioned the urgency of the task. The laconic menace in Lady Nevinson's text to his private mobile phone quickly put him right.

At about the same time, a motorcyclist from the Gendarmerie Nationale left the station at Rue Jean Monnet in Chartres en route for the headquarters of the DGSI on the rue Nélaton near the Eiffel Tower. He had been handed a small package personally by Colonel Aumonnier with the instruction, 'As quick as humanly possible. All lights on. Go like the wind.' To a 23-year-old police *motard*, this was too good an opportunity to miss. In the streets of Chartres, he kept his speed down, but once on the motorway to Paris he decided to put his Yamaha 1300 in its blue and yellow livery through its paces. The machine had a high power to weight ratio and was said to have a top speed of over 220 kilometres per hour. But he would have to be careful.

Although not formally under anyone's command in Paris, except the ambassador, Jacot was still properly subject to a number of diplomatic and military regulations. The most bureaucratic and rigidly enforced of these involved his official-issue Glock 17 pistol. He was required to take and pass an APWT, Annual Personal Weapons Test, each year, and/or within two months of arriving at a new posting. The test had to be conducted by an authorised instructor, who then had to sign a number of certificates required in London. In Paris, the only instructor qualified on Jacot's type of weapon was John Barkstead.

Barkstead was able to supervise one part of the test in Jacot's office. Easy enough – the regulations stated that Jacot's weapon, ammunition, magazines, shoulder holster and cleaning kit should be in good working order. The inspection was followed, naturally, by a glass of Manzanilla. But the second and third parts of the test had to be conducted on a firing range. The British Embassy, despite a maze of cellars and storerooms, didn't run to such a thing; so Barkstead booked a slot at the underground range of the DGSE, the French MI6, with whom he was on very good terms.

DGSE headquarters, appropriately for an organisation run by the French Ministry of Defence, was in a barracks in Paris's dingy Twentieth Arrondissement. From the windows its employees had a depressing view of the Père Lachaise cemetery. Barkstead drove them there. The security was tight, but after a few minutes they were escorted through the courtyard to the underground range complex behind the back of the building.

It was a cavern-like enclosed space where both *longs* and *shorts*, rifles and handguns, could be fired. It wasn't busy, and Barkstead had booked a double lane off to one side where he could put Jacot through his paces. The test required by the British authorities to allow a designated and trained individual to carry a Personal Protection Weapon, on and off duty, was hardly taxing – stripping and assembling the weapon within a fairly generous time slot; and a little snap shooting from standing and kneeling positions, including both an emergency and a tactical reload. Curiously, for an infantryman Jacot had never been much of a shot with a rifle – OK, but nothing special, no matter how hard he tried. But with a Browning 9mm pistol he had been a natural, and thanks to Paradis' relentless training, he was now just as deadly with a Glock 17.

'OK Jacot, stick the weapon on the table. Strip the weapon fully and then re-assemble it. I will time you. Get ready. Go.'

He had done this hundreds of times under Paradis' austere gaze – endless repetitions. After the first couple of weeks training, the good Sergent-chef had stopped giving him press-ups when he screwed up in some way; instead he had to strip and assemble his Glock. He was good at it even with his dodgy hands; *why not show off a little?* He shut his eyes. The gloved hands moved quickly, confidently, economically – first disassembling the weapon, laying out its constituent parts in the required order; and then putting it back together again, his fingers darting between the various parts of the gun like a factory worker filling boxes of chocolates on a production line. He opened his eyes again at the end of the procedure. Barkstead had given up timing him.

'Yes, well, it's clear you have been doing quite a lot of training recently.' Barkstead smiled. 'I've got the lanes for another hour or so, what about some fun instead of the bog-standard test?'

'What do you have in mind?'

'A little exercise we put some of our people through at the Fort. I'm sure the army has something similar.'

'Why not? Be odd though, not being shouted at by the Foreign Legion.'

Barkstead explained the exercise. Jacot was to stand about thirty yards away from the left hand target with his pistol ready, but holstered, safety catch to safe. Barkstead would stand the same distance from the right hand target, in the same weapon state and stance as Jacot, except that his Glock would hold a magazine with just a single round. As Barkstead brought his arm up to fire his single round, Jacot could begin his run towards the target, firing when close enough to get good hits, a grouping of at least three shots no more than 7 inches in diameter.

At the same time, Barkstead would conduct an emergency reload, take a magazine from his pocket, insert it into the weapon, cock it to get a round into the chamber, and then fire another single, accurate shot. If Jacot could achieve his kill before Barkstead fired his second shot – he would win.

Jacot stood in his lane, legs slightly bent, gloved hands loosely at his sides. Barkstead looked over towards him and said, 'Ready.' Pulling his own Glock from the shoulder holster underneath his right arm, Barkstead fired a single shot and then began the process of reloading.

Jacot's feet didn't move. Drawing his weapon in a smooth arc, the foresight and backsight aligning perfectly, he fired: two shots into the head of the target and three into the centre of the body mass – followed as a flourish by the same into Barkstead's target. The Glock worked magically – its double action meant that the trigger did not have to be fully released to take another shot, giving better speed and accuracy.

After each shot, the gases released inside the firing chamber racked the slide of the weapon backwards, ejecting the spent shell-case, and then forwards – pushing a new round from the magazine into the firing chamber. In the process, the muzzle of the gun first flipped up above the correct firing position, and then was dragged down below it. The key to rapid, accurate shooting was not to fight the natural forces affecting the aim of the gun; but to time it right, and fire the next shot as the muzzle of the gun, on its journey between being too high and too low, was for a microsecond in the sweet spot. Jacot could do it instinctively.

Barkstead didn't bother firing his second shot. He just grinned at Jacot saying, 'What about a quick visit to Père Lachaise, and then a drink? Anyone you want to see in particular? I went to see Oscar Wilde when I was young, on a school trip to Paris – just to annoy the master in charge of us. But haven't been here since.'

'Molière. I have got Molière on the mind. Did him at school and I'm hoping to see one of his plays next week.'

'All right, Jacot. There are maps at all the entrances and signposts to the graves of the famous. It's best to go in through one of the side entrances, according to my contacts here, not the main one.' They strolled amicably along the street. 'It's a great tourist destination – Chopin and Piaf are in there somewhere, and Proust. The most popular is Jim Morrison, the American pop star. Apparently, fans still hold vigils at his grave. As you are a professional soldier it's worth pointing out that the whole place was a battlefield during the uprising of the Communards. I got a potted history over coffee when I booked the range.'

They climbed a steep set of steps leading off the street, paying the entry fee at a rustic kiosk at the top. Like many urban cemeteries it provided a refuge from the hustle and bustle of city life to all kinds of animals, particularly birds. The area was quiet, except for the distant hum of traffic and the sound of birdsong.

As they walked towards Molière's tomb, they passed other tourists, most trying to read the maps in the back of tourist guides. Barkstead made a constant stream of wry observations about the French – good ones, sometimes with an intelligence flavour. Spies were trained to be good observers, and Barkstead had a penetrating, non-Francophile understanding of the French that Jacot found amusing.

They met just a single mourner, a smartly dressed, middle-aged man standing in front of a newly-dug grave, marked temporarily with a plain wooden cross. As they approached him on the path he seemed to be deep in contemplation, but as they got closer they could hear him talking softly. They both stopped and stood still – out of respect. The man, oblivious to their presence, continued talking for a couple of minutes. Then he put two cigarettes in his mouth and lit them. Leaning forward, he placed one on the cross. After raising his hat in farewell, he walked away, drawing deeply on the remaining cigarette.

'One for the living, one for the dead,' said Barkstead.

Standing in front of Molière's imposing tomb, they said nothing. A few yards away a stonemason was working on a new headstone, spelling out the name of someone recently dead. They heard a lark twittering nearby; one long note first, and then a number of small, chirrupy notes following on – a cheery sound for a cemetery, and a suitable tribute to the great playwright himself. For all the melancholy and pity at the human condition that suffused his plays, Molière's longest and strongest note was laughter. They smiled at each other. The lark continued twittering. For a few moments the sound of the stonemason's mallet and chisel matched exactly the timing of the lark's song – one hard strike, followed by a number of smaller taps. They both shivered and turned to leave the cemetery.

'Time for that drink,' said Jacot.

21b rue Bonaparte, Paris, 6ème

The photographs had come through onto his Magenta phone, about 500 or so from Brookwood's iPhone and computer. Slightly more from Norton's, and, apparently, one of his children had just sent some additional undiscovered images through to the Cabinet Office that were on their way.

Jacot poured himself a glass of *St Romain* and put the Dean Martin DVD Paradis had given him as a farewell present into his machine.

Connecting his phone to the large Apple screen on the desk by the windows overlooking the street, he began to scroll through the photographs. Amanda Brookwood's first. She had been a good-looking woman, with a charming smile and clearly infectious laugh. Most of the photographs from the period Jacot was interested in showed happy domestic scenes. Her two teenage sons figured prominently. There was a relaxed familiarity between them and their mother. Although in their late teens, there was lots of physical contact between children and parents – hugging, arms round shoulders. The Brookwoods had been a close and happy family.

Norton's series began easily enough with an Argyll reunion in Edinburgh – they could have been publicity stills from a recruiting film from the 1950s. Plenty of kilts, moustaches and whisky. Everyone having a good time.

There were a large number of Strasbourg. Of course he had gone to Strasbourg – his run was to Berne, just an hour and a half away and the cathedral would have drawn him in. Seven showed the west front of the cathedral as Jacot expected, given his interests. There were people milling around outside the cathedral. Jacot zoomed in on the figures. None appeared to be connected in any way to Norton – no contact body language or glances picked up in a photograph. And none re-appeared, as far as he could tell, in the photographs of the interior. He ran them on the screen again. Nothing.

He looked out of the window, sipped from his glass of wine and hummed along with Dean for a few seconds, an especially languid version of *Take me in your arms, I promise to be true* – one of the few he had not heard with Paradis.

He wasn't happy that he had extracted all the information from the photographs from Strasbourg. He would ask Aumonnier to check them out. The French Police would have sophisticated face recognition software and operators specially trained in picking up patterns of movement. It was a long shot though. Norton's visit to the cathedral looked routine enough. He had been an excellent photographer even with an iPhone 5. A couple of shots of the cathedral's majestic nave showed it exactly as Jacot remembered – ablaze with prophets, saints and kings but also in parts curiously stark, almost gloomy.

There were more images showing various details of the cathedral, including one of the cathedral's glorious single steeple, all the more poignant in that its companion had never been built – a powerful, single cry to Heaven but with the sadness and regret of being a surviving twin. There was a different group of people on the viewing platform with Norton – no one from the previous photos. Again, Aumonnier's people would check it for sure, but it seemed unlikely that Norton was being followed.

The series continued with a number of shots of Strasbourg's picturesque medieval streets; and then the front of a restaurant the *Maison d'Alsace*. Jacot Googled it – a traditional Alsatian restaurant, famous for its sauerkraut, with a wood-panelled interior and open fires. It must have seemed hugely cosy on a raw October day.

The five final photographs showed the inside of the restaurant, and must have been taken by a waiter or possibly another customer. Bingo! He had been right. Three were of Amanda Brookwood beside Norton. It was clear proof that they had met up in Strasbourg – not unexpected. A perfectly natural thing to do. But weird, thought Jacot, hugely weird, that the ambassador and the official foreign office line had been that they were unlikely to have crossed over. The fourth showed the pair looking up and smiling at what was obviously the maître d'hôtel, out of shot but whose hand could be seen resting on Norton's shoulder.

There was something odd about the photograph that triggered some kind of vague alarm at the back of his mind, but maddeningly just out of conscious reach.

Jacot had foolishly assumed that looking through the photos of the dead would be a merely routine business, perhaps tinged with a little embarrassment at prying into private, now ended lives. He hadn't minded the pictures of the Argyll reunion. They were a tough and unsentimental gang. No doubt they mourned Norton as a regiment – from the photographs he appeared to have been hugely popular with his old soldiers. But old soldiers took their chances, just like young ones. They would want justice and possibly revenge. There would be mourning, but no anguish.

Brookwood's photographs had been more disturbing. She had been a doting mother – the photos of her with her teenage sons showed a close-knit family – lots of hugging and messing around. Some teenage boys wouldn't let their mothers touch them, let alone submit to the embarrassment of even a private kiss, but these two clearly adored their mother. Jacot felt like a voyeur.

Dean Martin's smooth, silky voice had begun to jar with what he was doing. He switched him off and drained his glass, pouring another straight away. This happy family had been destroyed, almost casually it seemed. Jacot did not for a moment believe that Amanda Brookwood sheltered any dark secrets, say from her previous legal career, that would lead to her murder. She and Norton must have stumbled across something, perhaps without even realising it. Something so important and dangerous that they had to be killed.

He came most days after finishing his work at the French Foreign Office, a few minutes walk away on the Quai d'Orsay, just before closing, often slipping in as they were shutting up for the day. Not that the attendants ever complained. They called him 'Monsieur le vicomte' – he was after all the eighth vicomte de Chadbannes – a title of proudly Napoleonic creation. The red ribbon of the Légion d'honneur in his lapel button inspired additional respect and courtesy. Usually, he engaged in a little civilised banter. Occasionally, he made gentle criticism of some aspect of the administration of what was to him a near holy site. Female tourists in hotpants, 'Most disrespectful to the Emperor's memory.' Discarded sweet wrappers, 'Total disregard for His Imperial Majesty's dignity in death.' Floating cobwebs that descended from the dusty dome and brushed his skin silkily, but annoyingly, as he contemplated the life and mortal remains of his hero, 'The Chamberlain of the Imperial Household would have had a fit.' He always made such complaints with old-fashioned courtesy, and they were always listened to with grace by the staff at the Invalides, though they clearly thought him an eccentric.

Sometimes, they wouldn't know he was there at all – he could have spent the whole night in the place if he had wanted. The guards were easy enough to avoid as they did their final rounds. Perhaps he would stay overnight one day – mount vigil over his hero.

Gazing at the red porphyry tomb, he found a sense of peace and fulfillment, a sense of coming home, as indeed the Emperor had done in 1840 as he was laid to rest by the banks of the Seine, in accordance with his final wishes and those of the French people. Of all the scenes of Napoleon's life he found this the most affecting – his return, at last, to Paris.

In July 1821, as Parisian newspaper boys shouted out the news of Napoleon's death on St Helena, his old soldiers wept openly in the street. Some former Imperial Guardsmen were not convinced. 'Dead, like other people? What rubbish!' The great man was indeed dead. The English hadn't lied. They should know – they poisoned him and they would not allow him to return home, burying him on St Helena with the measly honours due to a mere general officer.

But on 15th December 1840 he came home – in a heavy snow storm, big flakes that you could hardly see through – just as he had fought at Eylau, his only winter battle. Of the twenty-six Marshals of the Empire, only four were there to meet him – death or disloyalty having removed the rest.

Moncey, bearer of Frederick the Great's sword in the glittering parade to celebrate the Prussian defeat at Jena, whose finest hour came defending Paris just before the first abdication. Oudinot, commander of the Grenadier corps, wounded thirty-four times and introduced to Tsar Alexander by Napoleon as 'The Bayard of the French Army'. The other two marshals had actually been present at Eylau. Grouchy, who had charged with his dragoons there – the only marshal created during the 100 Days, whose failure to march to the sound of the guns at Waterloo sealed his master's fate. And Soult, the infantry platoon sergeant who had wanted to be a baker, defeated at Corunna, later Napoleon's chief of staff at Waterloo and, curiously, the official French representative at Queen Victoria's coronation in 1837, where he exchanged quips with his old adversary from the Peninsula, Wellington. Chadbannes smiled. *How odd life could be.*

Just four out of twenty-six, and not the most distinguished. The two bravest, Ney and Murat, had both been executed by Bourbon firing squads – Ney in Paris and Murat in his erstwhile kingdom of Naples. As a final flourish, both men refused blindfolds and insisted on giving the order to fire themselves.

Perhaps of all their virtues, Napoleon and his marshals most impressed him by their contempt for death.

Jacot looked out into the square. He had first come to Paris many years before, just after leaving school. The journey then had been less easy and less glamorous – a smelly, faded British Rail train to Folkestone, followed by a smelly, faded ferry to Calais; and then a slow, clanking journey to the Gare du Nord. On arrival, it had been love at first sight. England in the 1970s had been a dowdy, dingy place, with grim food, still obsessed with the war, always looking back. Whereas in Paris the war had been firmly locked away, and the French never stinted on the money required to keep their capital in the style to which she was accustomed.

The food was different and exciting, and perhaps most important of all, Parisiennes seemed wonderful. After ten years in all boys boarding schools, Jacot was star-struck, sitting in strategically placed cafés to watch the girls go by. It had been forty years before – half the traditional human lifespan. His wistful, dreamy, harmless nostalgia was swiftly curtailed by the ghastly, inescapable fact that half a lifetime ago meant most of those beautiful young Parisiennes would now be grandmothers.

His gaze returned to the inside of the restaurant, his mind clicking back to the present, in particular the cheese on his plate and the generous shot of golden Calvados in the glass by his side. He enjoyed his meals there. Le patron had become a chum of his, making a great fuss of his requirements, always giving him the table he wanted and making sure the waiters gave him the best and promptest service. In return, Jacot tipped generously and at weekends insisted on buying le patron a drink.

Two femmes d'un certain âge were sitting diagonally opposite Jacot, side by side on a banquette, chatting amiably together. From time to time, they both looked surreptitiously at the man opposite them, lunching alone with a book. Mainly at his face but sometimes at his gloved hands.

Jacot took his own on-the-sly glances at the good-looking pair. Perhaps he had watched them admiringly walking in the street near here all those years before. He would have struggled with chat-up lines in those days. Not any more. Despite the inconvenience and the occasional bout of pain, sometimes intense, his burned, gloved hands had always proved a useful prop, never failing to attract the attention of the opposite sex. A well-dressed and handsome Frenchman came into the restaurant, kissed both the women sitting on the banquette, and sat down at their table. It was a bitter day. Jacot noticed from the corner of his eye that the cold had mottled and discoloured the man's ungloved hands like an old-age pensioner's. Both women seemed pleased to see him, and the man seemed intimate with both, bestowing light caresses and kisses equally between the two. After a few minutes and with some help from the women his hands had returned to normal.

Jacot wondered what the relationship between them was. The scene had a curiously erotic charge. But despite the presence of the handsome Frenchman, both women still looked surreptitiously from time to at Jacot. He could sense from long experience they were looking at his hands. He took a sip of Calvados and cut a slice of Brie. He looked again at the man's hands. He always noticed hands. *Oh s…! It was obvious or bloody well should have been. There were three people at that lunch in Strasbourg.* Jacot put down a 100 Euro note, no time for change, pushed the table away, and made quickly for the exit on the Place St Sulpice. *Please God, I hope I'm in time.*

Le patron, a little worried, followed him out to ask what might be the matter – was he unwell, or horror of horrors, was there something wrong with the food? Only to see him running at speed towards the rue Bonaparte at the end of the square.

Jacot ran in the direction of his flat a few hundred yards away, black gloves pumping the air. Le patron smiled – his dignified Welsh-by-absorption customer looked a little like a demented Parisian traffic police-man.

The impressions, thoughts, and feelings experienced during his near daily visits were not random. In the same way as one of the faithful might meditate on a particular aspect of Jesus' life, or the life of an individual disciple, Chadbannes drew inspiration from particular episodes in the life of the Emperor and the men who were his military disciples – the Marshals of the Empire.

Ah, Joachim Murat, his favourite. Napoleon's brother-in-law, King of Naples, the only marshal allowed to sit in the Emperor's presence. Glittering and gallant cavalry commander, with a penchant for over the top uniforms, and the leader of the greatest cavalry charge in history – at Eylau, in the snow. He teased his English friends about the exaggerated history of their cavalry, the charges at Waterloo, and the ludicrous disaster in the Crimea – a few squadrons at most. At Eylau, Murat led ninety squadrons of the reserve cavalry.

He liked to bring into his mind what it must have been like – the actual scene on February 8th 1807. Filthy, frozen weather in East Prussia. The French infantry assault against the Russians losing direction in the snowstorm; then taken terribly in the flank by the Russian artillery, deadly, enfilading fire that the disciplined French columns could do little about. Suddenly, unbelievably, between the Russian positions and Napoleon himself, nothing, no one. The drummers and buglers in his entourage sounded *A l'Empereur*, the tune that traditionally greeted him on parade – when sounded in battle it meant the Emperor's person was in danger. The cavalrymen of the Imperial Guard and his aides de camp drew their swords ready to defend him to the death. And then, Murat arrived, his new Polish-style uniform, all extravagant gold braid and ostrich feathers, contrasted starkly with both the snow and the plain green coat of a colonel in the chasseurs that Napoleon wore in battle.

Napoleon ordered him to attack immediately – not for victory but to prevent defeat. Murat personally led the attack, carrying just a gold cane. Chasseurs, horse grenadiers, Mameluks, mounted Imperial Guardsmen – 15,000 French cavalrymen moved in perfect formation across the snow and ice. As the charge was sounded, the commander of the horse grenadiers shouted to his men some of whom flinched at the Russian musketry fire, 'Heads up, by God! Those are bullets – not turds.'

The humblest soldier in Napoleon's Army had a more exciting, glorious, dignified, and fulfilled life than a middle grade French diplomat, close to retirement. He had had dreams of an ambassadorship, but it never materialised. His family knew of his passion for the First Empire but assumed he thought as a historian. If only they knew – in reality he dreamed of military glory.

Chadbannes could hear the heavy doors being closed – it was time to go. There was another man standing nearby – he wasn't the last visitor. There was still time. Gazing down once more at the tomb, he felt calm and at peace with the world. *Sacre Bleu!* One of those silky cobwebs had dropped down from the dome and was tickling his neck. He would complain again as he left, in the strongest terms. He brought up his right hand to brush it away. There was something silky around his neck but not the gossamer silk of a spider's web – the silk of the mulberry grub, real silk, woven into a black cord of great strength.

The man who had been standing nearby was now behind Chadbannes, pulling hard with both hands on the black cord. The victim would be unconscious within a few seconds as his brain was starved of blood and oxygen. Unconsciousness would be enough. The instrument of death was not to be soft silk but hard marble. The man heaved the body onto the low parapet and tipped the legs over the side. The eighth vicomte de Chadbannes fell head first hitting the garishly coloured marble floor with a dull thud.

Jacot took off his gloves and brought up the photographs from Strasbourg onto his screen. What was now clear to him from the photographs was that the table in the *Maison d'Alsace* had been set for three. Brookwood and Norton weren't waiting for their food, as he had initially assumed, but for another person. The penny only dropped when having lunch in his restaurant du quartier: as the two attractive women with whom he had exchanged glances were joined by a man, to make a party of three.

There was a message on his Magenta phone with a large attachment, announced by a peculiarly irritating noise that went on a fraction too long for his taste. The device was filled with state-of-the-art electronics and super-advanced algorithms, designed principally to thwart the American all seeing, all knowing National Security Agency. But it only made one noise to announce the arrival of a message from another Magenta phone – a kind of strangled chicken squawk. It couldn't be changed. The message was from Lady N with a large attachment. He should have taken the blasted thing with him to lunch.

Transferring the attachment to his large screen, he opened it. There were six additional photographs discovered by Amanda Brookwood's family stored on another device – all from the restaurant in Strasbourg. Two showed the third guest, the mystery guest at the lunch. Like Norton he was a man in his early 60s, smartly dressed, possibly ex-military, possibly ex-intelligence services. Probably not British, although it was difficult to tell these days. The old barriers of understated taste and tradition had been breaking down for some time. The man was wearing a wedding ring. There was something Gallic about him.

The next three photographs were general views of the restaurant, and the final snap showed Norton looking up at a man out of shot and shaking his hand. Norton's fingers were long but not slender, the nails bitten, with some nicotine discolouration on the first two fingers of the right hand. The other man's hand was partially obscured by the handshake, but Jacot could just make out a signet ring with some kind of letter engraved on it. He zoomed in but could not make out what it was. *Very European,* thought Jacot. Probably the maître d'hôtel, or the owner of the restaurant.

He returned to the photos of the mystery third man. Given that the other two guests at the lunch were now dead, almost certainly as a result of foul play, it was important to be able to identify this individual. Perhaps he could help with the investigation.

Jacot noticed something on mystery man's lapel and hit the zoom button. The red lapel ribbon of the Légion d'honneur. The man was French. Filled with a sense of foreboding, he found it difficult to think. But he must act fast. There was no time to ring Lady Nevinson – Gilles Navarre had a Magenta phone. He would have to go straight to him, even if it turned out to be false alarm.

The phone rang and rang. Jacot heard a faint voice and the sound of fumbling. 'Monsieur le Directeur, I am sorry to bother you on a Sunday.'

'Indeed, mon colonel.' The poor man sounded as though he was in the middle of a long lunch, but then again Navarre always seemed to be eating.

Jacot explained the situation.

'No, don't worry about going through the registry of the Légion d'honneur. The man would almost certainly belong to some ministry or other. In fact, if you think about what the two English at the lunch did for a living, it is likely that this individual is a French diplomatic courier. We do not have a specific corps as you; instead, someone at the Quai d'Orsay normally does it. Sometimes, my people do it. But Strasbourg is, naturellement, in France – so it would be a routine run. I will deal with it now. Just one thing, this man, do you think he is involved in the killings Madame la Baronesse has explained to me?'

'It's possible he is the killer. He is certainly a connection. But, to be frank, he may also be a possible victim. If someone has murdered the other two at the lunch in Strasbourg then it seems to me the third person at the table might also be at risk.'

Navarre swore, a mild, cosy, domestic oath by Paradis' standards and it clearly wasn't about a lunch cut short – he understood the implications. 'I will act now. Stand by your phone and please alert Lady Nevinson.' The connection was broken abruptly.

Jacot returned to the photographs. Missing a possibly vital or deadly fact was a risk that came with the job. To be fair, he couldn't have identified the third man until the new photographs arrived, but he still regarded it as a lapse.

He drafted a short text to Lady N who would be unamused by being disturbed at Sunday lunchtime by a chicken squawk, and went back to the photographs on his computer.

His eyes and attention were completely fixed on the screen as the latest photographs scrolled automatically in front of him – ten seconds for each image – repeating again and again, in case he had missed something. After a few minutes, he realised he had. Norton's expression in the photograph of him shaking hands with the presumed maître d'hôtel wasn't quite right. He tried to think back to his lunch with Norton in Aix a few weeks before. Yes, it was the same expression he made as Jacot ordered Calvados instead of whisky. *What was it?* A mixture of disbelief and distaste. Jacot remembered now. It had been play-acting, a piece of fun laughing at a Guardsman's Continental tastes. In the photograph, the expression was the same but somehow more earnest. Something had shocked Norton at that moment. He couldn't quite believe what he was seeing.

French Intelligence worked fast in an emergency. Navarre rang back less than an hour later. 'We identified the man. Too late I am afraid. At Napoleon's Tomb. My chief-of-staff will meet you there.'

The steps down to the tomb were poorly lit, just a strip of lighting at floor level on either side, like walking down into a basement nightclub. It was a long, claustrophobic staircase, but not steep. Jacot descended into what was usually, he remembered from previous visits, a hushed area in semi-darkness. He had always despised the reverential tone of the place – appropriate for a saint or holy man but hardly for General Bonaparte. At the bottom of the stairs, silhouetted against bright scene-of-crime spotlights he could see a tall man in his late thirties. His suit was too tight for the English taste, but he was a handsome figure with a full head of slightly curly hair, worn long. With a sinking heart, Jacot realised it was Jerome Dax, chief of staff to Navarre, also colleague and friend to Zaden.

Jealousy was not a constructive emotion. He hadn't felt it for many years, but he was feeling it now. While on their previous assignment, Zaden had taken him through some of the undercover operations she had been deployed on in Paris's teeming and restive Islamist suburbs – a depressing story: posing as a cleaning lady, putting up with harsh treatment, the threat of rape ever present and the possibility of a gruesome end always in the background. Dax had been her handler, confidant, and ultimately the man who would organise her rescue, if her identity were discovered. There was a bond between them that Jacot resented. Silly, really, like being a teenager all over again.

Dax was sullen, ushering Jacot with a flick of a many-ringed hand – as if he were a waiter – to the far side of the tomb where the body lay face down. There was no sign of any blood, but the neck and both wrists were lying at unnatural angles. 'We think it is the man in the photograph you sent Monsieur Navarre. Laurent de Chadbannes, a French diplomat on the verge of retirement who had served all over the world in mainly consular roles, and who in his last assignment undertook diplomatic courier missions.'

'That makes three couriers dead – two British and now a Frenchman.'

'Two of them on French soil and all, if your late-in-the-day interpretation is accurate, apparently connected by having lunch together in

Strasbourg a few months ago, again on French soil. The Elysée is in uproar.'

Jacot refused to rise to the clear insult. He would deal with Dax professionally – laced with a dash of Foot Guards hauteur. 'Three for lunch, and now three dead. Yes, I can see it would make the politicians uncomfortable. Lady Nevinson also is most displeased. She has an important appointment in London tomorrow morning, but I expect her in Paris after that.'

'Monsieur Navarre was most specific that you should see the body. The forensic people will produce their report as quickly as possible – later today. The *flics* are suggesting that de Chadbannes was somehow tipped over the side of the viewing gallery – it's quite low as you can see. According to the staff here, he often came in just before closing time to meditate at the Emperor's tomb. He was to many the greatest of all Frenchmen.'

'I thought he was Corsican.'

Dax ignored Jacot, bounding up the stairs. Jacot followed, his eyes fixed on Dax's pale brown, Cuban-heeled shoes, and reluctantly impressed by the lightness and fluidity of his movement.

On their way out, they passed a tomb much more to Jacot's taste – that of Marshal Foch, the victorious allied commander of the Great War. At the moment of maximum danger in March 1918 with the German armies on the point of a war-winning breakthrough – Foch was appointed Generalissimo on the Western Front. From then until the end of the war the French, British, American, and Portuguese armies served under his command. Foch was a great man who fought a war because he had to – not out of choice. He hated bloodshed. Field Marshal Haig, unsurprisingly, hated him.

The side chapel in which his body rested had horizon blue stained glass – the colour of the field uniform of the ordinary French soldier – eight of which in bronze supported the Marshal of France's coffin. A more soldierly tomb than that of Bonaparte, thought Jacot.

'Monsieur Navarre has convened a CPCO to deal with events.'

'Forgive me…'

'I am sorry Colonel Jacot, you may not have heard of it: a committee of the French government at the highest level – the acronym stands for Centre de Planification et de Conduire des Opérations. The same I think as your COBRA. For your information, you understand. To attend you would have to be a French general.'

'Mr Samuel, so soon, what a delight.' Lady Nevinson was still fully dressed. 'I thought I'd have my swim after you have left.'

'Er, yes, Lady Nevinson. Well, I do have something for you.'

She thought he looked much more nervous than on his last visit. Maybe he was going to hand over some hard intelligence rather than generalised waffle. 'Don't be frightened, Mr Samuel, I'm not going to have you arrested. In any case, and just between us, I have huge sympathy for your cause. I understand that you suspect a conspiracy behind the recent deaths of two of our Queen's Messengers. You do know that we lost a second one in France – run over while jogging. To further complicate matters a French courier was found dead yesterday in Paris. We are pretty sure they are connected – through a meeting in Strasbourg in October.'

'Our people in Paris have kept me up to date, Lady Nevinson. Ironically, it has made my job easier. A single suspicious death is one thing, but now three. They are as you say connected. AFI has them all in Strasbourg together, and there was some other communication, but please I never told you that.'

'I won't say a word. But why? Why would anyone kill such harmless people – they just carry messages?'

'We don't think they were killed because of their jobs. We don't know yet. We're working on it. But the trail looks as though it's leading to terrorism.'

'Doesn't it always?'

'Not this kind of terrorism, Lady Nevinson. This is different – much more sophisticated. It's forming up in France – we have some idea where. Part of it is heading for the UK.'

'And you suggest that this kind of terrorism may have highly placed sympathisers. It seems unlikely. Frankly, it's absurd.'

He swallowed and reached into his pocket, pulling out a small piece of paper. 'It comes from Elint – so we haven't broken any codes. I don't think in this case we could even if we tried. Our people merely observed the electronic activity. It's just what is there.' He handed over the paper.

'Eleven locations in four countries – France, Germany, Belgium.' He paused and swallowed.

'That's hardly surprising. The fourth country?'

He could see in her eyes that she knew. Her interruption had been a mechanism to buy a few seconds in which to steel herself for the blow. 'The United Kingdom, or to be more accurate England. Here's the list. The number alongside each location gives the number of mobile phones and or computers involved at each place.'

Lady Nevinson took the piece of paper and read it. 'Thank you, Mr Samuel, thank you. I am in your debt.' She stared at the list as if hypnotised. Oscar Samuel slipped out of the changing booth without saying good-bye. Ingoldsby, standing sentry just outside the changing rooms, nodded as he went by.

Early morning swimmers began to enter the pool, mostly middle-aged or elderly, who swam lengths in a gentle breaststroke or lazy crawl. Ingoldsby waited for Lady Nevinson's summons, or for her to start her swim. After five minutes he became worried and knocked on the door of her booth. There was no reply, and for one ghastly moment Ingoldsby panicked, drawing his gun and pushing open the door violently.

Lady Nevinson didn't react. She was staring at a piece of paper and looked close to tears.

'Sorry, sorry, Lady Nevinson. I just got a bad feeling for a second. Sorry.'

She looked up. 'Put the gun away, Ingoldsby. And don't worry; I'm grateful that you were concerned about my safety. Perhaps you are right to be.'

'Are you all right?'

'Not really. I don't think I'm in the mood for a swim anymore. The French diplomatic messenger murdered at Napoleon's Tomb is almost certainly connected to the two we have lost – Norton and Brookwood. Three murders. If what your Mr Samuel is suggesting is accurate then I think we are beginning to get an idea of what exactly is going on. Come back to my office with me now, please, Ingoldsby.'

Ingoldsby always felt a little nervous on his rare visits to Downing Street. Lady Nevinson escorted him in via the back entrance from the Cabinet Office on Whitehall and then up to her office on the second floor, over-looking the garden.

'Tell me, Ingoldsby, what do you know about *false-flagging?*'

In military terms, the first thing that springs to my mind would be the Battle of the Bulge – German troops putting on American uniforms and that sort of thing. In political terms, the Reichstag Fire. Not invented in the Twentieth Century, the idea was first used at sea during the Napoleonic Wars and is still a legitimate and legal act of war at sea, pro-vided the false-flag is hauled down, and the true identity of the ship declared before opening fire. I seem to remember Hornblower is end-lessly hauling down false-flags.'

'Last time I was in Paris, a city you and I are going to get to know better in the next few weeks, I was given a private tour by Gilles Navarre of the avenue de l'Observatoire where Mitterrand organised a little false flag operation in 1959 – his own attempted assassination.'

'Yes, Lady Nevinson, the Observatory Affair.'

She warmed to her theme. 'Mitterrand's scheme was extraordinary for the time. But the most extraordinary thing about it was that in the end he got away with it. It should have finished him, and would finish off any modern politician anywhere in civilised Europe. In a way, he owed his escape to General de Gaulle who refused to use the affair against him in the 1965 presidential election on the grounds that one day Mitterrand probably would be president of France.'

'The cynics suggest that Mitterrand actually got the idea from de Gaulle in the first place – the theatricality of his triumphant arrival in Paris on 26 August 1944 which cemented and affirmed his leading posi-tion. In particular, the snipers inside Notre Dame – lots of bullets appar-ently fired at the general from pretty close range as he walked down the nave, but no hits. Plus conflicting accounts subsequently of who these snipers might have been. Very *grassy knoll,* if I might descend into slang for just a moment, Lady Nevinson.'

She continued, 'I've been thinking. Maybe Mitterrand getting away with it wasn't what impressed me most. It was how much more powerful such an episode would be now, in a world where few politicians have much of a backstory and where everyone appears obsessed with narrative and presentation. Say, you could rig a bogus assassination attempt by your political enemies, or better still a bogus terrorist attack on your supporters. Not only would you become something of a hero, but your political opponents would immediately become beyond the pale – people who use or support terrorism. Even more deliciously, there is no further need for wearisome, reasoned argument – your political opponents and their views become a matter for the police. If Samuel's piece of paper contains any truth bloody and sophisticated treason is about to flourish over us – golly, words from when I was at school. Shakespeare, but I can't remember which play. Any idea, Ingoldsby?'

'Familiar words, but it's gone from my memory too.'

'Jacot will know. I'll ask him. I'm weary, but it's back to Paris for me. That's where the action is going to be.'

Jacot entered Gilles Navarre's outer office and stood in front of the chief of staff's desk, behind which Dax was sitting, sharply dressed in what Jacot would describe as *the French style*, and apparently studying a document intently. His hair also appeared to be in *the French style*. Jacot stood perfectly still and made no sound. After a minute, Dax deigned to look up.

'Oui?'

Jacot was impressed – so much disdain and arrogance in such a short word. 'Colonel Jacot, Renseignements Militaire Britannique, pour Monsieur le Directeur Navarre.'

Dax looked him up and down, slowly. 'We met, I think. Yes, the man who solved the puzzle late in the day.'

Jacot was having none of it, leaned over the desk, snatched what was clearly Navarre's appointments diary and pointed to the entry with a gloved finger. 'It says – urgent meeting with UK National Security Adviser and Colonel Jacot, I think.' He turned on his heels, and before the chief of staff could intervene, knocked on the door of Navarre's office and went in, shutting the door quickly and firmly behind him – without looking back and rather pleased with the episode.

Navarre's office was splendid, decorated in First Empire style. From the double height windows you could see the Eiffel Tower looming over the end of the rue Nélaton. Jacot stood briefly to attention. 'Monsieur le Directeur, Lady Nevinson.'

It was lunchtime, and the multiple crises faced by French Intelligence meant Navarre was glued to his desk, without the spare time for his usual lengthy and expensive lunches in some of Paris's best watering holes. A small trolley had been set up next to the desk, covered in the most gorgeous looking sandwiches that he was eagerly consuming, at the same time as issuing instructions into the telephone. A large glass of red wine stood by the telephone, and he sipped from it during his conversation. In a well-upholstered chair by the window, was Lady Nevinson – tired, but looking a million dollars in navy blue silk. She was drinking a glass of champagne.

She smiled. Jacot noticed that as Navarre spoke animatedly into the phone, his eyes roved equally between the array of sandwiches and Lady Nevinson's legs. He wondered if they were having an affair. After all, as young diplomats in Saigon many years before, they had almost certainly been lovers. Lady N had almost admitted it during his last mission.

Putting down the phone, Navarre waved Jacot to a chair and pressed a plate and glass on him, gesturing to the sandwiches and the bottle of the DGSI's own red Burgundy on the trolley. Jacot helped himself. He wasn't at all surprised that Lady Nevinson was suddenly in Paris again, the epicentre of the current terrorism crisis. Navarre as well as being a personal friend ran his own Magenta network.

Navarre got up from his First Empire bureau plat – an expansive flat-topped desk with a green leather writing surface, inlaid with golden Napoleonic bees, and covered in a cascade of gilt decoration. More like a dressing table in a luxury hotel than the desk of France's top secret policeman, thought Jacot. Navarre began to pace the room, agitated and anxious.

'Mon colonel, you may be able to help me with some advice. I know, or I think I know, that a large cache of arms and explosives has just been delivered to a French provincial town a couple of hours from Paris – not a big town, just an ordinary town. It is for use throughout Europe, including the UK. The information comes from an agency that is sometimes allied to us, sometimes not. You understand?' Jacot nodded at the well-understood coded reference to the Israelis, but said nothing. Navarre continued, 'It was passed in London to Madame la Baronesse and transmitted to me by her with the originator's permission. Not officially and not necessarily with the knowledge of the people running the agency. You understand?'

'Yes, Monsieur le Directeur, perfectly.'

'Finally, in case you had not arrived there already, this intelligence also suggests that there is a connexion between the group behind these explosives and the murders of Madame Brookwood, Colonel Norton and the vicomte de Chadbannes. So, for now, simple. Find the explosives and we have a chance to get to the people behind. What do you say, mon colonel?'

'Isn't it a matter for the French police and your agency?' said Jacot. Lady Nevinson glared at him.

Navarre gave a wry smile and shrugged. 'It's not that sort of information; it's not that sort of terrorism; and to be honest we are not that sort of agency.'

'Ah, I see,' replied Jacot. Lady Nevinson rolled her eyes. 'I understand now. Yes, I have some experience of searching for arms mainly in the rural areas of Northern Ireland – South Armagh, County Fermanagh and East Tyrone.'

'Quite, quite.' Navarre retrieved a sandwich from the trolley, peered at its contents, bit into it with his large teeth and began pacing again, pausing only to take another sip of his Burgundy and smile at Nevinson. 'You see I know that the weapons have been buried somewhere near to but outside the town – but I don't know exactly where.'

Jacot had one further question, 'Will the weapons be used by the same people who hid them?'

Navarre flashed his teeth and grabbed another sandwich. They were extremely good, rare roast beef on brioche bread with just a touch of French mustard. Jacot took another one himself. 'No, we don't think so. They have been hidden so another group can use them. It's like a cut out, n'est ce pas?'

'In that case it might just be possible to find them. Have you heard of a technical intelligence term that Lady Nevinson would certainly be familiar with – *Winthropping*?'

'*Winthropping*,' he rolled the word round his mouth. No, but please go on.' He refilled Jacot's glass of Burgundy.

'Well, Winthrop was a young engineer officer with the British Army in Northern Ireland in the early, difficult years, the bad years. He ran a search team, mainly rural, in the same areas that I operated in fifteen or so years later. Searching for weapons was a bit of a hit and miss thing in those days. Sometimes, we had good intelligence, sometimes not. Sometimes, our hunches worked, sometimes not. But Winthrop had extraordinary results.' Jacot sipped from his glass. The wine was silky smooth. 'He came up trumps time and time again. At first, everyone thought he had just got lucky. He seemed to find arms caches by instinct. But, of course, he had a system. He didn't realise it fully but it was certainly a system.' Navarre looked alert. 'The beauty of it was that it was simple. Let me explain. Say, Monsieur le Directeur, you wanted to take Madame Navarre and your children on a picnic.' Navarre looked pleased. 'And say, you had a hamper prepared by *Fauchon*.'

Navarre suddenly looked a little shifty and glanced at the sandwiches. 'Fauchon make the best beef sandwiches in Paris, but it is getting more difficult to put them on "incidental expenses".' He glanced at Lady Nevinson for re-assurance.

Jacot continued, 'But your official duties meant that you could not be at the picnic at the start, and you want to surprise your family with the beautiful hamper. One thing you could do would be to hide it near their chosen location, and then give your wife instructions on how to find it.'

'I see.'

'Let's imagine that you planned your picnic at Versailles. The hamper has to be hidden well – otherwise someone might make off with it, but not so well hidden that your family would be unable to find it. What kind of instructions would you give to Madame Navarre and the children, bearing in mind that they must be simple?'

Navarre glanced at Nevinson again. He was clearly intrigued, thought Jacot. Or was he was thinking about taking Lady N on a picnic? 'Well, I would explain to her the general area the hamper would be in, then probably more specific instructions about the exact area... the third rhododendron bush along from the statue of Louis XIV or something like that.'

'Exactly. Winthrop's great insight was that we all look for hidden treasure in more or less the same way. In order to find something that has been hidden for us, we need a series of markers – a primary one to put us in the general area; and then a secondary one, possibly with some kind of discreet sign on it – a scratch on a stone in the wall, say, to guide us to the exact spot. It obviously gets a little more complicated if we are dealing with terrorists. They will be under great mental pressure, believing the police or your agents to be around every corner. They will almost certainly be in a car and want to recover their treasure at night. And they don't want to spend hours trekking over muddy fields. There are other considerations – the ground will not usually be waterlogged, and the cache or *hide* which was our technical term, has to be easy to find for a man in the know, and difficult to find for an outsider. Finally, it has to be somewhere near the action – no point in hiding stuff at the top of an inaccessible mountain. If you give me an approximate location – I'll find it for you.'

Navarre looked at him and smiled a little wearily. 'It's somewhere in the fôret de Senonches, the nearest really big forest to Paris.' Returning to his desk he unrolled a map, 'Here, about thirty kilometres west of Chartres. An old Resistance stronghold too dense and too vast for the Germans to patrol properly.'

'I'll need a bit more than that, I am afraid,' said Jacot.

'Yes, yes, mon colonel,' replied Navarre, handing over a thick A4 file. 'Our signals people have done some preliminary work even liaising with the forestry people down there. There are two crucial areas of interest – all marked on the maps.'

Lady Nevinson shifted in her chair and said, 'What about a partner and some sort of backup? I don't want him on his own.'

'The nearest person we have is Aumonnier at the Gendarmerie Nationale Station in Chartres. He will provide backup, if necessary, and one of his men will assist you. You have met, I know.'

'If I may make a suggestion,' said Jacot, 'searching for weapons is a military speciality. Perhaps someone from the French Army with recent experience in Afghanistan or North Africa would be ideal. Indeed, I understand the French Army have been training Afghans in search techniques.'

Navarre nodded. 'Well, you have just spent some time training with one of the best units we have. Let's get someone from the Légion étrangère.'

'I was thinking of Sergent-chef Paradis the man who supervised my training.'

Navarre looked doubtful, 'Is he a French citizen? Many of the sous-officiers are not, especially if they have troubles with the authorities at home. They get French citizenship when they complete their engagement. This operation must be led by someone who is already French. That would be a problem.'

'I don't think he is French by birth, but he was wounded in Afghanistan.'

Lady Nevinson stirred, 'I don't see what that has to do with it.'

'Actually, with greatest respect Madame la Baronnesse your colonel is right. He would be *Français par le sang versé* – French by spilled blood. In which case, I would have no objection and no one else could have any objection – the man is fully French. Let me not do it on the phone. We need to appear unhurried – that life is normal. I meet frequently with the French military – I think I am due at the Ministry of Defence tomorrow sometime. Paradis, the man is called, you say. Colonel, be prepared to move in forty-eight hours.'

Jacot nodded, finished his Burgundy, grabbed another sandwich and headed for the door trying to disguise his immense relief that he wouldn't have to cancel his date with Zaden the following night. Coming in as he left, was Jerome Dax whom Navarre introduced as his new chief of staff. Lady Nevinson looked up approvingly. Gilles had mentioned him to her – he had achieved great things in the Islamist infested suburbs of Paris. He was destined for the top of the DGSI and would spend a year in Navarre's private office to broaden his horizons. 'A little too political, perhaps,' was Navarre's only criticism.

Dax smiled and shook Jacot firmly by the hand, very firmly. All Gallic charm towards *les rosbifs* now he was in front of his boss. Jacot could feel the rings on the man's fingers exerting pressure on his wafer thin skin grafts. This up and coming French intelligence agent seemed to be dripping in jewellery. He was smoothly good-looking – no wonder Lady Nevinson liked him. He greeted Nevinson and then Navarre effusively. They were clearly pleased to see him.

Jacot shimmered out as quickly as he could, casting a disapproving farewell glance at the young man's suit – too shiny – his elegant hair-style – rather more than Jacot was left with these days and his rings – ghastly. His natural lifelong Francophilia briefly suspended.

Molière had worked his magic thoroughly. Both he and Monica had laughed their way through *Le Bourgeois Gentilhomme*. Lully's music, despite his earlier doubts, was charming. Jacot got most of the jokes, and when he didn't, he laughed anyway. The only difficulty was that his hands had been hurting all day. They just ached for no particular reason, and the skin grafts felt paper-thin. Occasionally, the weather set them off, particularly thunderstorms, and they seemed to be in the offing throughout the day. Even picking up his glass of champagne during the interval had hurt. But he was determined to conceal it, surreptitiously downing a mouthful of painkillers while Monica was concentrating on the play – to no avail; the source of the pain was too deep. He would just have to put up with it. Perhaps more champagne would help.

They walked from the Comédie Française through the Tuileries Gardens, across the Pont Royale to the small restaurant in the rue de l'Université, recommended to Jacot by Paradis. 'Good food,' he had said, smiling. 'A little dance floor, aussi. Très intime.' Jacot had turned quickly away to avoid Paradis' lascivious grin. But in many ways, he was a man of good taste, so why not follow up the recommendation.

As it turned out, Paradis was right. The restaurant was dark and atmospheric with, as promised, a small dance-floor at the back. As they sat down at their table, a couple were swaying to gentle and very slow music that had probably been popular in France in the 1950s. A red wax candle in an earthenware holder lit up the table. The tablecloth was heavily starched white linen, worn through in some areas, but crisp and clean. The candles from the surrounding tables flickered. All was in shadow except Monica's face – large brown eyes set below a high forehead, beneath thick dark brown hair, almost the colour of melted plain chocolate. It lay close to her head in scalloped layers, cascading down to bare shoulders. Her white teeth briefly stuck to the glossy red lipstick on her mouth as she laughed. She laughed a good deal, as Jacot regaled her with an account of his time with the Legion. Her laugh was lower than her voice, almost masculine. He had not seen her since their adventures in Cambridge and Ely, but it seemed as if their last meeting had been only earlier that day.

They were drinking ice-cold champagne. It was an effort to look away from her face even for a few seconds, but as she raised her glass Jacot looked at her hands. Long fingers, but stronger-looking than most women's, the nails cut short and unpainted, and no rings; as he expected in a woman who carried a gun. He chose a white Burgundy to go with their chicken casserole. And then back to champagne, while sharing a bowl of strawberries covered in cream, and the sweet wild strawberry liqueur, *Fraise des Bois*. The sound track continued softly throughout as they ate. The great Dean Martin appeared from time to time, as expected, much to Monica's amusement. She was in a playful mood and clearly pleased to be with him.

'Come on, mon colonel, tell me your favourite film,' she said mockingly, putting a strawberry into her mouth and then licking the sticky *Fraise des Bois* from her lips. 'I can tell a lot about a man from his favourite film.'

Jacot was torn between saying something clever, and the truth. '*Kind Hearts and Coronets*,' he said truthfully. 'It's a comedy about a man who murders his way to inheriting a dukedom and a fortune, bumping off, in various colourful ways, all the relatives who stand between him and his goal.'

She looked at him doubtfully. 'Is just one killing ever funny? How can many killings be funnier, and of his family too?' She was still. She didn't make a movement with her hands or head to back up her argument. Instead, her eyes opened wider, briefly, as if to underline her views, and then went back to their normal position. It was an unusual mannerism, thought Jacot, but bewitching and delightful.

'No, no, I assure you it's funny. One thing I didn't mention – the same famous British actor plays all the murdered relatives: uncles, great aunts, and cousins. The humour comes through because you know they are not real people, but cardboard cutouts. Also the methods of killing cannot be taken seriously: a hot air balloon shot down with a bow and arrow from an office window, a pot of caviar with a small bomb inside that goes off as some tedious military bore shoves his knife into it. It is so far removed from real life that it is safe to laugh. Trust me, it's great stuff. Very like Molière, in fact.'

She laughed. 'We will watch it together. You can explain.'

'And yours?'

'Mine?' She looked sad and shrugged. 'Mine would be *Des Hommes et des Dieux*. It's about a group of Trappist monks living in a remote spot in Algeria in the 1990s, based on a true story: how they live and pray, help the local community; and how they face death at the hands of Islamist fanatics. It sounds odd, but it's beautiful and uplifting.'

Jacot spoke softly, 'I know. I've seen it. The soundtrack gives it great power – the last supper scene as they share food and wine and prepare for abduction and death…'

'*Swan Lake* is the music to that. It's nearly unbearable but the calmness and serenity of the monks as they are about to meet the end...' Her eyes played their lovely trick of opening wider again.

They were silent, looking at the candle on their table and each other.

'OK, we have done films. You can have another one, Dan.'

Jacot warmed to the game. 'A question we always used to ask at school – who is your hero?'

'The Emperor Constantine.'

'Which one? There were many.'

'You're such a know-all.' She giggled. 'The last one, Constantine XI, who died fighting on the walls of Constantinople with his knights as it fell to the Ottomans – just a few hours after the final celebration of Mass in the Hagia Sophia. As the city fell, one account suggested that the Blessed Virgin herself was seen fighting on the ramparts. They never found his body. I think you call it, *Missing in action.*'

'In the American Army, and in Hollywood. In the British Army, the phrase is *Missing, presumed dead.* You can't be classified as such until no one has seen you for three days. It's the worst of all because it means you are almost certainly dead, but there is no body for the family to mourn and honour. Poor you, you do seem to dwell on gloomy things.'

'It's the job, I suppose. Recently, anyway. My turn. Your hero?'

Jacot smiled. 'I am sure you were briefed.'

She laughed. 'Monsieur Churchill, of course.'

'Waterloo could have been won on the playing fields of anywhere, but Churchill's defiance in 1940 owed something particular to Harrow on the Hill. Next time you are in London, I'll take you there and tell you the story. Favourite food?' he shot back.

'Strawberries,' she bit one in half, laughing. 'Et toi, cheri?'

'Corned beef sandwiches with pickle. Not fancy, delicatessen pickle – British Army-issue pickle.' Zaden made a face. 'Your turn, Monica. Favourite poem?'

'*Frère Jacques.* I suppose it's more a nursery rhyme or even a little song. But a poem also.' She hummed the tune, laughing. 'It was a sort of sound-track to my childhood. Which, before you ask, was happy. My father, who was barely in his twenties, had supported the French so he had to leave at independence. But he worked for a French bank that gave him a job in

Paris. He was lucky – "More like a posting, than exile", is how he remembers it.'

'Nothing from your Algerian and Arab heritage?'

'I'm French, and of Berber not Arab heritage as you put it – you can tell by the name. Anything with a Z in it is usually Berber. And I'm a Roman Catholic. So, my heritage is European. And your poem?'

'Me, *The Soldier,* by Rupert Brooke. "If I should die, think only this of me, that there's some corner of a foreign field that is forever England." We learned it on our first term at school. It's what every British soldier thinks about as he is about to die, or so they say.'

'And you, all those years ago?'

He smiled. 'I wasn't thinking in quite those plaque-in-the-school-chapel terms.'

'You haven't answered the question.'

'I needed a drink,' he laughed.

She didn't laugh but just looked at him for a few moments. 'OK, what is your favourite drink?' She took a long sip of champagne.

'Manzanilla. A very dry sherry made close to the sea and with a salty tang. You?'

'French girls like champagne: smart, expensive, tasty champagne, if possible. Song, your favourite song? No, not a song from your school; the briefers played me some before I came to London – like a Victorian music hall. A normal song that makes people feel things. That they dance to.'

Jacot pushed back his chair and walked over to the bar for a whispered conversation with the barman in charge of the sound system. He wanted not just a particular song, but a particular song by a particular singer. Luckily, the singer was French Canadian and well known in France. After a few seconds, the barman had found the right track. Coming back, Jacot stood formally at the table holding out his right hand. 'Mademoiselle Zaden? L'honneur est le mien.' He eased her chair away from the table and placing his hand on the small of her back, guided her gently to the empty dance floor.

The initial hiss from the speakers was followed by the gentle sound of an acoustic guitar being plucked – sparse, plain – the opening chords of *La Vie en Rose.* Followed by the husky voice of the French Canadian singer, Daniela Andrade.

Zaden had loomed large in his imagination, but in real life, she was shorter and smaller than he remembered. She leaned her head against his shoulder, the glorious mass of brown hair smelt of lemons and thyme.

Her hands slid slowly down the back of his smoking jacket, flowing gently with the nap of the thick green velvet, part adjustment, part caress. She started giggling on discovering the shoulder holster with his Glock 17.

'Lady Nevinson insists.' Jacot was relieved. She was too French to understand *Kind Hearts and Coronets* but for the important things seemed equipped with a near-British humour.

He pulled her even closer, pressing the small of her back with his gloved hands. During dinner, they had hurt, badly. Normally, during these episodes Jacot sought cold for comfort, placing them in an open fridge or around a jug full of ice. But the warmth of her skin coming strongly through the black silk of his gloves, seemed to soften away the pain. He pressed hard to absorb as much of her warmth as he could. They weren't dancing anymore, just standing still listening to the music.

They walked arm in arm along the river. Just as they turned into the rue Bonaparte it started to rain; not run-of-the-mill, everyday, northern European rain, but a downpour of tropical ferocity, announced by great flashes of lightning accompanied by raucous thunder, the sound magnified by the narrowness of the street. Everyone ran for cover, taking refuge where they could, inside a shop or underneath an awning. But Jacot and Zaden kept walking and laughing, the natural human reaction to being soaked by freezing rain entirely suspended.

Jacot realised that Monica was getting cold. He could feel her shiver from time to time. Taking off his now damp smoking jacket, he placed it over her shoulders. Smiling, she held onto him tight as they walked in step together down the street. Suddenly, she squealed and pushed Jacot into a doorway. 'The gun, the gun!'

'The gun. Of course. S....' Jacot quickly unbuckled the shoulder holster, no longer concealed by the smoking jacket, and Zaden jammed the whole apparatus into her handbag, laughing.

They strolled on together down the rue Bonaparte. Teasingly, she was determined to get his gloves off. 'I want to hold your hand, you, not some piece of silk and leather. I think we know each other well enough, mon colonel, for you to take your gloves off.'

Jacot feigned playful offence at her mocking tone, keeping his hands firmly in his pockets. The other people in the street were too occupied by the rain to notice them – just as well, they looked as though they were trying to mug each other. They skirmished affectionately for several yards. Now Jacot appeared to be pushing her forward. 'No, go ahead. I will walk just behind.'

'Why?' she asked, pouting and pretending to sulk.

'Why do you think?'

She walked ahead swinging her hips suggestively, from time to time turning round to giggle. Her blue cotton dress clung to her figure – the wet material glued to her curves, some patches almost transparent. As she turned her head sharply, droplets of water flicked off her hair onto Jacot, just a step behind. He could smell her – fresh lemons and thyme, as always. It was lovely. He looked and looked at her, hypnotised by the walking rhythm of her body. The next time she turned her head, he grabbed an arm and pulled her towards him, sliding his gloved hands onto her hips, feeling the warm, wet cotton of her dress.

She placed her hands on top of his. With a flick of each wrist, she undid the buttons on his gloves, pulling them off and dropping them to the ground. She took both his hands, gently but firmly, and pressed them to her face.

The rain continued to fall, dripping through her thick brown hair onto the red scar tissue of his hands, lightly scenting them with the smell of fresh lemons and thyme.

'Mon colonel,' Paradis' voice boomed out of the videophone. 'Sorry to be early.'

'Don't worry, come on up. Hang on, why don't you go next door and get the croissants? I have a daily order…under my own name.'

'Oui, mon colonel.'

Jacot was already dressed. He was going down to the area west of Chartres with Paradis to begin searching for the explosives, as ordered by Navarre and Nevinson.

Paradis bounded into the flat, armed with fresh croissants. Jacot gave him some strong black coffee, and they had their breakfast in companionable silence. Looking around inquisitively, Paradis admired the portrait hanging in the sitting room, CRW Nevinson's *Brigade Headquarters*, a striking rendition of a depressed, harassed looking Great War staff officer in a deep dugout. 'It's good, mon colonel. He is a desk officer and looks unhappy.' He grinned, sniffing the air looking puzzled. He then sniffed Jacot. 'It is your scent, nest-ce-pas?'

'Yes, Extract of Limes from Trumpers, the famous London shop.'

'It is good, very good.'

They drank more coffee, and afterwards at Paradis' suggestion, stripped and cleaned their weapons, both Glock 17s. Jacot's was always clean and well oiled, but Paradis was right – weapons should be cleaned every day, and before every operation. They had no idea what would face them while they *Winthropped* around the Beauce. Paradis produced another weapon, a revolver that looked similar to a .357 Magnum.

'It's a Manhurin MR73, carried by some kinds of policemen in France, the heavier type of *flic*, shall we say. It's the French version of Clint Eastwood's Magnum. Come, keep your fingers nimble. Strip her down, clean her up and then re-assemble. I will time you.'

Jacot took just under five minutes even though it was an unfamiliar weapon, his hands working perfectly. They hadn't hurt since he put his arms round Monica the night before.

'So, she left early? Les femmes do not usually smell of limes,' said

Paradis.

Jacot ignored the question, grabbed his kit and made for the door. Paradis followed, crest-fallen. It was always a risk prying into the lives of senior officers. But he had meant no harm, after all Jacot had sought his advice over a restaurant.

They walked a couple of streets west of the rue Bonaparte where for security's sake Paradis had parked the vehicle, a plain white van, the sort preferred by farmers taking their produce to market – that is everywhere in French provincial towns and on country roads. It had no rear windows, but instead, over-large wing mirrors, giving the driver and passenger a good view to the back, and a sophisticated looking audio system to which Paradis' white iPod was already attached. He grinned, handing Jacot the keys. Jacot would drive, and Paradis would navigate.

For the first few minutes Jacot said nothing, concentrating on the Parisian traffic. But as they hit the Périphérique he realised that he had been rude to Paradis. It was a breach of manners. Anyway, who was he going to discuss the whole shambles with, Lady N? Paradis and he were friends, both men of the world. 'Chef Paradis, I am sorry. Thank you for suggesting Chez Rolfe's. Just the ticket. She didn't leave early. She never came back at all. Her mobile phone rang just at the wrong moment.'

'Mon colonel, these things happen. Modern professional girls are busy. Remember your phrase, *Tel Aviv*, that your Welsh soldiers use for c'est la vie. We liked that in the sous-officiers mess. What sort of a woman are we considering? How old is she?'

'Thirty-six, I think.'

'Exactement, she is probably becoming senior in her job. What does she do? A model, an artist, a dress designer? Something glamorous. French, English, Italian? Me, I like Italian ladies.' Paradis' no nonsense approach made it sound as though they were discussing food.

'She works for the DGSI,' said Jacot.

'Tu rigoles ou quoi? What?' Paradis laughed as they hurtled down the motorway towards Chartres.

'She's a French security official.'

'But that's OK. After all, vous êtes un colonel de la garde royale Celtique.'

'That's not the problem, I think. When she got the phone call she was picked up by a DGSI man with whom she looked on very friendly, possibly intimate terms. You can tell by the body language. We had both had quite a lot to drink.'

Paradis was silent for a few seconds. 'You have a rival then?'

'He's a very good-looking rising star in the DGSI. French, at least ten to twelve years younger than me, if not more. I've done a little digging – he is heavily allied to a particular political party. Something we don't allow in England. He has got a full head of hair. And as far as I can tell, twenty per cent of his skin area was not incinerated by the Argentine Naval Air Force when he was nineteen.'

Jacot could feel Paradis looking at him. He took his eyes off the road briefly and met his stern gaze.

'Sorry.' They both laughed. He was sure Paradis knew what he was going to say, but he said it all the same. 'The burns have generally been an advantage, chef, with the ladies. They like the gloves and if they are not keen on the rest of it… it's normally too late. Or I turn the lights off.'

Paradis who would be happy to talk about his own sexual adventures all day laughed, 'Paradis prefers the lights on.'

'Me too, actually, but skin grafts can be a little off-putting. Anyway, we had had quite a lot of champagne and she looked pretty mucko-chummo with this fellow.'

'Mucko-chummo?'

'Friendly, very friendly. In this case too friendly.'

'Does he have a name?'

'Jerome Dax. He took me round the murder scene at Napoleon's tomb. He's Navarre's chief of staff – the man with the big desk in the room outside his office.'

Paradis laughed again. 'Zut, alors. Il est vraiment une couille de loup.'

'What?'

'I have seen this man in Monsieur Navarre's office. He is twice as good-looking as both of us put together, even me. He wears lovely suits and has little interest in sous-officiers in the Legion. As you say, he has lots of hair and no burns. Il va faire voir chez les Grecs.'

'Definitely an annoying individual – he was slow to remember me. But please I can't understand your Legion slang.'

'It's a standard insult, suggesting the man is a homosexual.'

'If only. He looked rather heterosexual to me and rather interested in his female colleague. Thank you, Paradis. It is off my chest. I will keep you informed of any developments. One final thing that will amuse you I think since we are talking about military slang. When, shall we say, you are expecting or hoping to make love to a woman…' Paradis grinned enthusiastically. '…And you don't.' Paradis' tone switched to a polite and merely academic interest, as if nothing similar had ever happened to him. 'Then next day you are in an army lorry or armoured personnel carrier, on a long convoy, and you are thinking of this girl. Comment on dit?'

Paradis was laughing now. 'In the Legion we would say *attraper la gaule* or *bander à cause des vibrations.'*

'Yes, chef Paradis, these things are sent to try us. French is usually a more elegant language than my own, particularly for matters of the heart. But in this case we have a much better phrase in the British Army, more expressive and succinct – *convoy cock.'*

Paradis beat the dashboard with his hands in pure pleasure. 'Magnifique, maximum magnifique. I will communicate this with the sous-officiers at Aubagne, as soon as I can,' he chuckled. *'Convoy cock,'* he repeated to make sure he had got it right. Then once more, this time trying to mimic Jacot's voice, *'Convoy cock!'*

Jacot drove on, boosted by Paradis' reaction. *Bander à cause de vibrations,* indeed. *The academics who policed the French language against creeping Anglicisation better get cracking. Convoy cock* was about to take French Army slang by storm.

'Good, mon colonel. If necessary, we will make a plan about your lady friend. Paradis will help – I have great experience of women. But now we need a plan for our task. Incidentally, I should thank you for my promotion. I am now an acting adjudant-chef – given to me just before coming to Paris. You have until now, mon colonel, addressed me as chef Paradis, or simply *chef* – both correct and you as an officier de la garde royale have always been most correct. But from now on I am *mon adjudant*, mon colonel. Just to update you – I received a full briefing. The three murders, the ground, the intelligence, everything.'

'Which was why, mon adjudant, you were in…'

'Monsieur Navarre's office. Oui, mon colonel.'

They had both conducted *map recces*, marking likely spots in the areas indicated by Navarre for explosives caches based on Winthrop's principles which Jacot had explained in great detail. Paradis had experience of searching for arms and ammunition in both Afghanistan and the Sahel, and they had come up with a remarkably similar plan of action. Their first target area was some fields and orchards that straddled a crossroads about twenty miles west of Chartres. Because of security concerns, they would have to search by night. First of all, they would get established in Chartres itself.

Jacot drove fast down the motorway. It was exhilarating and Dean Martin, as ever with Paradis, provided the background music. Jacot asked Paradis where he was staying.

'At the Gendarmerie station,' he replied.

'Look, let me get you a room in a decent hotel. Lady Nevinson handed over too many Euros for me to spend. You don't want to be stuck in a police station. Believe me, I have lived in a number in Northern

Ireland. Officious, overweight policemen and bad food.'

'Mon colonel, you are too kind. But a police station is an entirely appropriate location for a warrant officer of the Legion.'

Jacot dropped Adjudant-chef Paradis at the Gendarmerie station and then, taking care to park the van in a different street, installed himself in the Hotel Éliane. After lunch he went to bed. It was going to be a long night.

As dusk began to fall, he texted Paradis to get ready for pick-up and left the hotel by the main entrance. On his way to the car he passed the West Front of the cathedral and cast his eye over the carved figures. On his last visit he had been distracted by Norton's death and keen to get inside to say his prayers, missing the exterior splendours. The figures were extraordinary – full of zest and vigour, stylised, but somehow real and alive. Above the West Door itself was a representation of St John the Divine's vision of Christ in Glory sitting on His heavenly throne. A boy at Harrow in the 1970s would hear passages from the Bible twice a day – once in the morning at Chapel, and again in the evening at House Prayers, always in those days the King James Bible. The verse jumped into his mind; it was the sort of thing schoolboys remembered:

And he that sat was to look upon like a jasper and a sardine stone: and there was a rainbow round about the throne, in sight like unto an emerald.

No time to linger, sadly. He had to collect Paradis. The Glock 17 with a full magazine felt heavy in his shoulder holster – no round in the chamber, safety catch on.

They left Chartres on the D24 heading west for Senonches, the small town that gave its name to the surrounding forest, Jacot at the wheel. The aim of the trip was to conduct a preliminary reconnaissance of the area, to get a sense of what it would look like to an individual trying to find an explosives cache – at night – the most probable time for such activity. On both sides of the road, the landscape was flat as far as the eye could see. The setting sun lit up the fertile grain lands of the Beauce gloriously, forcing Jacot to squint through the windscreen.

Both of them checked the side mirrors to ensure that they weren't being followed. You could never be too careful in this business was Paradis' sensible rule of thumb. Paradis was keen to show his recent pupil that he practised what he preached; and Jacot was keen to show how much he had learned under Paradis' tough but encouraging stewardship.

They stopped to check their maps in the village of Digny. Afterwards, Paradis bought a couple of ham baguettes from the local café. Jacot inspected the war memorial outside the church; sadly unexceptional for a French village in recording the extraordinary number of its male inhabitants who had died in the Great War, but unusual in that the bust of a *Poilu* on the top of the memorial was in a coloured bronze as close as the sculptor could get to *bleu d'horizon* in metal. The *Poilu* held a gathered Tricolour in his arms, as if cradling a child, echoed beneath by the stark inscription, all that needed to be said, *La Commune de Digny A Ses Enfants*.

As darkness took hold, they set off again at high speed; the surrounding countryside began to feel different. They had crossed the boundary between the flat, grain growing Beauce and moved into the Perche region, dotted with ponds and thick forest. The fôret de Senonches crouched everywhere on the horizon.

It felt to Jacot like a routine enough reconnaissance at the very start of what promised to be a lengthy and dull search operation. But then looking in the mirror, Paradis stiffened, spouting a series of untranslatable Legion curses, 'We are being followed.'

Jacot checked the mirror on his side. It was difficult to tell in the dark, but for the last couple of miles since a roundabout outside the previous town, a set of car headlights had followed about two hundred yards behind. It didn't mean a tail, but it could be, and if Paradis' instincts didn't like it...

'Allez, allez. Go faster, much faster.' There was an edge to Paradis' voice.

Jacot was already rolling along at quite a pace, but put his foot on the accelerator. Their speed picked up – 80, 90,100,110 kilometres per hour. It was dark, and although the road was straight enough, Jacot had to concentrate. He could feel his heart racing.

'More, just a bit more, mon colonel.' The speedometer moved slowly up to 120 kms per hour, the engine of the humble van straining at top revolutions. Jacot was beginning to sweat. The car behind them was still there. Paradis issued his instructions. 'Next time we can't see the headlights behind us turn our lights off. Please, please do not indicate and take the next turning either left or right. Then stop. You understand? Let's hope there is no one on the side road. No, no, don't cut your speed yet. Don't worry, I will say when.'

This was hard work even with Dean Martin soothingly audible above the engine noise, hammering along at over 80 miles per hour in an antiquated and rather flimsy van, down a pitch-dark, French provincial road. He would have to identify the turning with his headlights on, at full speed it would seem, slow down drastically, cut his lights and then make the turn in the dark – hoping there were no other cars on the side road.

Paradis' eyes were fixed on the side mirror. 'OK, there are no lights. As soon as you can.'

About a hundred yards further on – ahead on the right side of the road the headlights picked out a white wall of some kind, with what looked like a minor road going off to the right. *Thank God*, at least he could see to line it up, and it meant he didn't have to cross the road. He pumped the brakes as hard as he dared, was about to put his indicator on through instinct when luckily Paradis patted his hand away from the lever. He killed the lights once he was lined up, and made the turn. The car skidded a little, but Jacot quickly corrected. It wasn't elegant, but he got the van round although he slightly clipped a hedge. They came to a stop.

His eyes fixed on the wing mirror, Paradis made his Glock ready and turned off the music. The headlights of the following car flashed by on the main road. 'I think we go back to Chartres and leave it for the night. Maybe it was nothing, but best to be sure. The road we came on is a bit obvious.' He looked at the map for a minute. 'We'll go back this way. I'll read the map.'

Jacot drove down small country roads for a few minutes, Paradis giving clear and timely directions. They emerged onto a bigger road, deserted at this time of night and were making good time back to Chartres. Paradis relaxed, turned on the music, and said he was looking forward to a nightcap back at the police station.

Jacot noticed the road dipping slightly and narrowing just before a railway bridge. He slowed down. There were no lights ahead. Nothing coming the other way. Jacot was about to accelerate through the dip underneath the bridge when he realised something was not quite right. His headlights seemed to be reflecting back at him.

He slammed the brakes on, the car skidding, Paradis swearing. He had been doing about 50 miles per hour, – so it was going to take fifty yards to stop, minimum. As the car skidded the full horror of the situation was becoming apparent to Jacot – a heavy lorry was parked across the road just the other side of the railway bridge, a white cement lorry with the word *Lafarge* written in black on the cement mixer. Even if he had wanted to avoid it or hit it side on, he couldn't. They were going in bonnet first, head on. He sensed Paradis bracing himself.

'Head back, hard,' was the last thing Jacot heard before impact. The side of the lorry seemed almost to leap up from the road and throw itself against their flimsy van. The bonnet of the van crumpled like so much kitchen foil. The windscreen shattered. They stopped. The impact had turned Dean Martin up to full volume, and *How Do You Like Your Eggs in the Morning?* blared into the darkness.

'Out the back, allons, allons.'

'Bloody seatbelt's stuck.' Paradis leaned over and cut Jacot's seatbelt with a knife.

They scrambled into the back of the van; the floor sloped steeply upwards. Kicking open the back doors, they threw themselves out onto the ground as the shooting started – automatic fire, lots of it, chewing up the front seats of their van. *The stupid bastards couldn't see.* They'd assumed the impact had either killed or incapacitated them. Jacot and Paradis ran for their lives by instinct and dived behind a stone wall. The firing stopped for a moment. So did the music. From behind their wall about thirty yards from the site of the crash they heard the doors of the cement lorry opening.

Paradis touched Jacot's arm and whispered short instructions in French – the language of command in the Legion. Jacot was used to Paradis' instructions but quickly ran it through his head in English, just to make sure. 'Two magazines each. You double tap and I will fire single shots. I will cover your re-load. After four volleys on the second magazine we go. I'll give them a couple from the Manhurin to keep their heads down. You left, me right. Watch for a cut-off. Meet up later. On my command. Do you understand?'

'Oui, mon adjudant.'

'Alors, mon colonel.'

They rose like a couple of Jacks in the Box with faulty springs – a powerful movement of the thighs and arms propelled both men upwards, so their heads and right arms were just above the top of the wall. They opened fire in the general direction of the cement lorry. Jacot, as instructed, fired two bullets each time in quick succession, the Glock making its characteristic light, metallic, clinking sound as he fired. Every third shot came from Paradis' Manhurin – a full-throated, deafening thump produced by its heavy calibre. Counting the rounds, Jacot changed magazine, his left hand with the new magazine passing the previous one in a smooth movement rehearsed many times. Paradis was firing rapidly now. They were producing sustained and accurate fire, fast. Nothing was coming back – the quick fight-back had surprised their opponents. After four final volleys they bugged out – running into the dark, desperate to get away and hide themselves in the night. Dean seemed to come alive once more crooning at top volume, *In the Cool, Cool, Cool of the Evening*. A burst of automatic fire from the lorry finally silenced him.

Jacot stayed in cover as much as possible, running along a hedge line, keeping at right angles to the road in case Paradis was correct, and there were cut-offs in place.

He wasn't sure how far he ran but eventually came to another road, dashed across it and ran up a small hill on the other side. Once at the top, where he couldn't be surprised, he threw himself down flat among some bushes and small trees and started to get his breath back. There was no more shooting – Paradis had successfully gone to ground as well. They had both pressed the alarm buttons on their phones after the ambush. Back up would be on its way.

Jacot ran through in his mind what he had been taught about ambushes at the School of Infantry long ago. Vehicle ambushes consist of three elements. A *killing zone* and two *cut-offs* – one on the way in to the killing zone, to give timely warning of the approach of the target; and, usually, one on the way out, in case the intended victims manage to drive through.

It had been professionally organised but sloppily conceived – a crucial flaw in the detail. The crux of the plan relied on the victims being either killed by the impact, or so shocked by it that they would still be in their seats to be finished off. *Belt and braces, belt and braces,* thought Jacot.

Clearly, whoever was behind it didn't mind littering the French countryside with bullets and wasn't particularly worried about hiring, or more probably, stealing a cement lorry.

After a few minutes lying low his phone vibrated with a text from Paradis:

Five out of ten – failed the course. Maximum mistake. They parked the lorry side on. No headlights on the killing zone. The Gendarmerie Nationale are on their way. Are you OK?

He texted back:

All in one piece. Could do with a drink. I'm about 700 metres south of the ambush – on a hill by a small road.

Paradis replied:

Stay down. We'll pick you up. Somebody knew we were here.

The police car dropped Jacot at his flat in the rue Bonaparte. He was tired and battered by the strenuous events of the previous night. More than that, he was appalled at the thought that his recce with Paradis had been compromised. Luckily, his hands hadn't been damaged but he had a huge bruise across his body from the seatbelt and a nasty cut on his leg from the broken glass – all fixed up in the gendarmerie station at Chartres. Lady Nevinson had summoned him for three o'clock that afternoon so plenty of time for some *Egyptian PT,* as young officers had called sleep all those years ago. It was funny that some slang always remained in the head. *Egyptian PT* was exactly what he needed. Four hours of it should be enough. He drank two huge shots of Calvados and set his alarm clock.

On waking, he took a long shower, successfully keeping his bandaged leg dry by covering it in a roll of kitchen wrap. He sprayed himself in Trumper's West Indian Extract of Limes – the strong and distinctive aromatic smell lifting his spirits and soothing his muscles, although it stung like hell on the bruise.

He decided to walk to the embassy, or rather the British Ambassador's Residence next door, where Lady N seemed to have established a temporary HQ. There must be something really nasty behind the deaths of the three diplomatic messengers to keep her in Paris. It only took half an hour, if he kept his head down and avoided being distracted by the sights of the City of Light.

'Colonel Jacot?'

'Yes, sorry, drifted off there for a moment. It was a long night.'

'Lady Nevinson is waiting for you in the Ambassador's study.'

The uniformed footman led him up the cantilevered staircase to the left of the hall and on to the first floor, a piano nobile, where the major rooms of the house were to be found. A long corridor ran the length of the house with rooms overlooking the Residence's glorious gardens on the left, and those with the more prosaic view of the courtyard on the right.

The footman opened a door on the right and showed Jacot into a room with floor to ceiling bookcases.

This afternoon she was in a green silk dress, *eau de nil* was the technical term. It didn't suit her – she had the wrong colouring, thought Jacot. Still, she looked fabulous and was clearly in a good mood. Annoyingly, she didn't seem at all put out by the difficulties and dangers of the previous night. Waving him to a chair, she then, to his surprise, placed a cup of coffee on the small table next to him and half-patted his arm. These were signs for her of real concern, and Jacot was mollified. Sitting down at the desk, she read from a report on the previous night's incident.

'Nothing, absolutely nothing, from the two vans or the cement lorry.'

'Two vans as well. All we saw was the cement lorry. We left rather hurriedly, as you might imagine, Lady N.'

'Two vans – one about a hundred yards to the front; the other the same distance behind. Look, the DGSI kindly sent over this smart diagram and some photos.' She handed Jacot the plan of the incident prepared by the police.

'The vans were *cut-offs* in the jargon, Lady N. If you survive the first contact, as we did, the cut-offs finish you off as you are trying to escape, but they positioned them incorrectly. It was a fairly Janet and John mistake to make.'

'Lucky for you I'd say,' she smiled. 'Lots of detail here. Vans hired last week near Metz by two French nationals holding Euro driving licences that check out on the computer, but don't seem to belong to real people. Paid for by a credit card from a Luxembourg bank, not unusual in eastern France. Looks as if it was cloned rather than stolen – transaction takes place in the first half of the month with weeks to run before a statement is due. CCTV cameras outside the rental office show nothing – there was a fault that morning. All in all, that part of it was a professional job.'

She skipped a few paragraphs and then continued, 'Rear van set on fire in situ after you and Paradis made your escape. The cement lorry was pretty much unscathed except for the windows. Well, every single window. Looks as though you and Paradis managed to give as good as you got. The front van probably undamaged. Some blood on the road – Rhesus O Positive – but not too much, no haemorrhaging or anything like that. We believe they put the injured individual in the front van and then took off. '

Jacot sipped his coffee.

'I don't want to upset you, Colonel, but you and your Foreign Legion friend were merely involved in a road-traffic accident last night, officially that is. If you were to return to the scene today you would find nothing – maybe some burn marks in the grass.'

'I don't understand. It was brazen attempt to bump us off.'

'Much as I like you a random attempt to "bump you off" as you put it would not normally be a sufficient reason for me to leave London and set up shop here.'

'I see. This is becoming bigger and more off-balance-sheet by the minute. How's the ambassador taking it?'

'He left this morning. The Foreign Secretary is holding a conference at Chevening his country residence next week. He has kindly and suddenly brought it forward for some pre-consultation. It's followed by another conference at some ghastly FCO think tank. All our ambassadors to EU countries will be attending. I doubt they will be doing any thinking, just foaming at the mouth about events on both sides of the Atlantic. Anyway, going back to the man you or Paradis shot…'

'Paradis, I think should have the honour. He's a better shot than me.'

'We think he was taken to Brussels – vanished into a private clinic.'

'But surely, Lady N, the Belgian authorities…'

'Why on earth would we want to let the Belgian authorities know we know? Sorry, I sound that like that mad American who worked for President Bush. What makes you think that the Belgian authorities would want to do anything…other than tell their friends? I'm afraid this is all leading to the "wow finish" – an operation that both Gilles and I thought was watertight, isn't.' She paused, lowering her voice. 'The fact that it isn't is now more important than solving the three murders or interdicting those explosives, although we will still have to do that – or rather you and Paradis will still have to do that. Do you understand what I'm saying? I can hardly bring myself to put it so plainly, but there it is.'

She tidied up the report, slipped it back into its folder and laid it on her desk. 'It's early, but I think I owe you a drink. Calvados, isn't it? Good for the nerves. I think the ambassador has a very smart version. Then I have more to tell you. Nothing for me just yet.' She leaned back from the desk and watched him.

He got up, moved to the drinks tray beside the desk, and had a look at what there was available. Her Majesty's temporarily absent Ambassador had some very smart Calvados indeed – three different types. Jacot liked the look of a near caramel-coloured version in a bottle containing a *pomme prisonnier* – the presence of an apple inside the bottle always enhanced the flavour. He poured himself a large slug and sat down again.

'Okay. Let's keep going. I've got some pain-killers if you need them.'

'The Calvados will work for now, Lady N. But thank you.'

'There's another catch. We had planned to get the hardware you are going to need from the French. But Navarre is nervous about any further compromise – their political system as you may have noticed is in uproar. The possibility of another leak would be too great. We'll have to get them from someone we know we can trust. Ingoldsby is rounding up the weapons and ammunition you and Paradis will need.'

'Just me and Paradis?'

'Just you and Paradis. The Foreign Legion has been told that Paradis was hurt last night in your car accident and will need to stay in Paris for a while. All the official military medical paperwork has been properly filed, in case anyone starts asking questions. You might want to chat to him before you fly to London early tomorrow.'

'I'm going to London?'

'A plane will fly you to London at eight in the morning from Villacoublay – the French airbase outside Paris – to RAF Northolt. Cars are arranged. You are to meet Ingoldsby – have a decent lunch or something. This could be a long haul, and you look a bit shaken up. He will take you back to Northolt with the weapons. The plane will fly you back tomorrow evening with the weapons in a diplomatic pouch. They will be stored here. Take what you need when you and Paradis deploy back to the forest. Given what happened last night you'll need more than your sidearms. While you are in London Paradis is getting further briefings from Navarre's people.'

'You are too kind, Lady N.'

'Please, please, you've got to find the explosives and soon. You've got a few days at most. Winthrop must come good. Once we have a fix on where they are we can start planning to hit back.'

'As you wish, Lady N.' Jacot noticed the police file on her desk and next to it a tube of expensive looking paper tied in a red ribbon. She smiled at him, and it seemed the time for small talk while he drank his Calvados. 'Have you been given an honorary degree?'

For a moment she seemed puzzled. 'No, no. One lives in hope. It's a suggested design for my coat of arms. As you know the prime minister insisted I took a peerage, but I never got round to the fun bits like a coat of arms.' She unravelled the parchment and showed him. 'It's beautiful, but I'm not sure it's quite right yet. I was going to fax it back to the College of Arms with some suggested changes.' She laughed. 'You know what girls are like – it's like choosing new curtains for your house.'

Jacot looked at the parchment. He was expecting something gaudy but beneath her full title, Baroness Nevinson of Church Stretton in the Marcher County of Shropshire, was a plain shield with a single ever-open eye in gold bang in the centre. Beneath was a motto in English, *Scatter all our enemies*. He rather approved and said so. 'The motto is especially fine,

Lady N.'

'Thank you.'

'Although the phrase is familiar, I'm embarrassed to admit that I can't quite place it.'

'Unusual for you, Colonel. "He made the winds and waters rise to scatter all my enemies" – Elizabeth I on the Armada.'

'Ingoldsby would approve. Might I redeem my ignorance with an apposite quotation from one of her courtiers, Sir John Harington?

Treason doth never prosper: what's the reason?
For if it prosper, none dare call it treason.'

Lady Nevinson suddenly looked her age. A wave of tiredness washed over her. 'I think that puts it rather well.'

Jacot continued admiring the parchment and quickly changed the subject. 'Who put all this together for you?'

'Sir Peregrine Pelham, Beaumaris King of Arms – he is responsible for Wales, parts of the West and what they still call *The Marcher Counties* – Cheshire, and Shropshire where I originally hail from. Have you heard of him?'

He sipped at his Calvados – better not to drink it too fast in front of her. 'We were at the same school and played football together, I seem to remember.'

'Football? You surprise me, Colonel.'

It wasn't that sort of football but best not put the good lady right. He took another sip of the Calvados – wonderful stuff, well above his pay grade. Something was stirring at the back of his mind – *something in the photographs from Strasbourg or was it something from tea with the ambassador?*

Jacot asked the government driver who met him at RAF Northolt to drive straight to the College of Arms in the shadow of St Paul's Cathedral. He had never had cause to go there before but knew its near neighbour, St Benet's, Paul's Wharf, well. It was the only church in London offering Divine Service in Welsh. From time to time while living in London, he shook off his West End habits and came here for Evensong, his favourite service. There was always something about this quiet, restrained, reflective act of worship that he found hugely re-assuring. The effect was magnified by the words of the traditional Anglican Liturgy – but not in Elizabethan English – instead in Welsh, most of which he could understand. At the time Jesus walked the Earth speaking Aramaic, most Britons spoke a form of Welsh – so they said, particularly after any victory at the Millennium Stadium over the English. To top it all, St Benet's was a Wren church rebuilt by him on the site of a medieval predecessor consumed in the Great Fire.

Early for his appointment, he went inside for a few moments' contemplation and prayer. The interior was a fine example of Wren's best work: light, airy, elegant, uncluttered and above all untouched in the Blitz. Most of the original fittings were still in place. The banners of the bigwigs of the College of Arms, whose official church it was as well, added a dash of chivalric colour. He knelt and said the Lord's Prayer in Welsh. There was no one else in the church and so he spoke aloud, 'Ein Tad, yr hwnyn y nefoedd....' When he had finished he popped a twenty-pound note in the collection box as he went out. He strode up the hill and across the road to the College of Arms.

An ex-military looking usher in a cherry-coloured uniform escorted him to an office on the first floor. Perhaps living a life against a background of gold and silver, and the gorgeous, rich colours of heraldry, made the man immune to the extraordinary colour of his uniform – very cherry. Jacot wondered if he could get away with a smoking jacket of the same violent colour when he next went to his tailor. The usher knocked at a highly polished and venerably aged oak door, emblazoned with the words *Beaumaris King of Arms*, and five red and gold Welsh Dragons grouped in ascending size, smallest on the left tallest on the right. A voice sounded, the usher opened the door and Jacot found himself in the presence of Beaumaris King of Arms.

'Peregrine, how nice to see you. Just one thing I should make clear, Lady Nevinson doesn't know I'm here, and I would be grateful if you didn't mention my visit to her.'

'Oh God, Jacot, not you as well. We don't sell them or help people buy them – we simply handle the procedure once Her Majesty or the prime minister has decided to give you one. Still, I'm not sure it's going to be easy for a mere colonel, even in the Celtic Guards.'

'What on earth are you talking about, Perry?' said Jacot.

'You don't want a title of some sort? Oh, thank God. Sorry. The first thing people do who are on the make is swear you to secrecy – in case it doesn't come to pass. It used to be marvellous working here; even the rough diamonds one dealt with were only after a coat of arms for their masonic lodge or obscure professional association. Or a town, even. I once did a wonderful design for a Canadian town somewhere in the Arctic Circle. Consisted mainly of Grizzly Bears in various poses against a background of ice. Huge fee and they were hugely pleased. These days, though... I just can't describe some of the people who come to me.... Would you like a drink, old boy?'

They reminisced about their days at school, drank gin, and even at one point sang a few verses of *Forty Years On*, Harrow's most famous song, in honour of the fact that they had left the school nearly forty years before.

'Actually, when I'm not involved in heraldic stuff, and it's not as grim as I made out, I am writing a history of Harrow Football. We were both rather good, if I remember rightly. Much more fun than that other, oafish, Midlands game. Played by physical freaks these days. The England team look like Bulgarian weight lifters of old – and about as nimble on their feet. The best thing about the World Cup was that lovely song. But don't let me bang on. Pleasure though it is – why, exactly, are you here?'

Jacot enjoyed watching Rugby and had enjoyed playing it in his youth. But he smiled. Most of what Peregrine Pelham said was for effect, even as a schoolboy. Jacot also enjoyed Harrow Football and from time to time ventured up to the Hill to visit a string of godsons and nephews who passed through the school. Occasionally, he even turned out for the Old Boys' team. It was a game that suited his injuries – not much handling of the ball, and by long established tradition it had always been permissible to wear gloves. If you fell or were pushed over, the thick mud of the pitches cushioned the impact. 'I am here on a matter of national security, and I need your help. The reason I don't want Lady Nevinson to know is that like your failed candidates for peerages and knighthoods I may end up looking stupid if I'm on the wrong track.'

'Go on.' Sir Peregrine Pelham looked serious. 'Whatever you need, of course. Peering into our records can be a bit tricky, but I am sure I can arrange for it to be done discreetly.'

'You may be surprised. I don't want to snoop into the embarrassing social climbing secrets of the great and the good. Nor am I interested in the process of how people get titles. What I really need is some advice, a verdict even, involving your core skill – heraldry. I want you to look at a photograph.' Jacot took an A5 sized photograph from his inner jacket pocket – a blown up version of the crucial lunch at Strasbourg.

As Jacot drew out the photograph, Pelham caught sight of the shoulder holster. 'Blimey, armed in London. I knew you worked for Lady Nevinson, and that there had been some trouble recently. Lots of chat at Cambridge High Tables. But guns….it must be serious.'

'It is serious, Perry. I need you to keep absolutely quiet about this – schtum. Don't worry, I don't approve of people who seek professional advice without paying for it. A fee of a thousand guineas was paid into your business account this morning with the reference *Advice to Cabinet Office*. I'm afraid it's taxable.'

Pelham laughed. Jacot unfolded the A5 photograph, arranged the right way up for Pelham's professional inspection, and pushed it across the desk. Pelham took a pair of reading glasses from a case on the desk and put them on. He looked at the photograph for what seemed to Jacot like a long time. Looking up he said, 'No, that's not quite right,' and pushed the photograph back across the desk. 'You were looking at it the wrong way up – heraldically speaking, of course.'

'Ah, Jacot.'

He looked up and saw Richard Ingoldsby, one of the most non-descript men to look at he had ever seen. He wasn't shabby or down at heel, in fact he was smartly dressed, but in a way that was instantly for-gettable. His face was normal enough, but a few minutes after saying good-bye you would be pushed to come up with an accurate description of it. Ideal as an extra in a film – you could use him again and again and no one would notice. Ideal also as a man who followed, stalked was a better word, his prey. He was Lady Nevinson's man at MI5.

Ingoldsby sat down at the table; like all who knew Jacot well, he avoided shaking hands, instead half-patting him on the shoulder.

'How nice to see you, Ingoldsby. I am already tucking into a cocktail – a wonderful thing called a French 75 after their Great War artillery piece. Gin, lemon juice and fizzy water. And then, some Muscadet, the Chablis is a little too expensive for these straitened times.'

'Yes, yes, absolutely. A French 75, why not? Didn't know military intel-ligence patronised this establishment, although it is always convenient for us at Albert Embankment.'

Jacot smiled and waved his hand at the mural by Rex Whistler that dominated the restaurant, almost hemming in their corner table. 'Rex Whistler was an officer in my regiment, and I always feel at home here. Poor man. Could have been a war artist but insisted he wanted to fight. Killed by a mortar outside Caen, his tank battalion's first casualty of the Normandy campaign. Rotten luck.'

Ingoldsby tucked into his French 75. 'Actually, I did know that Whistler was one of yours,' he said, looking round. 'Haven't been here for ages, it's been restored well. The mural is glorious, the greenest thing I have ever seen indoors. Emerald green, and that peculiar colour like sage leaves. It's like having lunch in a wood.'

Jacot warmed to the theme, 'It's called, *The Pursuit of Rare Meats,* and is all about a group of seven, including a princess, a colonel and a pantry boy who set out in search of a good lunch. The regiment had so many of his paintings it's like being back in the mess.'

Ingoldsby finished his 75 and moved onto the Muscadet. 'This wine is rather good. Used to drink a lot of it when I was first starting out in the service.' He looked round the room again, but not this time to admire the mural. It was early for lunch, and luckily no one was sitting near them. 'I got a text yesterday, a Magenta text from Lady Nevinson. Most secret, highest priority. Don't get them very often, even less often with a shopping list attached. Tell me, Dan, what exactly is going on?'

Their smoked salmon and capers arrived, along with another carafe of Muscadet. Jacot took Ingoldsby through the weapon searching operation he would carry out with Paradis, explaining that in Navarre's words 'an aggressive security and intelligence operation' would kick off once the bombs were located. The DGSI expected them to be moved soon, probably to the headquarters of the terrorist group where they would be prepared for immediate use.

Ingoldsby asked a few questions and told a story about his days as an agent handler in West Belfast. They were both having lemon sole that came with a fritter made from vegetables easily available during the Second World War. It was delicious, and there was a pause in the conversation as they concentrated on the food. 'What sort of political extremists are we talking about?'

'Well, not our bearded chums, certainly,' replied Jacot.

'Who else is there?'

'Lots of people, as you know, Ingoldsby, haven't gone away. These guys are certainly for real. A splendidly diverse group: some kind of Eastern European hybrid, part neo-Nazi, part organised crime, part plain thuggishness, even some Kosovars – just as prepared to kill for money as ideology. There have always been individuals or even whole agencies prepared to employ these kinds of people – deniable operations. We both know that our dirty work, the very dirty work, isn't handled on our behalf by men and women in suits who go to Vauxhall Cross or your office just along the Embankment here to get their orders.'

'Yes, well obviously you are right. All kinds of frightful people emerging from the East. Makes you nostalgic for the Berlin Wall. But these matters are tightly controlled.'

Jacot briefly explained what had been troubling him.

'Oh, for God's sake, please, no,' Ingoldsby wailed and drank an entire glass of Muscadet. 'I had been praying that what you and Lady Nevinson are onto was a matter for G Branch. Happy to help with the hardware, naturally, but something for them, not me. You know their responsibilities – "counter-terrorism international, except Irish". But if what you say is true, this is a D Branch matter. It seemed to rally him. 'But don't worry, treason is my special subject. Who knows?'

'Just you, for now. It came to me last night when I was admiring Lady N's heraldic stuff to do with her peerage, but I didn't say anything. Anyway, I made a quick visit to the College of Arms an hour ago with a photograph of the fatal lunch at Strasbourg. My heraldic chum made everything clear. The original tip off came from your friend Mr Samuel. Put us on the trail, but it was not specific. This nails it. I'll tell Lady N tonight, and Paradis. The poor man was furious after we got hit outside Chartres. He'll understand why now.'

'And are you sure?'

'Ingoldsby, you are a professional spy. Are we ever sure of anything?'

'No, no, of course not. Sorry. It's just too depressing if it's true. The odd traitor is always a risk. Keeps chaps like me gainfully employed, but what you seem to be suggesting is institutional treason. What the hell, let's have another carafe, but Jacot – let's enjoy it slowly.'

'We need to identify these traitors, and as you say it's your special subject. There have always been people like you, Ingoldsby, flushing these bastards out.'

Ingoldsby thought Jacot looked distracted and tense. Maybe it was a reaction to the incident outside Chartres. Lady Nevinson's text hadn't been quite as terse as he suggested to Jacot – she had outlined what had happened. He wondered how many French 75s had been consumed before his arrival. He decided to lighten the conversation.

'The powers that be aren't too keen on the term traitor these days – something that happens in Shakespeare plays, not in real life. I suppose we have our origins in the turbulence of the Elizabethan era, the first time we came under threat from foreign intelligence services, or rather individuals in the service of foreign kings and potentates. We used to read about Walsingham and the Elizabethan spymasters for historical amusement: the atmosphere in which they operated – the loyalty of many Englishmen lavished secretly on the Pope or the King of Spain rather than Good Queen Bess – seemed a historical anomaly as long gone and weird as bear-baiting, or frost fairs on the Thames. But these days…'

Jacot ignored the new theme. Looking round at the magnificent mural he said, 'I visited his grave. Always gets to me, military graves and their inscriptions. There's one in the same graveyard as Rex that stays in the mind. You know, lots of great bits from the Bible in English and Welsh and the Latin poets – trying to sweeten the pill. The next of kin could choose. A few rows away from Rex the grave of a young Guardsman, aged 17, said simply: *Much missed by his Mam and all at home.* Rex's parents took the traditional route with a moving, startling Biblical quotation. Unusual:

And they shall be mine, saith the Lord of hosts, in that day when I make up my jewels.'

Ingoldsby nodded and dredged up his residual knowledge from school and university days. 'Malachi, isn't it? The last and dullest of the Old Testament prophets. It gets darker and more frightening towards the end. I can only remember, to be honest, because in most Bibles he comes on the page before St Matthew. What a beautiful thing to put on your son's grave.'

'Yes, and you are right, it gets darker and frankly more to my taste towards the end:

And they shall be mine, saith the Lord of hosts, in that day when I make up my jewels; and I will spare them, as man spareth his own son that serveth him. Then shall ye return, and discern between the righteous and the wicked, between him that serveth God and him that serveth him not.'

Jacot's eyes flashed as he reached the climax:

'For, behold, the day cometh, that shall burn as an oven; and all the proud, yea, and all that do wickedly, shall be stubble: and the day that cometh shall burn them up, saith the Lord of hosts, that it shall leave them neither root nor branch.'

Ingoldsby nodded a little nervously. 'You are right – it is my job to discern between the righteous and the wicked, but I just hope in this case you are very much wrong.' Jacot was clearly in a strange mood. He was known to be devout. But the glint in the eye wasn't religious; it was a glimpse of hatred – never a useful emotion in intelligence work. But then again he was a Guardsman, not a member of the Security Service. Ingoldsby's phone buzzed and he looked at the message. 'The kit's all packed. Will you please check it all at the office? I'll accompany you back to Northolt.'

Ingoldsby had always liked him, but he was definitely too close to Lady Nevinson. Some said he had never been quite himself again after being blown up all those years ago.

'It's a General Purpose Machine Gun, firing 7.62mm in disintegrating link belts of 100. Effective range anything out to 1600 metres. Cyclical rate of fire 850 rounds per minute.' Jacot was proudly showing off the weapons he had brought back from England – stored in the hôtel de Charost's cellars.

Paradis was impressed. 'It is a thing of beauty, nest-ce pas?' He lay down on the floor, extended the tripod and tucked the weapon into his shoulder, checking the feel of it. 'But we won't need it in the next few days. It's just for the operation, right, mon colonel?'

'Absolutely, mon adjudant; for that special occasion we have a thousand rounds of four-bit as we call it – every fourth bullet tracer.' He pointed to the green plastic ammunition boxes. 'Tupperware for real men.'

Paradis grinned, 'Just in case. But for now a *long* as you say, each, will be enough.' He picked up one of a pair of Heckler and Koch MP5s that Ingoldsby had 'borrowed' from the Metropolitan Police. 'If only we had had these earlier in the week we could have chewed up those bastards in their ambush.'

'We didn't do too badly with what we had, I seem to remember. In any case, by cocking up the ambush they left a trail that has helped Lady Nevinson and Monsieur Navarre. And, er, mon adjudant, we have discovered, we think, who gave us away.' Jacot explained the visit to the College of Arms and the photograph from Strasbourg. He thought it best to do it before they were on the move to Chartres.

Paradis exploded into a volley of curses. Just as well they were in the cellars, thought Jacot. The curses kept coming eventually tailing off into the comparatively civilised, 'J'en ai vraiment plein les coquilles.'

'Quite.' Jacot replied calmly. 'But think, mon adjudant, if we can find the explosives we can roll the whole network up. Not just a bunch of terrorists, although that in itself will be a pleasure, but the people behind them. Remember we think they organised the murders – my colonel friend, the French diplomat and Madame Brookwood. Three families bereaved. They're working on the plan now.'

They loaded up the car in the courtyard of the hôtel de Charost hidden from the street by the impressive gatehouse with its bombproof gates. Jacot was nervous. Navarre's people had given them the very latest and now reasonably precise intelligence. Paradis and he knew what they were doing. They would find the explosives, but would they find them in time?

Once they had got the hang of the target area, some twenty miles west of Chartres, by driving around it, Paradis and Jacot agreed to split the most likely locations between them, and search on foot, individually. The DGSI had identified two specific areas and briefed Paradis in detail.

Before dawn each day Jacot would leave his hotel in Chartres using the back or side entrances and walk to the Gendarmerie Nationale station to pick up the van and Paradis – who always seemed extraordinarily cheery for so early in the morning, bounding out of the front door, armed with two packed lunches, prepared by his new best friend – the police station cook. Jacot managed to listen to a little Mozart during the first few minutes of the journey, before Paradis grew restless, switching to his own easy-listening menu on the van's sound system. Jacot didn't mind, he rather enjoyed a diet of husky-voiced French crooners interspersed with a little Frank and Dean. It gave the whole wearisome operation a retro road movie feel.

It was hard work, following hedge lines and stone walls, peering into every gap, testing loose stones, trying to stay out of sight. The fields were filled with sheep and cattle, growing fat on the luscious grass of the region. The sheep were not a problem, except that they tended to bolt en masse at the approach of a human being. The local breed of cattle was a different proposition. Bred for beef, they were magnificent looking, but bad tempered. Jacot was used to avoiding cows in England, particularly if there was a dog in tow. But these creatures were something else.

The weather was grim, and by the time they met up just before twilight on the first night, both men were soaked to the skin and weary. As soon as they got into the van, hidden in some trees, they turned the heating on full and laid out their maps on the dashboard. They discussed their routes and findings – not that they had found anything of great interest.

Paradis suggested, 'We need to refine our search further. Evergreen trees only. They must be clever enough to know that we could use satellites and drones so they would need year round cover. It'll cut the task in half and we are against the clock. I'll speak to the local forestry people again to see if we can get a different map that will help more.'

'What about asking Navarre for a drone or an overflight using infrared? We used stuff like that against the IRA.'

'Not just yet, mon colonel. I feel we are close, and any air activity might alert a watcher or sentry of some kind to our interest. Let's just concentrate on evergreen areas. I'll go into Senonches now – everything will still be open.'

'Best of luck.'

Paradis gave a broad smile, 'There will almost certainly be a young lady in the national park office in the town. Pas difficile.'

'Oh, and get some more chocolate biscuits while you're there.' Jacot wondered how long he might be gone.

'D'accord, mon colonel.' Paradis disappeared with the van. Jacot took up a position overlooking the road, weapon at his side – the fruits of Ingoldsby's procurement talents, a Heckler and Koch MP5SD assault rifle – completely silent, producing no discernable muzzle flash. Just in case. He ran through in his mind what he had confirmed on his London visit. Turning against your own people. Monstrous, awful. What made his blood run cold was that without the presumably unforeseen necessity of having to kill the three diplomatic messengers in a hurry, and an uncharacteristically helpful Mossad – the whole thing would have been missed. *How far had the rot spread?* The job he and Paradis had in this phase and the next was clear enough. He wondered what Lady Nevinson and Navarre were planning. They both had wonderfully devious minds – so did Ingoldsby. Something subtle, clever and, he hoped, deadly.

After an hour Paradis returned with a series of high quality colour print outs showing tree cover by season and species. He grinned as he spread them out in the van, 'It's even better than I thought. We knew this was a Resistance area in the war, but the young lady, actually there were two, said the area we are in now, just off the road to Belhomert was notorious as a place for hidden supplies, especially weapons and ammunition dropped by the British before D Day.'

'It makes sense,' said Jacot looking at the map. There is a road with forest cover either side most of the way from Senonches to La Loupe – the epicentre of the local Resistance. Bad for the Germans, and good for the Maquis. Easy to get stuff in and out, particularly at night. Can't see the Wehrmacht wanting to patrol this area – not in 1944 anyway.'

'No decent chocolate biscuits, but I got you something I know you like.' Paradis handed over a couple of Mars Bars. They laughed. They had been friends already but the shared experience of the ambush had brought them even closer. Paradis had also been gratifyingly impressed by the hardware produced by Ingoldsby – not just the weaponry but the packaging as well – everything stored snugly in specially constructed dark green leather Bergans. The clock was ticking – they would sleep in the forest.

They started at dawn. Mid afternoon Jacot came across the lid of a milk churn jammed into a cavity in a stone wall. Paradis was right – they were close. Jacot nosed around. No sign of a milk churn but there was a depression just below the wall, filled with mud that might have held some sort of container. *Clever, very clever.* The location was in the corner of a field made extremely muddy by cattle, encircled by a moat of stinking mud. No casual walker would have come anywhere near it.

Bingo, thought Jacot. *Winthropping* was an excellent technique, but his great breakthroughs in the 1970s had generally come about after he came to understand the preferences and quirks of a small group of IRA quartermasters, particularly in South Armagh. Some preferred trees as markers, some telegraph poles. Some liked stashing stuff inside walls, others preferred burying. Each quartermaster had a signature technique. Some of the most brazen hid their grisly supplies in plain sight. The storeman for this terrorist group was clearly a burier. The IRA had used milk churns – they could be easily made waterproof and animal proof. Whoever the quartermaster of this particular group was, he liked to keep his cache away from prying eyes by sticking it in the muddiest part of a field, close to a stone wall and preferably protected by the bad-tempered local cattle and their generous effluent.

Jacot explained all this at their huddled conference in the van that evening. With the aid of maps and some aerial photographs they decided to mount covert night surveillance on one of the key road junctions. They would rest and prepare in Chartres during the day and insert the Observation Post the following night.

Unusually, Paradis seemed in no hurry to return to the dubious delights of the Gendarmerie Nationale Station, so they went for a drink near the cathedral.

'Kronenbourg, beer of the Legion.' Paradis looked intently at the glasses on the table in front of them. He drank the first glass in one go. Jacot did the same. 'Do you know that on Camerone Day, 30 April, each year, this beer is given to every Legionnaire wherever he is serving? It's our great festival commemorating the battle in Mexico in 1863 when sixty-two Legionnaires and three officers,' Paradis smiled 'held off thousands of Mexican soldiers including artillery and cavalry for a whole day. By mid-afternoon, only five were left alive. I will invite you one year, mon colonel to the grand parade at Aubagne. I had a case of Kronenbourg dropped to my patrol in Chad. Nothing from headquarters for days, and then some blow-waved pilot from the l'armée de l'air comes up on the net asking for us to activate the homing beacon. Half an hour later the Transall makes a low and accurate pass – we could see the Legion despatcher – out comes a container with a chute. Inside, Kronenbourg, ice cold, and lobster cocktails. Oh, and a note from the Commandant of the Legion wishing us well.'

Two more beers arrived. Paradis lifted his in a toast, 'L'Amour, mon colonel. L'Amour. To Love.' He gave a wonderful combination grin and leer and then winked knowingly. The beer disappeared. Paradis seemed able to pour it down his throat without even swallowing.

Jacot moved uneasily in his chair. They hadn't discussed Zaden since their first trip down from Paris. Paradis was his confidant, indeed his only male friend in France, but he felt reluctant to talk about her just then. Naturally it was about sex, at least in part, but he didn't want to discuss it entirely in those terms. Paradis was a wise man and a natural leader, but he tended to live his life from the waist down. Waist down matters were always discussed in waist down terms. At that moment he realised. No wonder Paradis had proved such a genial companion over the past few days. No wonder he didn't want to put up in the best hotel in Chartres at the expense of the hard-pressed British taxpayer.

'My congratulations mon adjudant. Let me guess.' It was obvious. It should have been obvious all along. 'Don't tell me, the lovely lady on the front desk. Or is it the cook?'

Paradis grinned broadly. 'Not the cook. The cook is a man. His national service was the highlight of his life – hence the packed lunches as you call them. It is, as you say, the beautiful lady on the front desk, Christine.' Jacot remembered their first day at the rue Jean Monnet, and smiled. Christine was striking.

Paradis sighed. Like all first class NCOs he had an extraordinary range of signals with which to demonstrate approval and disapproval, slightly muted when dealing with his British mature student. Sighing was one of his tools, especially during weapon handling sessions. It was highly effective at communicating finely graded shades of disappointment, ranging from a mild, let-down irritation through to full on exasperation, accompanied by Paradis' most powerful critical verdict, *maximum mistake*. He would have made a good actor. But this sigh was different, without impatience or sarcasm – the poor man had clearly fallen for the shapely gendarme.

Jacot could feel himself blushing. During his recent adventures in

Cambridge, and while training with the Legion he had thought long and hard about Monica Zaden. Sometimes, it was a conscious process. *Was it for real? What were his chances? What was his plan of action?* Sometimes her image, or the sound of her laugh, oddly lower than her voice, would come into his mind unbidden. More often, the thyme-scented countryside of the Midi where Paradis put him through his paces would remind him of her smell, a subtle combination of fresh lemons and thyme. But throughout, he had forgotten how ridiculous middle-aged passion could seem to outsiders, and now he had remembered.

They drank on in companionable silence, Jacot switching to white wine.

It was a freezing night, about minus four Centigrade. Paradis had constructed the observation post, not much more than a poncho stretched between two branches, with a waterproof groundsheet. He had sighted it cleverly behind a bank that gave them protection from the wind, and stopped any accidental noise they might make from alerting anyone close to the target, about 200 metres away. It was a gamble, but an informed one. The target was a junction – not of metalled roads, but of muddy paths, hardly ever used and partly overgrown, but easily passable in a Land-Rover type vehicle. The junction itself was a mere fifty yards from the Senonches-Belhomert road. Once at the junction, any traveller or treasure hunter had four further paths to choose from – all disappearing into the deep forest. It was along one of these the day before that Jacot had come across the milk-churn lid. As a bonus, and unusually for this part of the forest, most of the trees were evergreen.

'Mmm, mon colonel. Has it ever occurred to you that none of us is French, originally? I was born a subject of the Queen of the Netherlands. I am Legion now, loyal to France, a citizen of the French Republic because of my wounds in Afghanistan. You are an Englishman.'

Jacot didn't reply.

'Mon colonel, have you ever wondered why?'

Jacot had been staring at the stars, enjoying the night. He started. 'Mon adjudant, it is a long standing habit of mine not to discuss the human condition without immediate access to industrial quantities of alcohol, or unless I am sitting close to a very pretty girl. I'm afraid that hunkered down in this remote forest keeping an eye on a muddy track, we seem to be lacking both. Don't take it personally. Although, come to think of it I have got a small flask of something we call in the British Army *Gunfire*.'

'Comment?'

'A mixture of brandy and port. Guaranteed to keep both the cold and the vast edges drear of the universe at bay.' He rummaged in his Bergan and passed a large silver hip flask to Paradis.

'More like a hot water-bottle than a hip flask,' Paradis grinned, his white teeth flashing in the darkness, and took a large mouthful. 'Magnifique. No, I wasn't about to consider what you call the mysteries of life, but the mystery of why an adjudant-chef in the Légion étrangère and a colonel in the regiment de la garde royale Celtique are hiding in a forest twenty miles from Chartres, looking for a cache of terrorist explosives.'

'Well, I offered to help Navarre and Lady Nevinson agreed – so here I am. Thanks to a good old British technique, and our very sharp eyes, we seem on the point of finding what we were looking for.'

'Plus some experience in Afghanistan. They hide stuff in trees there. Neither of us is important in the scheme of things and here we are dealing with a crucial matter of British and French internal security – half the targets are in England. If there are explosives or weapons in that milk churn it is a very big deal. Is it not odd, do you think that the place isn't crawling with Navarre's men, plus every counter-terrorist policeman, plus the equivalent from England?'

'If what I told you in Paris is right,' said Jacot taking a long pull at the flask 'then maybe people like us are the only ones that Monsieur Navarre and Madame la Baronesse can trust. I do what she tells me, and you do what the Legion tells you. We both, more than anything else, love our countries. Some would see us fools, but it also makes us reliable.' The alcoholic harshness of the Armagnac, and the cloying sweetness of the Port were the ideal combination to produce both warmth and a comforting buzz. It was a freezing night deep in the forêt de Senonches. 'For my part, I'd rather be here than behind a desk. My official job is pretty humdrum, and as I told you after our excitements last week, I'm only in Paris because things were getting a little too hot in London.'

Paradis nodded. 'Oh, yes. When you were rescued by the Chasseurs Alpins.' Jacot had given him a full account after the ambush. He had murmured approvingly at the account of Jacot's rooftop escape from Cambridge, questioning him closely about the topography of the university town. Paradis clearly enjoyed the idea of rooftop escapes, but as for being rescued by Chasseurs Alpins – that was clearly a fate no Legionnaire could tolerate. 'Tell me how the dinner went?'

'Pretty well, I thought. *Le Bourgeois Gentilhomme* was charming and funny and the original music by Lully gave the whole performance a kind of infectious happiness, the effect Molière was probably after when he wrote it for Louis XIV. We drank a lot of champagne before it started, and in the interval. Chez Rolfe's was just right, thank you – a romantic atmosphere. We played a game of asking each other our favourite things.'

'What sort of things?'

'Oh, favourite songs, films, food.'

Paradis was silent. 'There's something you're not saying, mon colonel.'

'Well, there was a difficult moment when I described my favourite poem, a fairly standard text by a Great War poet about dying, and what people should think of dead soldiers. Every English schoolboy used to learn it by heart. It's beautiful and comforting and rather English, but somehow the conversation took a twist I wasn't expecting.'

Paradis took a gulp from the hip-flask. 'And?'

'She asked me what I had been thinking of all those years ago.'

'Mon colonel, you took her hand, looked into her eyes, told her, and then kissed her, softly. Giving the disguised but distinct impression that the best thing about cheating death all those years ago is that you are now sitting in Chez Rolfe's with her. Reassure me, mon colonel, that you did this.'

'Well, no, mon adjudant. No one has ever asked me that question before. I didn't know what to say so I brushed it off with a joke about needing a drink.'

Paradis shook his head. 'Maximum mistake. Mon colonel, let me give you a piece of advice. When a beautiful girl you have taken out to dinner asks you what you were thinking about as you thought you were dying in a war – even a small war many years ago – she is trying to enter your world. It is polite not to give her a throwaway answer. What were you thinking about?'

Jacot took a long pull at the hip flask. 'Do you really want to know?'

'I too have been blown up, my friend. I know what it's like. And no, no one has ever asked me that question either. I will listen. You tell me and then I will share with you my experience.'

'Faces, three faces. When I made it into the open air on deck the first thing I saw was a man being propped up against the bulkhead by a medic and another Guardsman helping him. His eyes were open, staring right at me intently, the face composed, calm but somehow not quite right. He looked unharmed but couldn't move for some reason. The medic checked him over and spoke to him. There was no response. The medic got out a syringe and was trying to find a vein. The Guardsman helping him took off the casualty's beret and they realised that much of the back of his head had gone – shrapnel, probably. He was dead. The front of his face was just a mask – there was nothing behind it.

The medic and the Guardsman grabbed his identity discs and moved on. The eyes still stared at me. I wanted to close them, but the ship we were on, the *Oliver Cromwell*, lurched alarmingly just at that moment and he toppled over onto his side. As what was left of his head slid down the bulkhead, leaving not blood but a trail of clear, sticky liquid, the eyes closed. We thought the whole ship was about to explode – we could hear tons of ammunition detonating in the hold. I thought I had better get off, if I could.'

Paradis was silent for a moment. 'The second face, mon colonel?'

'The second face was that of a brother officer, crouching a few feet further onto the main deck. Side on to me at first, like looking at someone depicted on a postage stamp. With the fire and the explosions it was very noisy, and so he was shouting into the radio, the radio volume was turned up full – I could hear what was being said. It was a message from the picquet ship, look-out ship is a better term, far to our west looking out for Argentine aircraft: *Four enemy aircraft sighted low west of Beaver Island.* The voice on the radio was tense, surprised. Then this officer turned. I could see his face full on. There was no expression – he just closed his eyes. I remember his skin changed colour to a dull grey. He knew what Beaver Island meant – so did I. More aircraft heading for us, and they were near. There wasn't going to be enough time to get everyone off. I looked away – I didn't want him to know that I understood the same thing he had understood. It was over. Short of a miracle, we would all meet a fiery death in the next few minutes.'

Suddenly, Paradis placed his hand over Jacot's mouth. They both sat absolutely still for a moment and then both eased forward to their night vision goggles, set up on tripods at the forward edge of the observation post.

A car passed by on the main road, slowly. They couldn't hear its engine against the background of the wind and rain. But the reflection of the headlights in the trees was moving slower than it should have been. The natural instinct of any normal driver on a straight, well-metalled road at that time of night and in that weather, would be to press on to the next sign of civilisation and human habitation as quickly as he could. The car went past the turning to the track. A minute or so later it came back, same headlight reflection, same slow speed. It stopped. Annoyingly, they wouldn't be able to see it unless it turned off the main road. Paradis cursed under his breath. After a few minutes the car moved away, this time at a more normal speed.

'We can't risk it, mon colonel. According to Aumonnier, the intelligence said that they weren't ready to move yet. I'm not so sure. We need to find it tonight. You stay here. Warn me if anyone turns off the road. Show me on the map again where you walked yesterday, and tell me once more what you think his markers are.' Paradis disconnected his night-vision goggles from the tripod and slung them round his neck. 'I will leave my MP5 with you. I will take my pistol.' They talked and looked at the map by torchlight for a few minutes. 'Paradis will find it tonight, I promise.' Jacot proffered the flask. Paradis took a large swallow and disappeared silently into the night.

Jacot waited without anxiety. Rain sodden nights in remote spots and people like Paradis were a good match. He returned just before dawn grinning and nodding – it was enough. 'Second path, unfortunately, or I would have got back earlier. But the markers exactly as you suspected: muddiest part of a field, close to a stone wall, plenty of cattle and not too far along the track.'

Jacot got the breakfast on – the small gas burner giving out some welcome heat – eggs, sausages, baked beans (not particularly easy to buy in Paris) and slices of baguette fried in the sausage fat. Plus very hot, very real coffee. Paradis looked at the packet, *Hédiard,* and smiled.

Once it was all ready, Jacot served up producing a small travel bottle of *Henderson's Relish.* 'Try it, mon adjudant, it's from the north of England, where they understand how to flavour sausages.' Paradis was clearly ravenous after his long night. Although he had spent several hours in the teeth of the elements messing around in muddy fields, he was curiously clean and dry.

After breakfast, Paradis explained exactly what he had found, 'A milk churn, almost certainly, possibly with an anti-handling device. I left it. I have someone on standby who understands these things. He will come tonight. I've told Paris – Monsieur Navarre wants to make me an officer! Give me four hours, mon colonel.' He climbed into his sleeping bag.

The following night Jacot and Paradis waited in a layby about 10 kilometres from the target. It was another wild night, pouring with freezing rain, and the wind buffeted the side of their van. They had dozed much of the day.

Paradis' Magenta phone rang, and soon after a motorcycle arrived in the layby.

'He's here. He'll come with us.'

The wind howled. Paradis got out of the van and walked towards the dismounting motorcyclist – a small, lightly built man, even in his bulky leathers, who briefly stood to attention as Paradis approached him. The two men then embraced, the back door of the van opened and in they climbed. The motorcyclist, water dripping from his black leathers, and a small reinforced steel suitcase in his hand, removed his helmet and leant forward to shake Jacot's hand. Paradis introduced him 'Sergent-chef Piquet, 1er Régiment étranger de genie: our bomb disposal man on our last tour of Afghanistan. No English, but the best in the business.' Jacot passed back a towel and a cup of hot coffee. The man smiled but said nothing. Jacot was on the point of offering him a slug of Gunfire, when he remembered that although alcohol had many uses in many situations, explosives ordnance disposal was not one of them.

Paradis completed the detailed briefing. Jacot started the engine, slipped the van into gear and moved on to the main road. Even with the windscreen wipers at manic speed, it was difficult to see properly, but it suited them. Above all, they didn't want to be discovered. Few people would venture out on such a foul night.

They parked up in the woods behind their Observation Post and moved tactically in Indian file towards the target. Paradis led, his Glock 17 drawn. Piquet followed, still in his leathers and clutching his small suitcase, looking, thought Jacot, a little like an escaped prisoner of war. Jacot brought up the rear, carrying his MP5 and a large rucksack that banged painfully against his hips.

Jacot's main job was to remain on the path as a sentry while the others did what they had to do to the explosives. But first, he had a small and unpleasant task to perform, digging in a short electric fence to protect Paradis and his friend from the aggressive local cattle. The mud in the corner of the field stank, and cowpats oozed over his boots as he drove the metal stakes into the ground. It only took a couple of minutes, but by the end he was wet through and covered in evil-smelling mud. Paradis and Piquet were huddled the other side of the wall unpacking their equipment underneath a poncho. Jacot climbed into the lane, indicating that he had finished. Paradis nodded. He and Piquet vaulted the low stone wall. Used to the army bomb disposal people in Northern Ireland who wore heavy protective clothing, Jacot was surprised to see that Piquet wore no protective equipment at all, just a headband with a powerful infrared spotlight torch.

Jacot took position with a good view of the approaches on either side and perched with his back to the wall. From time to time he looked through the infrared sight of his MP5 conducting a 360-degree check around the area. The smell of cow-dung seeped up from his warm, damp trousers.

It was going to be a long night. After nearly an hour, Paradis joined him in the lane. 'We need to move away, mon colonel. He is into the milk churn and is about to take apart one of the bombs. If he makes a mistake…' They moved fifty yards down the lane. 'He will be some time, I will perform my other task now.' Paradis moved silently off down to the entrance of the narrow lane, carrying a small rucksack. The rain, mercifully, stopped. Paradis re-appeared after half an hour, but it was another two hours before Piquet himself appeared. After a quick cigarette underneath the poncho, and a muttered conversation in heavily accented French, he took Paradis back to the milk churn.

Piquet had explained to Paradis and Jacot in the fugged up van the kind of bombs intelligence reckoned they were dealing with. Like most bomb disposal people Piquet had a fascination, even a grudging affection, for all things explosive. Jacot had been able to follow most of the conversation which was in Legion French. A kilogramme of C4, with nearly twice the power of old fashioned dynamite, causes a lot of damage just on its own. As little as 500 grammes, the size of a pat of butter, is enough to blow up a car. As a substance C4 is fairly harmless and reasonably stable. Made from standard military explosive, mixed with upmarket plasticine to make it malleable and a splash of motor oil to keep it stable. Drop it, and not much happens. Set fire to it, and it produces an oily flame like a British army hexamine burner. In Vietnam GIs sometimes used it for cooking. But send an electrical charge into a detonator encased in it, and the C4 starts its rapid chemical journey from solid into gas, sending out a powerful shock wave travelling at 8,000 metres per second. At this point Piquet had slipped into broken English and gesticulated violently, 'You can hide, but you can't run!'

Jacot remembered his days on the Falls Road. Irish terrorists had used similar bombs – with pieces of scrap metal in the mix rather than shiny, machined ball bearings – what the IRA used to call *dockyard confetti* – since much of it was gathered up in Belfast's great shipyards. The sort of thing modern soldiers fighting counter-insurgency wars feared more than anything else. Except that the bombs hidden in the forest weren't for use against soldiers in a far away war, but against civilians on the streets of Western Europe.

Dawn had just begun to break, the weak, winter sun peeping through the milky mist that clung to the valleys in this part of France. They weren't much more than a hundred miles from Paris, but it felt remote. The thick fir trees that clustered and dominated in this part of the forest gave Jacot a hemmed in, claustrophobic feel. It was a difficult-to-find and concealed spot, unless you knew what you were looking for.

Paradis and Piquet were finished, at last. As it was nearly light, they both lit up cigarettes in the open and started walking towards the van. Jacot clambered over the wall to recover his makeshift cattle fence. As he walked back to the wall, the metal stakes of the fence and its battery banging against his hips once again, he took care to disguise his boot prints trailing a branch behind him. Conveniently, the cattle were now following him into the corner of the field and the rain had returned. In the almost impossible event that any traces of the operation had been left behind, they would soon be smothered in water, mud and cow dung.

Jacot drove the van away at speed. It stank inside: all three of them caked in mud and worse. But after a night in the open they were too cold to open the windows. Gradually, on their way to reunite Piquet with his motorcycle, they warmed up and the unpleasant fug in the van was diluted by a little fresh air and the evocative smell of Gauloises, the pungent and unfiltered Caporal rather than Disque Bleu; and the sweet and sharp smell of Armagnac mixed with vintage port from Jacot's hip flask.

Jacot insisted on booking a room in the hotel for Paradis. He didn't argue. They rested, cleaned up and went for lunch in a restaurant recommended by the hotel, the other side of town from the cathedral. Paradis had submitted a short report to Aumonnier for onward and immediate submission to Navarre. Jacot had had a brief conversation with Lady Nevinson. The intelligence wheels would be grinding in Paris, but he and Paradis had the day off as they awaited further orders.

They lunched lavishly, *courtesy of the taxpayer Britannique*, as Paradis enjoyed saying every time the waiter approached to take an additional order for food and wine. Jacot had convinced himself that somehow the looming and probably very large bill was *a reasonable operational expense*. They were both pleased with themselves, Paradis especially so – after a text message of praise from Navarre that mentioned a letter being drafted to the commanding general of the Foreign Legion in Aubagne.

'I must ask you, but if you don't want to say… the third face, mon colonel? You never told me about the third face – we were cut off by that suspicious car.'

Jacot was taken off guard. 'Someone I felt close to.'

'A woman?'

'A woman. A crowd of dying men isn't company.'

'I know what you mean. English?'

'It wasn't the moment for Latinas.'

Paradis laughed and drank more wine. 'The English sense of humour!'

'An image of her was somewhere in my mind as soon as the explosion happened, but when I heard the Beaver Island message I think my mind decided that it preferred the image of this girl rather than the reality of what was going to happen to me in the next few minutes. It was strange – I could function and see in reality – but her face came to saturate everything, smiling, looking straight at me. I couldn't work out why her hair wasn't on fire.'

'When I was at school on St Maarten we were taught that the Greeks and Romans placed a coin in the mouths of the dead as a farewell gift and to pay the ferryman across the river into the underworld. Maybe soldiers get a farewell vision of a beautiful girl instead. I too was thinking of a woman, strongly, when it seemed all was over. No one ever says…'

'You have listened to me, mon adjudant. How was it for you?'

'We walked into a complex ambush. A string of buried 155mm shells left over from the Soviet occupation – all with pressure pads. Unlike a Western minefield designed to slow down and sometimes channel the enemy, the one we walked into was simply designed to kill as many of us as possible. A young Legionnaire in my patrol stepped on a pressure pad, and four booby traps went off together, one set in the wall behind me. I was blown into the air, spinning. As my body turned, I remember a splash on the back of my neck – like a barber spraying your hair with warm water, except it wasn't. I went up and up into the air and as I span I could see where my young Legionnaire had been standing. One minute a person, the next nothing but meaty red mist. *Mort au champ d'honneur* is our formula. He was my *binome*. What do you call it in England?'

'Buddy. Oppo. We have the same system – everybody has a pair.'

They sat in silence for a few minutes, drinking slowly.

Paradis spoke first, 'I feel guilty sometimes; instead of a woman I should have been thinking about my binome. He was my responsibility.'

'Does it come back?'

'Sometimes, in the night, mon colonel. And you?'

'Sometimes, in the night, mon adjudant.'

'The girl?'

'Always the girl.'

'Not everyone is so lucky. A flashback with a happy ending you might say,' said Paradis solemnly. Jacot started to laugh. Paradis remained silent. 'Is it funny?'

'In polite company *happy ending* is the same as *bien se terminer*, but amongst the rough soldiery like you and me it has a sexual meaning.'

Paradis loved it and laughed and laughed, saying *le happy ending* over and over again, mimicking Jacot's voice. Jacot's mood lightened – *another one for the sous-officiers mess at Aubagne.*

Navarre had summed it up, 'Now, we wait, we wait. At the moment it's just a hidden supply of terrorist explosives. Once they move it – we can strike. It will be soon, I promise. You must live your normal lives to avoid suspicion. Paradis, you must return to your regiment. We have prepared a cover story. The injuries you sustained in a car crash are now much better – keep a bandage on somewhere. You, Colonel must return to the embassy. All of us must return to our jobs – to normality. We must pretend. But be ready to move quickly.'

Jacot tried to preserve some semblance of a normal life, but it was difficult – every day was like being in the interval of a marvellous concert or opera – he couldn't wait for the curtain to go up again.

He was pleased at the state of his fitness achieved under the watchful eyes of the Legion's physical training instructors and was determined to keep it up. Twice a week, he ran back from work, although it meant disregarding Lady Nevinson's orders on being armed at all times. He very much doubted anyone would have a crack at him on the rue du Faubourg Saint-Honoré – official government Paris was swarming with armed gendarmes and soldiers. But once away from the security bubble, he varied his routes, choosing a different bridge to cross the Seine each time, and approaching his flat in the rue Bonaparte from a different direction. At the weekend, he normally took a longer run and did a few exercises on the Champ de Mars in the shadow of the Eiffel Tower.

He had picked up a good speed one Saturday afternoon. The gravelled paths were easy and bouncy to run on. He did a few sets of press-ups – a strangely civilised experience without someone shouting, 'En position' – the Legion's instruction to prepare for more press-ups than he had ever imagined were possible. But he wasn't as young as he used to be and decided to sit down on a bench to get his breath back. A sunny afternoon, the Champ de Mars was filled with joggers and families pleased to be out in the winter sunshine.

Jacot watched as balloon sellers circulated, their bunches of helium-filled balloons swaying gently in the breeze. Small children squealed with delight as their parents offered to buy them balloons, solemnly choosing with great care their favourite colour. A family passed by his bench with two small daughters gripping onto their newly bought balloons with grim concentration – blue and red. As they moved off slowly towards the Eiffel Tower, the little girl holding the blue one stumbled. Her father scooped her up before she fell, but the blue balloon shot up into the sky. The little girl shrieked and cried, inconsolable at the loss of her lovely blue balloon. Her slightly older sister came over to hold her hand. At the same time, she let her red balloon fly into the sky just a few seconds behind and a few feet lower than the blue one. The two sisters watched both balloons blow away, gaining height as they flew towards the Seine and the Eiffel Tower. They pointed and laughed.

It was time for the run home. A glorious day – he would vary his route by running to the street market on the rue Cler. He would need a rest half way, and there were always new things to see, smell, taste, and buy.

He enjoyed being physically fit again. Lighter, faster on his feet, more alert, he once again experienced the emotional highs that he had found in running long distances as a young man.

Accelerating down the rue de Grenelle, he could smell the market from a hundred yards away. It specialised in provincial produce – cured meats, exotic vegetables, and hard-to-find, obscure eaux-de-vie from La France Profonde.

Jacot stopped running as he turned into the rue Cler and stood close to a wall for a few minutes to rest. Once he had his breath back, he began to walk the length of the street. It was always exciting, different from London, wonderfully French. The musty, woody scent of dried champignons from Burgundy mingled with lavender and herbs from the Midi, and the sharp animal pong of mountain goats cheeses, piled high on wooden tables covered with straw – smelling like *angels' feet* according to one over-the-top food critic.

Some of the stalls sold a huge array of spices from France's former colonies in North Africa and South East Asia. The market mixed the exotic with the familiar, combining to produce a smell that was comforting – something the many children who passed through it with their mothers on their way back from school would remember with affection as part of the routine of their childhood.

Just as Jacot remembered vividly the smells and textures of his youth, often replayed in his sleeping mind: the heavy earth smell of the mud on the games pitches at the foot of Harrow on the Hill; and its feel, glutinous and granular at the same time; the exotic aromas of the food stalls in the alleyways of Hong Kong, and the coconut smell and slipperiness of sun tan oil beside the South China Sea.

Jacot had always been a dreamer – even as a young man he had dreamed vividly at night, in colour, and with full sound effects. Pop music, picnics, swimming, sports matches, pretty girls – the sights and sounds of growing up.

He loved the rue Cler, lapping up the sounds and sensations as he walked slowly past the stalls, buying two things he hadn't seen before – black rice from the Camargue and bulbs of garlic, almost violet in colour, from the Dordogne. Even though he was in the middle of a run, he began to feel hungry.

A young man in a chef's hat and apron was offering hot dogs for sale at an open-air food stall. Not the plastic Americanised version, but a proper French hot dog made from strong pork sausage encased in half a baguette. He wouldn't run all the way back but buy a hot dog and a beer from the stall.

He joined the short queue – his mouth watering at the prospect of the pork sausages sizzling and bubbling on the improvised barbecue in front of him. Just as he was about to be served, the gas burner under the barbecue spluttered sending a wave of hot air mingled with kerosene towards Jacot. The young man cooking the sausages grabbed a damp cloth to turn the gas down, but part of it caught on the flame.

Jacot turned away and ran, retching. He dropped the brown paper packages of black rice and violet garlic. He had to get away. He ran and ran, not taking any notice of the direction, stopping only to be sick. The smell of a damp street trader's cloth catching alight, combined with the smell of kerosene and barbecuing pork sausages exactly reproduced the smell of damp and unwashed soldiers burning alive after a missile strike all those years before.

He made it back to his flat – he wasn't sure how. It was coming and he dreaded it. He drank a large glass of Calvados to steady his nerves and another.

After being trapped and badly burned when an Exocet missile hit the troop carrying ship RFA *Oliver Cromwell* during the Falklands War, a new set of dreams had entered his repertoire, outstaying their welcome even into his sixth decade. They remained vivid, etched into his mind, or soul, as Jacot himself would have it.

The most unsettling and persistent of them was more flashback than dream. It could come in the day, unannounced, set off by the smell of hot metal, or the saltiness of a cold sea carried on the wind. He used to stay inside on the ferry trips across the Channel during his Rhine Army days. But more often, it came at night – rarely in middle age, but stronger, more vivid, exhausting: the smell of flesh burning, the sound of men screaming – nearly impossible to blot out.

Being with other people didn't help – in any case during his pleasant posting in Paris who could he turn to and with what message? 'Please come on over and hold my hand while I have a flashback – RSVP.' Lady Nevinson would send someone. But what would she think afterwards? At the very least, she would insist on some long, no-expense spared course of psychotherapy. And would she still want him on her staff if he were a little off-kilter? Paradis would come too. He understood more than anyone else after their heart to heart in the forest, and his own experiences in Afghanistan. Zaden also. If they were going to be lovers at some point, as he hoped, he would have to tell her. But the bottom line was that he preferred being alone. There was something slightly weird about the experience – so persistent, so vivid, after so many years that he kept it to himself. The truth of it was – he was ashamed, ashamed of his weakness. Discipline should be enough to get him through.

Self-medication had always been the norm, consisting mainly of impressively large quantities of alcohol. In the British Army of the Rhine, Jacot remembered often drinking a bottle of Veuve Clicquot in his bath, followed by sherry or gin at the cocktail hour, and then a bottle of Claret with dinner. In the cold German winters, he would continue the movement with Kummel or especially his favourite prop, Calvados.

Refining the process over the years, experience had confirmed that alcohol was crucial. It usually took two or three bottles of wine, the best wines he could find because they made the experience more pleasurable and left him with less of a hangover. Followed by the best Calvados available. He would kick off with the Cristal Rosé that he had been reserving for Zaden – ice cold. He would order another bottle next week.

If he could stay awake through the night, and fall into a deep, drunken sleep once the sun was coming up – he found that he could sometimes keep the gathering demons at bay, but not always. The small hours were the time of maximum danger – if he fell asleep at that point the dreams were likely to come with great ferocity.

He had experimented with various methods to stay awake until dawn. Coffee and the other highly caffeinated drinks available on the market kept him awake well enough for a time, but they were designed for the sober, and he couldn't be sure that they wouldn't be overcome by the alcohol just at the crucial moment. Amphetamines were easy enough to buy, perfectly legal in some forms, and worked well for staying awake. But one of their side effects was to produce a strong sense of unease, nervousness even – not at all helpful. Sometimes, more rigorous medication was required.

XLIII

Le patron stood behind his zinc-topped bar polishing glasses in an absent-minded way. He liked clean glasses as a Parisian restaurateur should, but the habit was also a legacy of his military service – the orderliness of a barrack room, and the plain but highly polished steel of the cook house with military chefs in their immaculate white overalls, appealed to his inner soul. He hadn't enjoyed his short, compulsory time in the army in the early 1970s. It had all seemed pointless; most of his fellow conscripts either didn't want to be in the army at all, or would much rather have been a few years older and caught the tail end of the Algerian War.

But the sense of order behind military life remained a great comfort to him in his maturity, perhaps as a subconscious barrier against the increasing disorder of the world around him – especially recently. Even Paris was no longer safe from the madness. He liked to believe that he kept a smart establishment – and he took great joy, not just in the compliments he received about the food, but the appreciative glances from many of his customers at the perfectly white linen, glistening knives and forks, and glasses of various types that sparkled on the tables.

The immaculately dressed Welsh colonel who came in several times a week had been kind enough to express his approval frequently, always beginning his remarks with the formal, 'Monsieur le patron.' On discovering he was a serving colonel in the British Army on attachment to the embassy in Paris le patron insisted on calling him 'Mon colonel' in return. He felt it added tone to his establishment. They had got to know one another, often chatting over a glass of Calvados. Le patron felt they had become friends.

As it was a Saturday, it was highly likely that he might turn up for lunch. And le patron would experience both the pleasure of serving a regular and satisfied customer, and the sense of mystery that surrounded him, reinforced after each occasion as he cleared away the numerous empty glasses at the end of a meal – unlike the thousands of other customers he had served during his professional life, the good colonel left no fingerprints.

It had been a quiet morning – a few customers only and just warm enough on a mild late winter's day like this to sit outside. The Place Saint Sulpice was looking at its best – the horse chestnut trees adorned with sprigs of early bright pink blossom, giving the square a carnival, slightly camp air. With the French doors of the restaurant partly open, he could hear the splashing of the fountain in the square. Normally referred to simply as the St Sulpice Fountain, some of his customers still gave it its original and now old-fashioned name, The Fountain of the Four Bishops – from the statues of four famous episcopal preachers adorning the compass points. Despite staring at the statues from his usual position at the bar for many years, he could never remember who exactly they had been. Except for the one closest to his restaurant, Bossuet – every French schoolchild knew about him. France's greatest preacher, who had scandalised all of Versailles with the opening sentence of his eulogy at the funeral of Louis XIV, 'Only God is great.'

He turned towards the glass racks in the bar, re-arranging the glasses, and making sure that all the bottles were positioned in line, labels forward. He bent down to pick up a fresh, crisply laundered bar towel and turned back to face the square. Just time for a drink before the first lunchtime customers arrived. Pouring himself a scant half-inch of Calvados from his private bottle beneath the bar, he began to admire the view again, just as a familiar figure entered the restaurant. But instead of his usual suit, the Welsh colonel was dressed in plain grey trousers, a white linen shirt, half undone at the front, and white running shoes. He had clearly been taking some strenuous exercise, as his face was red, and the linen shirt damp in places. He eased himself onto stool and rested his bare hands on the coolness of the zinc bar top; but said nothing.

It was the first time le patron had seen him without his trademark gloves; and it became clear why he wore them all the time. The hands had been badly burned; skin grafts on the backs had taken well enough but were of a different texture and colour from the unburned skin on the wrists. None of the fingers had nails. The tips of some were missing, giving them a curiously pointed appearance as if they had been half-sharpened in a pencil sharpener. He could see other burnt patches on the body, partly hidden by the linen shirt. The Welsh colonel seemed agitated, the hands shaking slightly. Le patron poured him a very large Calvados that Jacot drained in a gulp, and then another one, plus another half inch for himself.

'Mon colonel?'

'Monsieur le patron, an Exocet in the Falklands. A French missile,' said Jacot looking at the hands clasped firmly around the glass of Calvados. 'But don't worry, President Mitterrand was a good friend to us and made sure no further deliveries were made. Did you know he was the first foreign leader to ring Mrs Thatcher and offer unconditional support?'

Le patron could see that something was wrong, possibly, he was in pain. Pouring him another drink, he gently suggested, 'Perhaps you should go back to your flat and come back for lunch, or later for dinner. We have an excellent Navarin of spring lamb tonight, with a cherry clafoutis afterwards, and I have some new cheese from Normandy – just in.'

'Sometimes it comes back in the night. All of it.'

'The Falklands?'

'Yes, a flashback. What's the word in French?'

'The same,' le patron smiled, 'le flashback, as in le weekend. I'm not sure there is a word for it in Breton. You don't look well. What about a doctor? There is a big military hospital in Paris – they will have someone who deals with these things. You need something to help you sleep? Have a few drinks and then take something. Sleep always helps.'

Jacot laughed, 'Sleep, f...... sleep. It's the worst thing. If I can stay awake through the night then it's not so bad – like being on sentry duty against myself. This stuff helps,' he gestured with his full glass and then drained it, 'but it makes it harder to stay awake.'

'What do you need mon colonel? A woman? Some pills? A nurse? I will make the arrangements, and then you should go home. I can send some food round later, if you would like.'

Jacot gulped at his Calvados. 'They don't happen very often these days, but when they do they seem stronger, out of control. If I play it right, I can avoid the full force. Over the years, I have experimented. Large quantities of alcohol backed up by a small quantity of... cocaine. Not too much.' It was a strange thing to ask.

Le patron seemed unsurprised, shrugging his shoulders in an open-minded and tolerant way, 'When do you need it?'

'Before dark.'

'One of our waiters will drop it round. 21b rue Bonaparte?' Jacot nodded and got up to go. 'Wait, wait.' Le patron took a bottle from the fridge under the bar. 'Our best white Burgundy – from me with my compliments. I hope it helps. Now, mon colonel, go home.'

XLIV

Rue Bonaparte, Paris, 6ème

Encased in a thick overcoat and wearing a hat to protect against the drizzle, the figure moved silently south along the rue Bonaparte. In the dawn twilight and from behind, it would have been difficult for a casual passerby to decide whether it was a man or a woman. The figure crossed the Boulevard St Germain, heading in the direction of the River Seine at some speed and then stopped to look up at a set of windows above a smart-looking patisserie – they were wide open.

Head down, the figure crossed to a doorway beside the patisserie and pressed one of the buttons on the entry phone system. There was no reply. The figure stood absolutely still in the quiet, empty street as if listening intently. Then in a flurry of movement opened the door and stepped inside.

The armoured door on Jacot's first floor flat was shut, but not locked or bolted, and was easily opened by sliding a thin but strong piece of plastic into the mechanism.

As the door clicked open, the figure drew a gun from the pocket of the thick overcoat. There was another faint metallic sound as the safety catch on the weapon was clicked off.

The smell was overpowering, even with the windows in the sitting room wide open – limes, not quite the smell of fresh limes, but very nearly so. It permeated everything. Some sort of strong scent been sprinkled and sprayed throughout the flat.

Jacot was asleep, or possibly unconscious, in an armchair close to the window, dressed only in a thick, light-blue towelling dressing gown that was clearly damp – his hands ungloved, the right hand lying across the body, burned side up. An empty bottle lay at his feet. The figure crossed the sitting room quietly, gun at the ready. The smell of limes got stronger – the dressing gown was soaked in the scent. There was a second smell as well – less strong and less sharp than the limes – apples. The figure shut the windows. Jacot didn't stir at all.

The figure stood still, as if deciding what to do; and then leaned over Jacot picking up his right wrist and moving it across his body, turning it over palm side up. For just a second it looked as if Jacot was trying to wave in his sleep or stupor. Just above the burn marks the figure searched for a pulse. Better to be sure.

Jacot sat on a leather sofa facing Lady Nevinson who was ensconced in a high backed leather armchair beside the fireplace – the fire was burning brightly, casting a comforting and luminous glow over the room. He felt ghastly, really rough. He kept his hands on his thighs, pushing them down. They were shaking, and he didn't want Lady Nevinson to see. In an effort to distract himself from his throbbing head and close to heaving stomach, he looked round the room. Originally the bedroom of Pauline Bonaparte's estranged, heroically tolerant, Italian husband, Wellington had turned it into a gloomy study. Duff Cooper, Churchill's ambassador after the Liberation, had it transformed into an elegant and cheery library, generously donating his book collection. He had been a Grenadier in the Great War and the room had the masculine feel of a Guards Officers' Mess – Jacot felt at home. He could smell the fire and a trace of cigar smoke, now mixed in with Nevinson's scent. Something rather lovely and citrussy thought Jacot – her Scandinavian pine forest period seemed, thankfully, to be over. He started to feel better.

'There's someone I need you to meet,' said Lady Nevinson. 'It's the last piece of the jigsaw. Gilles tells me that his people are expecting the move very soon. Once that happens I want you and Paradis to make any final adjustments and brief us on the plan.'

A timid and intermittent knocking sound came from the bookshelf just behind Lady Nevinson. Very odd, he thought. Builders perhaps, or a ghost. She looked at Jacot and smiled. Getting up, she moved behind the chair and pulled a small brass lever – the bookcase hinged open. It was a secret door, the sort of contraption much enjoyed by tourists going round a medieval manor house or castle. In the opening stood a young man in his late twenties. Nevinson dragged him in by the arm, pushed him into an armchair, introduced him and told Jacot to pour the coffee – all in one elegant and continuous movement.

'Vince is from Government Communications Headquarters,' said Lady Nevinson looking at the young man with maternal benevolence. Vincent Potter looked rather bemused, thought Jacot, as he handed him a cup of coffee.

'How interesting,' said Jacot. 'What do you specialise in?'

'Ultra-secure communications systems,' Vince replied. 'Well, actually, ultra-ultra-secure communications systems. Highly encrypted ones that rely on tricks so you don't even know they are really there.' He smiled shyly and took a small hesitant sip of his coffee, like a teenager drinking alcohol for the first time in front of his parents.

Nevinson went on, 'Vince completed his doctorate in computer sciences at Cambridge at the age of twenty-two. He is so clever that he spent a year at Fort Meade helping our American allies with their eavesdropping activities. He is one of the technicians behind Magenta.' She beamed at Potter.

'Actually, that's not quite right. I wasn't one of the clever men and women who dreamt up Magenta, and I was only on the project at the very end. My job wasn't to construct it – it's a brilliant programme. Brilliant. My job was to try to break into it.'

Jacot took a large mouthful of coffee, his fourth cup of the morning then quickly put down the cup and saucer that he was finding difficult to hold still. 'I thought it was unbreakable.'

Vince grinned broadly, 'No code system that involves more than a few communicants, if I can put it like that, is unbreakable, Colonel. Just as no ship is unsinkable. Even if a system is perfect – not every user will be. Think of the German signallers who began every coded message with *Heil Hitler*! Or the central basic but imperceptible flaw underlying every Enigma machine – no letter could be encoded as itself.' He seemed to have grown up now, sipping frequently from his coffee, reminding Jacot of an old lag explaining the finer points of safe cracking. 'There is always a way in, some chink or weakness that a man like myself can exploit. Although, to be frank, Magenta is difficult for reasons that I won't, of course, explain. So far, it looks secure from the Americans – its primary purpose. My guess is Fort Meade will break it eventually. Absolute secrecy is only attainable through the one-time pad – a random text agreed between just a very small group of recipients that is then encoded using simple number substitution.'

Lady Nevinson set the scene, 'Vince is here not to give us a workshop on code-breaking but to help us with a specific task – breaking into the mobile network I mentioned to you during our last discussion.'

'Let's get on with it then and crack the thing, Vince. These punters are using a highly encrypted mobile phone network, not KGB nostalgia one-time pads,' said Jacot.

'You would think. Trouble is the key to the encryption appears to be similar to a one-time pad – it changes all the time. Not every day, like the rotors on an Enigma set, but every few minutes. Let me explain more. With a one-time pad sometimes the text can be from the same edition of a book or magazine – sometimes it is produced in pads, a bit like stacks of bingo cards. Every card is unique, but issued in matching numbered sets to the group. The encrypted cipher will be the same length as the plain text usually, but other than that it carries no additional information for the code-breaker. Multiply that a hundred times and you can imagine the scale of our problem. Even Turing would have failed. Unless you know the key, you can't make head or tail of it no matter what computing power you have at your disposal.'

Jacot became animated, 'There must be a way. We have some suspects – surely we can work something out from Mr Samuel's list. Can't we break into their houses or offices and have a rummage round? See if we can work out if they are using *Pride and Prejudice* as a key or find the *bingo cards* and photograph them. At least we could work out what they were saying for a few minutes – that might help. We need to know what these awful people are saying to each other so they can be sent for trial.'

Lady Nevinson glared at him. 'Been there; done that. Well, we've tried it, anyway. I had someone carry out a little reconnaissance on a possible suspect. Trouble is the individual we are interested in has been in the intelligence services for half a lifetime and would soon pick up on our suspicions. It's not like having a quick look round some dingy semi in West Belfast. We are dealing with people who have a sixth-sense about search and surveillance, and highly trained visual memories. Put his collected Jane Austen back just a millimetre out…'

Potter intervened, 'It doesn't matter anyway – I simplified matters so I could explain. It's much more complex. Just understanding the mathematics behind the encryption is difficult enough – even for me. But there could be a way in. Depends what you want to know.'

Lady Nevinson was suddenly alert. 'Quickly, Colonel, more coffee for our genius.'

Just what he didn't want – shaking hands aren't good for pouring coffee. Jacot stood with his back to Lady Nevinson and managed more coffee for Potter without, he thought, giving himself away.

Potter went to the window and looked out into the courtyard. He seemed far away, thinking. Lady Nevinson and Jacot looked at each other but remained silent.

Potter turned from the window, took out a notebook and scribbled into it. He seemed to have forgotten there were two other people in the room in the middle of a conversation with him. He was whispering to himself. Then he looked up, slightly surprised to see the others.

'So sorry, Lady Nevinson. I was just thinking – do you actually need to know what these *awful people*, as Colonel Jacot calls them, are actually saying to each other? Because code breaking always involves, well, code-breaking, have we got ahead of ourselves? There are lots of other interesting things we could do – not as revealing, but certainly useful. Instead of decryption, impossible anyway, what about traffic pattern analysis – not what the *awful people* are saying to each other but merely which *awful people* are talking to which other *awful people*.'

'Could you do that?' said Jacot.

'Yes, I think so. That's what I wanted to tell you, Lady Nevinson. We might just be able to map their network under certain circumstances – with a bit of luck. Actually, even that's going to be a pretty staggering technical achievement. Last time I came to see you I explained the apparently insuperable difficulties behind tracking so-called *Tanzsignal* or *dancing signal* networks – whereby a mobile phone signal won't necessarily be attracted to the nearest mast.

'*Tanzsignal?*'

'*Tanzsignal*, Colonel. It has a German name because as with so many other technological tricks the technique was first developed by them in the closing stages of the war – as a way of making their night-fighters confusing to radar. I won't trouble you with the mathematics, but it gave them an edge. Unlike most of the high-end technology – bagged by the Americans and Russians in the chaos of defeat – this stuff was hidden away and resurfaced later in Berlin on the boundary between the British and French sectors.

'The target network we are interested in seems to use a version of this technology, as does updated Magenta. A simple idea, but it makes it very difficult to track the signal. Nearly impossible, really. You see the *awful people,* as Lady Nevinson describes them, seem to have thought of everything. What they say is secure – and it is. And who they are talking to is secure, or very nearly so.'

Lady Nevinson put down her cup slowly. 'Vince, the good colonel and I deal everyday with words that must communicate precisely what they mean. Did you say "very nearly so"?'

'I did, Lady Nevinson. I think I've found a way. It won't be easy, and I can't guarantee anything, and there is a big practical problem we still have to solve. But the system, like every other system, has a central basic but imperceptible flaw. It's secure from traffic pattern analysis – unless we can arrange to have simultaneous line of sight on a number of targets at a known time when we can predict they will talk to each other.'

'Oh well, I am sure we can arrange that,' said Lady Nevinson. 'Shouldn't be a problem, Vince.'

'Well, I don't want to be gloomy, but if you want simultaneous coverage of Paris, London and Brussels – we are going to need a visual horizon of more than 250 miles. And, er, well, the visual horizon if you were to stand on the top of Mount Everest at 29,000 feet is… let me work it out…209 miles. 40,000 feet would give you…262 and a bit miles. And we are going to need a lot of sophisticated electronic kit.' Vince took Nevinson and Jacot in detail through what was going to be involved. 'There is only one way it can be done. We are going to have to get our hands on an AWACS aircraft – you know the one with the huge Star Trek dish on the top. We have them, so do the French.'

Lady Nevinson looked a little deflated. But she rallied. 'I'll speak to Gilles.' She walked through the little secret door into what looked like a tiny pantry and made the call. Jacot and Potter both inspected the gorgeous rosewood and gilt bookshelves.

'Everything's fake in here, except the books. So Lady Nevinson told me. Just after the war there was no money to make a proper library so the ambassador's hugely glamorous wife begged, borrowed and cajoled to get it done.' Potter tapped on what looked like a finely turned rosewood column. 'See, it's not expensive wood but hollow iron – a plumber's pipe painted and tarted up. The shelves themselves painted pine.'

Jacot ran his hand along a shelf. 'Good Lord, you're right. And now I look closely at this bust of the lovely Pauline – it's not marble but a plaster cast made to look like marble. The whole thing is a visual trick but lovely all the same.'

'Plus a secret way into the ambassador's most private room – for assignations. The then ambassador had an eye for the ladies. Appropriate, don't you think, Colonel?'

'Quite.'

Lady Nevinson emerged. 'You know, gentlemen, the French organise themselves somewhat better than we do. To get an AWACS re-tasked at home would take weeks of bureaucratic horror. It took Gilles a couple of minutes through the president's military staff. The deal is we'll pay for the mission – not a problem. And supply half the technical people. I'll have to persuade the Chief of the Air Staff. The prospect has filled me with gloom. I know it's a lot to ask, Colonel, and you turned your back long ago against such things, but please, just to make it easier, do tell me one of your wonderfully snobbish jokes about the Royal Air Force. Not the one about the Air Board drinking *Blue Nun* – I've heard that before. Something new.'

'Lady N, I have always admired the RAF and, as you say, the dim snobberies of a young Guards Officer are far behind me.'

'Come on Jacot.' She smiled eagerly. Potter looked non-plussed.

'All right, as long as you don't repeat it, Lady N.' He paused for effect. 'Every time you read an air vice-marshal's obituary...you discover the name of a new public school.'

The cattle lowed loudly, pressing against the dry stone wall. It was a stormy night, again. The eastern part of the département of Eure et Loir was experiencing a prolonged period of bad weather, with spectacular thunder and lightning more frequent than usual. Suddenly, in the dark night and noticed only by the cattle, a small hissing package was thrown over the wall. Seven seconds later it went off with a loud crack and a brilliant illumination, like a large firework. It was actually a British Army-issue, Mark 5 *Thunderflash,* used normally to simulate explosions during training, and kindly supplied by Her Majesty's Government to its then new best friend Colonel Gaddafi. The cattle bolted heading for the far side of the field.

Two thickset men climbed over the wall equipped with shovels, and muttering in a Balkan language that neither the cattle nor the local people would have recognised. A third, thickset man carrying a large weapon of some kind remained in the lane. It took them an hour to uncover a buried milk churn, that they then manhandled for a couple of hundred metres to a van untidily parked near the metalled road.

They carried the milk churn carefully, gingerly, like a human casualty on a stretcher, and loaded it into their van with infinite care. Rough men, they were uncharacteristically gentle in this task. They knew what was inside and its technical specifications: eight improvised explosive devices. Each bomb consisted of a 1kg core of the military explosive C4, with hundreds of shiny steel ball bearings pressed into the soft, slightly sticky explosive – like chocolate buttons pressed into the sponge of a child's birthday cake. The detonation mechanism was a British grenade fuse (from a batch of standard army issue L2A2 fragmentary grenades supplied to Colonel Gaddafi's special forces) attached to a mobile phone SIM card and a small battery. Dial the number from anywhere in the world within the lifetime of the battery, about a month from the bomb being primed, and it would explode.

One of the thickset men remained in the back of the van ensuring that the milk churn, carefully encased in blankets, did not experience any violent jolts. Perhaps he didn't know that C4 was completely chemically stable; same detail with British grenade detonators. Maybe he was aiming to protect the delicate fusing mechanism, fearful that somehow a SIM card might become detached from a battery as the van bounced along the rugged little lane.

The team recovering the milk churn did a professional job, disturbing no one except the cattle. No one saw them. No one rang the police. But the eyes and ears of the French Republic were present at the scene, nevertheless. Installing them had been Paradis' "other task". As the van drove into and out of the narrow lane, infrared cameras took photos of its number plate and then re-focussed automatically in an effort to get images of the men sitting in the front. The electronic images were then encrypted and transmitted along the mobile telephone network to the DGSI's own receiving aerial, sublimely placed just three hundred metres from their rue Nélaton headquarters, on the top of the Eiffel Tower.

Jacot stood outside the ante room on the first floor, waiting for Paradis. *Well, well, the operation had expanded.* What had started with a single GCHQ technician working in a garret above the Residence's guest quarters had now expanded to fill a suite of rooms on the first floor.

Lady Nevinson and Navarre had transformed three generously proportioned and historic rooms into an operations centre. The Ante Room opening off the top of the stairs was filled with communications equipment. Appropriately, the DGSI High Frequency radio communications were set up beneath the only non-Duke of Wellington portrait in the room, a full-length representation of Pauline Bonaparte: a version, as the label announced, of a portrait at Versailles. But more respectable, Jacot noticed – the Versailles version that he had seen recently on one of his weekend rambles covered her breasts in translucent gauze, leaving little to the imagination. In this version, there was still a good deal on offer, but her breasts were covered in non-see-through silk.

Sitting at a desk, conducting routine radio checks with the gendarmerie station at Chartres and filling in a DGSI signals log on standard, pale blue paper was, gratifyingly, Jerome Dax.

'*Funny,*' thought Jacot, '*the Americans have bright yellow paper everywhere, the French government and military prefer a kind of boudoir blue.*'

Lady Nevinson hinted a few days before that Dax had been pestering Navarre for days to take part in the operation, but Navarre had refused – the place for his chief of staff was to assist him in command and control, not run around provincial France catching terrorists. Dax looked harassed, disgruntled and very busy, recording all kinds of dull radio messages. Jacot watched discreetly, with pleasure.

On the other side of the room from Dax was a full-length portrait of the Duke of Wellington by Gérard. Viewed from a certain angle, His Grace seemed to be looking across at the lovely Pauline. Although he bought the hôtel de Charost from her, they never met. But there was an intimate, non-military connection between Wellington and her famous brother; during the short period of his Paris ambassadorship the Iron

Duke was romantically entangled with the beautiful Italian opera singer, Guiseppina Grassini, who had become Napoleon's mistress after his first great triumph at Marengo. Contemporaries thought this a low blow. It was one thing to defeat the Emperor in battle, quite another to steal one of his girlfriends when he was down on his luck.

Jacot and Paradis took up position either side of a large-scale map of their target area on a pull down screen. A three dimensional model had been laid out on the conference table. They would do things by the book – in the classic military way.

Jacot looked around – the room had an English feel; the patterned wallpaper could have been found in any English country house. The only French touch was the lemonwood furniture with Egyptian carvings, fashionable after Bonaparte's madcap expedition to Egypt, and possibly a gift from him to Pauline. The walls were decorated with prints of the Iron Duke. Their map covered a melancholy portrait of him in his dotage.

They both wore standard issue Foreign Legion uniform in the dark *Tenue Européenne* camouflage, but with no rank or unit insignia. Paradis, rather unnecessarily thought Jacot, was sporting a bayonet in a green canvas scabbard. They had set up the room earlier and waited for the attendees to arrive.

'Ah, Jacot.'

He turned round to see Richard Ingoldsby. 'Ah, Ingoldsby.'

'I came in through the garden gate off the avenue Gabriel. Pretty walk. Good cover from the trees.'

'One the Emperor himself took frequently for nocturnal visits to one of Pauline's ladies in waiting; or so the ambassador told me. How was the Eurostar?'

'Ever the straightforward Guardsman,' Ingoldsby laughed. 'It's not quite how it works – the Gare du Nord is a too public place. The Gare Montparnasse on a train from St Malo seemed a better idea.'

Vincent Potter shuffled in, making frantic calculations on a small pad, apparently in another world.

Paradis stood rigidly to attention as Carolet de Liron arrived from the Élysée. They exchanged a few words of military badinage. De Liron took his seat, promptly lighting up a Gitanes.

And then – the person both Jacot and Paradis had been waiting for more than anyone else, Monica Zaden walked through the door. She kissed Jacot on both cheeks who then introduced her to Paradis.

'Mademoiselle, enchanté.' Paradis leant over her hand, lightly kissing it. All the male eyes in the room followed her as she moved towards the conference table. 'Mademoiselle Monica Zaden from the DGSI will be in charge on the AWACS,' added Paradis.

Aumonnier followed – also in a field uniform.

As Navarre and Lady Nevinson entered everyone stood up, the soldiers standing to attention.

Paradis began the briefing – in English. 'Ground. The map on the wall gives the location inside the fôret de Senonches near the hamlet of Belhomert. You can see here the road between Senonches and Belhomert and the D24 running east to Chartres.' Theatrically, he drew the bayonet from its scabbard and used it as a pointer. He paused briefly as Jerome Dax entered by a side door and took a seat at the back. Moving over to the conference table in broad strides, his combat boots squeaking a little on the polished wooden floor, he explained the model and its scale. 'The red triangle shows the location of our overwatch position. We will insert covertly when we receive the signal from you, Monsieur Navarre, that all the members of the gang are in position.'

Jacot took over, 'Situation: according to intelligence eight men are due to rendezvous at this hut outside Belhomert in the fôret de Senoches in the next forty eight hours in order to make final arrangements and pick up explosives for four separate terrorist attacks – two in France and two in the United Kingdom. The method of attack is nail bombs – nails and other pieces of metal embedded in C4 military explosives. Initiated by mobile phone. These are anti-personnel attacks designed to kill people rather than damage buildings. The intelligence on their targets is precise so I will give it to you. In France: the first target is the European Court of Human Rights in Strasbourg; the second – the Institute of European Youth, also in Strasbourg. In the UK: the first target is the office of the European Union in London's Smith Square, very close to parliament; the second – the EU office in Edinburgh, just off the end of Princes Street, Edinburgh's Champs Élysée, if you like. The date of the attack is a week from today – on the European Day of Action – a day of popular demonstration against those forces opposed to the European ideal. There will be crowds of supporters outside those locations on the day.'

Navarre intervened. 'We understand that the explosions will be exactly coordinated – they will all go off together. Please go on, mon colonel.'

'Mission: to destroy the terrorist cell and its equipment in situ in the fôret de Senoches.' Jacot had to try hard to maintain eye contact with all the attendees at the briefing except for Dax at the back whom he ignored.

What he really wanted to do was look at Zaden.

Lady Nevinson was also keen to get a good look at Zaden, but it was difficult as they were both sitting on the same side of the conference table. They had met briefly in the DGSI safe house outside Ely, where Jacot had taken refuge during his previous assignment. She found out a little more about her subsequently through Navarre and Jacot. Navarre had revealed that she had had a tough time undercover for more than a year as a cleaning lady in some extremist hellhole suburb of Paris. In the end, she was able to size her up covertly through her reflection in a mirror on the opposite wall. She was smaller, more petite than Lady Nevinson had imagined. Olive skin, dark eyes, and an extraordinary mass of brown hair. Not much make up, but then if you looked like that you didn't need much.

Lady Nevinson made an effort to concentrate. Jacot had explained the plan in outline to her and it made sense. This part of it was more a military than an intelligence operation so she felt confident in leaving the details up to the military men. Jacot looked younger in his fitting French uniform, much smarter than the shapeless combat suits worn by British soldiers. Paradis, of whom she had heard a good deal from Jacot, was a magnificent figure. Tall, athletic, impressive – that much she expected but she hadn't realised he was black. Jacot never mentioned it. She felt a little embarrassed – *why would he?*

One by one, the other attendees explained their roles in the operation. At the end, Navarre summed up the command and control arrangements. 'This is a French operation, but run from the British Ambassador's Residence. We have the backing of the Elysée, and I have informed the Préfet of Eure et Loir as a courtesy.' He turned towards Lady Nevinson, 'That's the system in France. He can be trusted but is not aware of all the details. His deputy will attend when the operation enters the final phase. In Chartres, Aumonnier is in charge and if back up is needed the Gendarmerie Nationale will provide. Adjudant-chef Paradis and Colonel Jacot are wearing uniform for ease of identification. They will deploy tonight, after dark; and will take up position waiting for the go-ahead. It remains for me to wish you both good luck and a wonderful English word Madame la Baronesse has taught me, Godspeed.'

'They are assembled. We go tonight, mon colonel,' said Paradis, looking at his Magenta phone. 'The final orders from Paris will arrive with us in two hours, from Navarre and your Lady Nevinson. There will be some more equipment, a hot meal, and a third person, a gendarme from Chartres who will remain with our transport…in case. Just in case. Three is better than two, if there is trouble. Though I doubt it will be dangerous for us.'

'That's why I think we should draw lots,' said Jacot.

Paradis was silent for a moment. 'Like they do in a péloton d'exécution?'

'It is a firing squad. Well, péloton or squad is rather grand as there are just the two of us.'

'But I am in command. We are on French soil. You have agreed to follow my orders.'

Jacot sighed, 'It's not that. It's too much. Killing in hot blood is one thing, but this is a cold-blooded operation. They won't be given an opportunity to surrender. They won't be able to defend themselves. They won't have a chance. It will be an execution.'

'Their victims never had a chance – we know they have murdered before. And those bombs – Piquet explained clearly what they could do. You listened intently. They don't deserve a chance. That's why I am perfectly happy to do it. Anyway, it's my job.' Paradis looked offended.

'All right, and as you say, you are in command here.'

They had a couple of hours to wait and were well concealed in the trees. Dusk was falling over the forêt de Senonches. In the valley below them, the fading sunlight glistened off the long grass as it ruffled in the evening wind and danced on the water of a small stream. The distinctive local cattle lowed contentedly. It should have been a delightful and calming time of day – the cocktail hour was after all approaching fast. But inside the forest, where they would do what they had to do, the coming darkness felt to Jacot claustrophobic and menacing.

They had checked their weapons and equipment. Paradis was an absolute stickler for Legion discipline: everything should be checked, thoroughly, but only once, no more. The standard was serviceability, not spit and polish. So there was nothing much they could do except to wait for the order to go ahead which would come over the radio. As Jacot leaned back in his seat for a quick doze he could sense Paradis' restlessness. *Fair enough* he thought – what they had to do looked simple, easy even. But Jacot, while not a pessimist, was a firm believer in Murphy's Law – if something could go wrong, it probably would. He wasn't worried about the technical aspects. The French signals specialists and their GCHQ colleagues were highly expert. He had absolute faith in the French Foreign Legion and Paradis. But still…

'In the Celtic Guards how do you draw lots?'

Jacot came round from his light doze. 'I suppose we would toss a coin if it was between two people; draw straws if there were more. What about the Legion?'

Paradis laughed, 'We fight in the barrack room – that's how we decide these things. Very occasionally, the toss of a coin, but always three times, not as you do in England with just one. And always the same call for each man.'

'Do you want to do it? It's not about command, remember. If it's me who has to press the button, I will do so on your orders.'

'You give me the coin, you call, and I will toss three times is how we do it, mon colonel.'

'D'accord, mon adjudant.' Jacot rummaged in his pocket and drew out a two Euro coin. Paradis put down his weapon and squatted next to Jacot. Taking the coin he spun it high into the air.

Even a small routine action like this had a certain grace and confidence thought Jacot. Higher and higher went the coin. Jacot made his call, 'Heads.'

Rather than wait for the coin to drop, Paradis snatched it from the air and slapped it onto the back of his palm. 'Heads it is.' He repeated the process – this time the coin travelled even higher. 'Tails.'

The process was without tension – both men were happy enough to carry out what was going to be a grisly task. Both were prepared to take moral responsibility. But Jacot had been right: killing in cold blood went against their long-nurtured military instincts. It was better to let the gods decide who should administer the fatal blow.

'Last one, mon colonel.' Paradis threw the coin into the air with great strength – up and up it went, almost to the lower branches of the oak under which they were sheltering. *Trust Paradis to finish with a flourish.* Once again he snatched the coin from the air…'Tails!'

L
Base aérienne 702, Avord, Central France

The young officer from the l'armee de l'air watched a civilian helicopter land in the driving rain on the other side of the runway, disgorging from the sliding side door a woman in her mid-thirties. She turned to wave at the pilot as the helicopter lifted off to return to Paris 200 kms away. Escorted by an armed air force policeman, she walked the hundred metres to the waiting aircraft and began to climb the passenger gangway. As she came up the steps, the young officer rested his pre-flight check folder on his knees to get a better look. She was stunning – olive skin, a mass of brown hair, short skirt, leather boots and a black jacket. If he had been flying with his usual flight commander, he would have whistled quietly and made some lasciviously complimentary remarks – French Air Force pilots are as keen on a pretty girl as the next man.

But, unusually, the commander of this mission was the air force full colonel responsible for all the electronic warfare planes based at Avord – the elite Escadron de Détection et de Commandement Aéroporté. There were a variety of aircraft, but the most important were France's four E3SDA Sentry Boeing 707s, better known to the public through their English-language acronym, AWACS: Airborne Warning and Control System.

'Mon colonel, our guest from the DGSI is now boarding. Shall I ask her to join us for take-off?'

'Yes, do, and then get on with your checks. And if you want, you can handle the take-off.' The colonel chuckled to himself – he had caught a glimpse of their female passenger as well.

By the time Monica Zaden reached the top of the steps and the open door of the 707, the young co-pilot was waiting. Tall and slim, his figure was set off to advantage by a fitting, dark blue flight suit. On each shoulder the three gold bars indicating a captain in the French Air Force. Just above the left breast pocket, he wore the distinctive pilot's wings in the elegant art deco style favoured by the French, and on his right arm the squadron patch of an AWACS aircraft in silhouette against the French Tricolour. He was a handsome young man.

'Mademoiselle, welcome aboard call sign Romeo Alfa 005. Please, if you would like to see the take-off from the cockpit?'

'Thank you.'

The colonel, his grey hair cut en brosse, looked up from his checklist and nodded towards her.

Strapping herself into a seat, in between and slightly behind the pilots, she put on a set of headphones, the staccato professional chatter between the pilots and the control tower coming through them clearly, despite the noise of the engines. Then the colonel's voice came on, 'Mademoiselle, have you ever taken off in a military aircraft like this one before?'

'No,' she replied, pressing down the transmit switch on the microphone.

'Military engines are much more powerful. We taxi faster, take off shorter and faster, and climb much steeper than a civilian aircraft. The radar dome on top of the fuselage buffets, and makes a worrying noise like an overloaded roof rack on the motorway. Do not be alarmed.' He turned towards her and smiled, then touched the arm of his younger co-pilot, 'You have the aircraft.'

They waited for a few minutes; after a brief exchange with the control tower, they began to roll forward towards the runway, much faster, as the colonel had explained, than a civilian aircraft. The co-pilot turned hard right onto the runway, and then with his right hand pushed the throttles forward. She was pushed back into her seat. The engines certainly made more noise than their civilian counterparts. As the plane picked up speed, the colonel rested his left hand close to the throttles. It was so noisy she couldn't hear anything through her headphones.

Zaden looked at both the pilots from the back; each was in his way a classic French military type. The colonel, with his severely cut hair, aquiline nose, deep suntan and smelling faintly of pipe tobacco. The young co-pilot, with tightly curled brown hair, probably a little too long for air force regulations, and an almost puppyish sense of youthful energy – long, elegant hands, encased in pale blue leather flying gloves.

Both men looked strong with broad shoulders. As they reached take-off speed, the younger one pulled back on the controls and suddenly they were airborne. The plane shuddered, and Zaden noticed a rosary rattling from a switch to one side. Once they had been in the air for a few seconds, the colonel pushed the throttles forward again with his left hand as the co-pilot pulled back on the control column once more. The roar of the engines was almost unbearable. She was pressed back into her seat with great force. They were climbing fast and steep, bouncing around in the rain clouds.

It was exciting being in the cockpit of a military plane for take-off, and sexy. There was something very attractive about the two French airmen, and the unhurried, professional way they controlled their machine. She could sense the co-pilot had enjoyed his little demonstration of professional skill. Both men had a timeless quality too. She could have been in the cockpit of a transport on its way to Dien Bien Phu.

As they reached their cruising altitude, the door to the cockpit opened. Another air force colonel introduced himself and ushered her back to the body of the plane. It was more cramped in the fuselage than she had been expecting. Every spare centimetre was crammed with equipment and computers. The plane, she knew, could carry a team of 17 plus technicians and operators of various types. But on this trip there were two teams of five: half in the dark blue overalls of the armée de l'air, and half in the pale khaki of the Royal Air Force – each team supervised by a senior officer of their own service. They sat in two rows running across the aircraft – a pair of high definition computer screens on every console. The senior officer sat behind, again with two computer screens.

Sitting down at a spare seat, she was offered a headset that she put on. The French colonel explained the channels: Channel One, connected them to the flight deck; Channel Two, connected all the electronics specialists together; Channel Three, connected to the joint COBRA – CPCO at the hôtel de Charost; Channel Four, to the action party in the forêt de Senonches; Channel Five, to the Gendarmerie Nationale Station at Chartres.

'Mademoiselle, we can hear what is going on both in Paris and in the field, but only your station can transmit to those stations, the orders were specific on this,' – the French colonel exchanged a meaningful glance with his British colleague. 'We have installed an emergency cut-off button according to your instructions – the red one just behind your head. If you press that, all radio communications except your own cease. The pilot will still be able to talk to air-traffic control, but that's all. Everything else in and out stopped dead. Only you can listen and transmit.'

Zaden felt a little embarrassed at having asked for such a precaution. It was as if she didn't trust the others in the plane. But it was standard operating procedure. She noticed the French colonel exchanging another glance with the senior RAF officer.

'One last thing, Mademoiselle, there is no need for a call sign, the channel is highly encrypted, and is only connected to persons you know and who know you. Voilà.'

She heard Jerome Dax's soft and slightly husky voice responding to a radio check. She felt for him. Poor man, he had been desperate to be in the field or at least aboard this aircraft, but Monsieur Navarre refused – he was after all meant to be both gaining experience at the highest level and resting from the pressures of undercover work.

The senior RAF officer, wearing the four rings of a group captain, offered her some coffee. 'So how do you fit in to this operation?' he asked while adding sugar and milk to her cup.

'I work for the French security service: DGSI. President Hollande changed our name a couple of years ago but our function hasn't changed – the same as your MI5. Our director told me to come along for the ride. I'd rather be in the forêt de Senonches, frankly.'

'Yes, quite. Do you know the guys out there?'

'One of ours, Adjudant-chef Paradis, a surveillance and weapons expert from the Foreign Legion. And one of yours, Colonel Jacot…'

'From the NSA staff. Guardsman with burned hands. I heard he was in France. Met him somewhere or other once – spends more on a suit than I would on a summer holiday.' He looked her up and down. The individual armed services remained separate – dark blue, light blue and khaki: military intelligence though was different, both small in scale and highly integrated between the services – *Purple* was the militarily correct phrase. And very gossipy – rumours of a glamorous French lady spy on the London intelligence scene had been circulating for months.

'Yes, that's him. We worked together a few months ago. What's your role?'

'Electronic warfare at RAF Waddington – bleak little spot in Lincolnshire. Dambuster country. I'm rather a sad man, living, eating and breathing my strange craft. My real speciality is finding needles in haystacks. If I were twenty years younger, I'd probably be a computer hacker. My guess is we are going to need every trick in the book later.'

'It's not an easy mission, is it?'

He smiled, 'Well, it beats Afghanistan or Libya. I doubt very much whether anyone will want to shoot us down over northern Europe, or mortar our airfield as we get back, though these days you can never be sure. Flying out of Akrotiri recently has been more fun. Some of your chaps are usually there these days – we get croissants now for breakfast.'

'Your football fans sweetly sing the *Marseillaise*,' she hummed a few bars.

He could talk to her all day, but the clock was ticking, 'You are right – we will be using equipment that's not specifically designed for our task. We have done a lot of work on the software with your people, and the operators you see here are the best both our countries have in this field; so we are in with a good chance of getting something. Better start monitoring our computers. Any questions, just ask.'

The French and British technicians began to go through a series of checks. They had less than half an hour to go.

'Putain de Merde,' whispered Paradis, furious as he crawled through a deeply muddy patch of the forest. Jacot could only agree.

It was bitterly cold in the forêt de Senonches, and wet, taking them nearly an hour to crawl the final three or four hundred yards to their designated position, on a small bluff overlooking a forester's hut deep inside the forest. A miserable spot, but it was the best location they could find from which to observe the hut. Outside it were parked two grotty and run-down, four-wheel drive vehicles of the type much favoured by local farmers.

The DGSI had formed a detailed profile of the men inside – no names or addresses but the kind of terrorists they were – professional, security conscious, surveillance conscious. They never spoke on mobile phones – sticking to encrypted texts on frequently discarded handsets that became, in effect, electronic one-time pads. They rarely left their safe houses, and when they did, they went through full counter-surveillance drills each time.

Every vehicle they hired was checked in great detail for transponders, even the engine block and fuel tank. The seats inside the vehicles had been slashed – nothing could be hidden inside them no matter how clever or lucky their opponents were. No one could follow them. Only one man could contact them – and he had now issued the orders to go ahead. All that remained for the group to do was to prime and check their devices, and then place them to maximum effect at four locations in France and the UK – and then stand back and watch the chaos unfold. Half the money was already safely stashed in offshore bank accounts, and the other half would be transmitted electronically once the mission was accomplished.

Jacot could feel his hands going slowly numb. Not such a bad thing except the thawing out process was extremely painful. He felt good. He had loathed the IRA and the moral right they claimed to murder defenceless civilians. He felt the same about the eight men in the hut. Eight men who thought they were on the verge of wealth and leisure but who would all be dead within an hour. His only regret was that it was going to be quick – too quick.

Zaden was listening intently on the command channel. Through her headphones she heard Paradis confirming to Dax in Paris that he and Jacot were in position, waiting for the order to go ahead that would come from Navarre personally.

Switching to the aircraft's internal communications she announced abruptly, 'They are in position. Paris is ready. Are we good to go up here?'

The French colonel gave the thumbs up. She turned to the group captain who waved his hands, 'Hang on, hang on. I don't think we have London.'

'What do you mean?'

'For some reason our coverage of London is faint. I can't guarantee we'll be able to pick up the signals accurately. Everything else seems OK, but not London. If you give me twenty minutes or so I can fiddle with the software to enhance the signal, and we should be fine.'

'We don't have twenty minutes. We are on five minutes and counting,' she said sternly and with a hint of irritation.

The group captain was unperturbed, 'If you can't give us time, then we need a bit more height. Flying higher should do the trick – it's to do with the way the phone signals bounce around the atmosphere, and how our computers pick them up. But my guess is we are already at the limit for this kind of plane.'

The aircraft captain's voice came into their headphones – loud, 'We are at 41,000 feet, but I can take her higher. 41,000 is the official maximum, but I am happy to fly at 45,000 plus for a short time, though we will have to do it on oxygen. Oh, and we won't have much fuel to play around with. We may have to divert to a closer airfield for landing.'

'Is it safe?' asked Zaden.

'Up to a point,' he replied in a jokey tone. 'We will lack thrust at that height and the window for stable flight is narrow. You will hear the engines constantly being trimmed, and if we come close to stalling, I may have to put the aircraft into a dive. But, no problem.'

'OK, let's do it,' she spoke clearly into the microphone It was an order, the crew responded quickly.

The operators put on their oxygen masks – the group captain helped Zaden with hers, and made sure she was strapped in. 'This could get bumpy,' he smiled and then fitted his own mask. Zaden looked round the consoles – all the airmen were smiling.

Up in the cockpit both pilots peered at their instruments intently, the young co-pilot with nervousness. 'Bit of an understatement, mon colonel, "the window for stable flight is narrow" – they don't call it *coffin corner* for nothing. Too slow and we stall; too fast and the wings come off. Our safe window will be less than 20 knots.'

'I didn't tell you before, but the orders are signed by Colonel Carolet de Liron – intelligence adviser and personal aide de camp to the president, and countersigned by the chief of the air staff. We have to go ahead. Concentrate now, young man. Let's fly this aeroplane – it's what we are paid for. I have the aircraft. Autopilot off. Stall alarm off – I don't want it bleeping in my headphones – puts my teeth on edge.'

The engines roared, and the aircraft juddered into a steep climb.

The co-pilot concentrated on his immediate task – listing and displaying in the cockpit their possible diversion airfields, in case they couldn't make it back to Avord. If their fuel status became critical, there were four with sufficiently long runways that they could reach quickly and safely. He wrote down the locations, their French Air Force identification numbers, and the amount of fuel they would require to reach each one – on separate post-it notes that he stuck on the instrument console between himself and the colonel, furthest away at the top, nearest at the bottom.

As each one went out of safe range. His plan was to remove the post-it note, and get an acknowledgement from the colonel who was concentrating on flying. When he pulled the last post-it note, they would have to head immediately for the final, failsafe airfield – a French Air Force training establishment close to the Belgian border. They would be flying on fumes.

His other task was to keep a sharp eye on the fuel tanks – not just how much fuel they had but ensuring that the fuel was evenly distributed around the aircraft – stability was crucial at 45,000 feet plus. He would have to pump it around constantly. Being a co-pilot in these conditions was a full time job – even with the colonel actually flying the aircraft. He would only need a co-pilot if the aircraft stalled… it needed two men to pull a machine like this out of a stall – and he devoutly wished it wasn't going to happen. He had never carried out the manoeuvre on a full-sized aircraft for real – it was frightening enough in a simulator. He glanced at his rosary and then at the colonel.

He winked back, his hands moving the throttles by instinct. 'I'll buy you a drink when we land, young man, and as a special treat I think we deserve a cigarette once this oxygen is off. Maybe we should invite that glamorous lady from the DGSI into the cockpit again.'

The aircraft bounced, creaked and shuddered alarmingly as it clawed its way higher and higher into the sky, with less and less air to give its wings lift.

'46,000 feet. I can't fly her any higher,' the colonel's voice came over the intercom.

'London is live. London is now live.' The group captain was clearly relieved and gave Zaden a thumbs up. London was now in range.

Zaden was also relieved. Navarre had made clear to her that London was part of the problem. Switching to the command net, she alerted Paris that they were ready to go. Dax's voice came through her headset.

'Zaden, this is Dax, message acknowledged. Out to you. Hallo Paradis, stand by – final authorisation from the Elysée is about to come through. Monsieur Navarre will give the order. It will be his voice, over.'

'Roger, monsieur le colonel and I are ready. On Monsieur Navarre's command. We will keep an open microphone, out.'

She could hear static in her headphones for a few seconds. The signals operators were all staring intently at their screens. Each one had a particular sector to sweep, and once they had a fix they had been instructed to raise their right arms.

The French practised *Need to know*, the cardinal principle of intelligence work, just as much as the British, but as all the air force personnel of both countries aboard the aircraft had the highest possible security clearances, Navarre and Lady Nevinson had given instructions that they receive a partial background briefing. They both felt that some idea of the context would improve alertness and efficiency. The days of highly trained operators performing merely routine or clerical tasks were long over.

The captain of the aircraft, and the two air force signals intelligence officers were briefed in more depth. They understood the critical importance of the mission. But the only person on the aircraft who had the full picture was Zaden. And only Zaden could transmit on the command net where the action would unfold – just in case.

The RAF group captain and the French air force colonel both turned in their seats and nodded towards her – they were ready. Absorbed for the last hour with the technical challenges of the mission, they had not paid much attention to this glamorous and slightly mysterious woman. But now their glances lingered.

The First Empire chandelier dappled the highly polished, lemonwood table with tiny pools of light in the shape of bees; neither busy and buzzing, nor quite still – they seemed to be moving slowly in a coordinated dance. Lady Nevinson, briefly puzzled and surprised by the effect, looked up – the crystal drops of the chandelier, moving gently in the draft from the window, were in the shape of bees swarming towards the light; originally the symbol of the ancient kings of France, later appropriated by Napoleon as his personal symbol.

The chandelier, and many of Pauline Bonaparte's possessions in the Residence, had an uncluttered elegance and beauty that Lady Nevinson enjoyed, even envied. To decorate a room in her London flat in First Empire taste would be lovely. But she found Napoleon himself monstrous, and sometimes wondered if the aesthetics of his Empire, however pleasing to the modern eye, were no more than propaganda and coarseness. After all, if a modern dictator or oligarch festooned his palaces and yachts with golden or crystal bees they would be a laughing stock.

Lady Nevinson smiled to herself. Time enough for musing on Napoleon some other time – Jacot, she knew, shared her doubts about the man. But now she needed to focus all her energy on the task in hand. She was excited but also apprehensive. *Va Banque* – they were playing for the bank… So much could go wrong, and if the operation failed for any reason, she would be out of a job. Navarre as well. Poor Jacot would find himself manning a particularly pointless desk until his retirement. God knows what punishment the Foreign Legion would dream up for Paradis.

Seven chairs were set around the table; each place provided with one of Jacot's reversible, Anglo-French intelligence folders, the blue French side up, and a small bottle of mineral water – French mineral water as she had instructed. On a console table at the back of the room, beneath yet another portrait of the Iron Duke, coffee and sandwiches were laid out. Next to the food was a small steel briefcase, lying open to reveal a blue scrambler phone.

In deference both to French sensibilities and the realities of command, Frenchmen sat at both heads of the table. At one end, Monsieur le Directeur Navarre, and at the other, as demanded by French protocol, the sous-préfet of the département of Eure-et-Loir – his superior was technically in charge on the ground in Chartres.

On Navarre's right, was the chief of the military intelligence staff at the Elysée Palace, the uxorious and abstemious Colonel Carolet de Liron. In the uniform of the troupes des marines, he wore on the right shoulder a heavy gold wire aiguillette as a personal staff officer to the president. It twinkled like a Christmas decoration under the chandelier. At the other end of the table sat a general from the gendarmerie nationale's counter-terror division. A senior official from the DGSE flanked the sous-préfet. All the Frenchmen were smoking.

Lady Nevinson had positioned herself on Navarre's left with Barkstead next to her, who in his turn was next to the gendarmerie nationale general whom he seemed to know well.

She hoped that the strangeness of holding such a meeting in the British Ambassador's Residence would dominate the minds of most of the attendees – that they were part of an operation to destroy a terrorist gang and their explosive supplies – so secret, so sensitive that it had to be run from what was in effect foreign soil. She wanted them swept up in the theatre of the operation, unable to think too hard.

Navarre was at his most icily professional. 'Until now the details of this counter-terror operation have been on close hold with only a very few officials in Paris and London fully briefed. But now it is time to act we feel duty bound to bring in representatives from the intelligence services of both our countries, and so welcome Monsieur Barkstead who is the head of the British Intelligence station here in Paris, and of course declared to the French government.' He nodded politely at Barkstead. 'General Gasquin, the representative from the Gendarmerie Nationale – a specialist in counter-terror. Monsieur Pontarlier, the sous-préfet of Eure-et-Loir in whose département the operation will unfold, representing his superior who is in charge in Chartres. And finally, Monsieur Ornans, from the Boulevard Mortier.'

Navarre lit a cigarette. 'This meeting should be regarded formally by all attendees as a French controlled Centre de Planification et de Conduire des Opérations, in session, for reasons of the security of the republic, alongside elements of a British COBRA. The operation carries the authority of the president of the republic, expressed verbally, and the involvement of our British colleagues has been agreed between the British prime minister and Madame la Baronesse Nevinson, again verbally; as has the use of this embassy residence that for reasons I am about to explain has proved a, shall we say, more convenient option. There will be no minutes – no written record. But I would like you all to read the written brief in your folders – the facts, as we know them, and our intentions. Once you have absorbed this information, you will understand, I think, our arrangements, and why we prefer to operate from the British Ambassador's Residence. The folders will be collected at the end of the meeting and the contents destroyed.'

Nevinson looked round the table. The general from the gendarmerie, the DGSE agent, and Barkstead looked in their separate ways affronted and furious. The ultimate loss of face for an intelligence officer is to be left out of the loop; and men of their experience and seniority were used to being in the know.

Of the four newcomers, only the sous-préfet, a young man in his early thirties, seemed happy, if slightly overawed, at the proceedings. Navarre said he was a rising young *Enarque* who could be trusted and would do as he was told. She caught his eye and flashed him one of her most friendly smiles – the ones she sometimes bestowed on Colonel Jacot for his efforts. The young man blushed slightly, holding her gaze.

But no one was going to cause any trouble. The chief of France's internal intelligence service was a powerful man even in untroubled times, with the ear of the president. France's current difficulties, and the state of emergency meant that his word was law. And they all knew that Carolet de Liron briefed the president personally each morning, and was constantly at his side during any crisis. In the intelligence game, proximity to power trumped rank and organisational prestige.

As Navarre continued his briefing, the sous-préfet turned his head to look at the pictures on the wall – Wellington, over and over again, in his glory, including a magnificent panorama of the first Waterloo Dinner at Windsor Castle – a Who's Who of British generals and politicians who had bested the French. He caught Lady Nevinson's eye this time and gave a knowing, amused shrug. As a sous préfet he was a living embodiment of the Napoleonic system, but he got the joke and no doubt the irony too.

Dax appeared in the doorway – a very good-looking young man, thought Lady Nevinson, as she watched him move towards Navarre. He moved well – athletic, elegant, controlled, aware, alert. He spoke quietly to Navarre, giving off a sense of competence and purpose. As someone who exercised every day the heavy responsibility of trying to choose the right people to perform competently at the highest level, she understood why he had been selected for greater things. Beautifully dressed, she noticed, unpleasing perhaps to a Guardsman's eye, but in the modern style of contemporary France. As a woman, she understood also why, if her information was correct, Zaden was strongly attracted to this man.

He switched on the desk microphone and speaker in front of Navarre. On his way back to his electronics next door, he nodded briefly at Lady Nevinson. Paradis' voice came over the airwaves with a radio check. Navarre acknowledged, followed by Aumonnier in Chartres. They were nearly ready to go.

Carolet de Liron rose from his seat, walked to the console table, picked up the blue phone in the suitcase, and spoke softly into it. Lady Nevinson couldn't quite hear everything he said, but he stood to attention throughout, his left hand pressed palm open into the stripe of his uniform trousers. Replacing the handset, he turned and nodded at Navarre. 'Alors, we are to proceed.'

Navarre pressed the transmit button on the microphone, 'We have the go-ahead from the president of the republic. Paradis and Jacot execute your instructions immediately and keep an open microphone, over.'

'We will move now, out.' Paradis' voice was sombre, the stress of the moment revealing a slight Antillais lilt.

Navarre, Nevinson, and Carolet de Liron sat motionless, leaning in towards the microphone, eager for the action to take place. The others leant back in their chairs, with their heads down and turned away from the microphone, as if they had found themselves too close to the stage in an overloud pop concert. The sous-préfet looked relieved that the microphone was at the other end of the table. Barkstead turned and smiled at Lady N, but she could tell it was forced. She was hoping he was upset at being brought into the secret so late in the day, nothing more.

They listened in silence. The language used in the briefing papers they had just read was the language of intelligence and counter-terrorism, a specialised, emotion free patois. But they all understood that they were about to witness what was in plain language a mass execution.

They could hear Paradis and Jacot shift their positions – it sounded as though they were burrowing down into the ground. The click of safety catches coming off their weapons came clearly over the net. Next, a short muffled conversation between Paradis and Jacot. Then the electronic-metallic sound of a mobile phone being dialled slowly and deliberately – as if by a child or an old age pensioner determined not to make a mistake with the digits: eleven, twelve, thirteen, fourteen numbers in all – a mobile number with the +33 French prefix in front. There was absolute silence around the table – no one in the room breathed. Then the sound of the ringtone just for a second; followed by a huge, rattling, thumping noise. The state-of-the-art speakerphone in front of Navarre tipped over.

'F…! Are we sure they only had eight nail bombs?' Jacot's voice sounded shaky.

The speakerphone, hastily righted by Navarre, began to broadcast indistinct and muffled sounds – like someone chopping wood. 'It's gunfire,' said Carolet de Liron, 'incoming.' The signal went off air. A few seconds later they could hear again. Both Paradis and Jacot shouting at each other, and lots of shooting – what sounded like a large calibre machine gun being fired in short bursts, interspersed with a smaller calibre rifle.

'I can't f…… see him.'

'He's moving right to left – in the fir trees – à gauche, à gauche.' Paradis shouted fire control orders.

The machine gun went quiet. 'Stoppage,' shouted Jacot.

The smaller calibre weapon continued firing. The sound of Jacot's stoppage drills came through the speaker. The clunking noise of the breech case being opened, the tinkle of cartridges being cleared from the feed tray, the slap of the cartridge belt hitting the feed tray, the click as the weapon was re-cocked. 'Gun cleared,' Jacot shouted at the top of his voice.

The machine gun fired three sustained bursts of forty to fifty rounds. Those round the table winced.

'Check fire, mon colonel, he is down.'

Navarre grabbed the speakerphone and addressed Paradis in rapid French. To the horror of those round the table, it appeared that one of the terrorists had somehow made a run for it.

Lady Nevinson grabbed the handset in front of her, 'Jacot, what the hell is going on?'

Jacot sounded calm and perhaps less out of breath than Lady Nevinson would have liked. 'It's OK, we've got him.'

'What do you mean you have got him? The whole point of the operation is that there shouldn't be anyone left to get. My God, is it that difficult for two professional soldiers to blow up a hut full of terrorists? Even the machine gun doesn't work properly. You're like two gorillas in the bloody mist.' Lady Nevinson was furious. She turned to Barkstead and pushed the microphone towards him. 'You tell him – you're a professional.'

Barkstead grinned. 'Jacot, Barkstead here. I am afraid the National Security Adviser is right. Rookie mistake – there can't be any survivors. It's not how these things work, as I am sure you understand.'

'Sod off, Barkstead. Out.' Jacot's voice, sarcastic, aggressive, offended and slightly slurred, came over the net loud and clear. Then in more muffled tones, 'Here, mon adjudant, take the microphone. I don't think I can handle yet another bollocking from Lady N, and no doubt that useless lounge lizard Navarre will want a word with you.'

Navarre held his head in his hands. Nevinson looked angrier than before, if that was possible.

Barkstead's face turned a mottled, puse colour with rage. 'Lady Nevinson I must protest. This is what happens if you conduct intelligence operations on your private account without the proper people. To be candid – not only have they screwed up what should have been a simple operation, but Jacot sounds as if he has been drinking, as he often does in my view.'

'Scandaleux. Outrageous.' Sounds of anger and dissent surrounded Lady Nevinson.

'You could be right, Barkstead. I'll deal with him when he gets back to Paris.'

'Thank you, Lady Nevinson. Really, you should leave these things to the professionals. Lady Nevinson's face wore an odd expression – behind the anger there was almost relief. Barkstead wondered what kind of pressure had been put on her to mount this operation.

Navarre took back the microphone with an air of offended dignity. At the same time, Dax appeared in the doorway. They nodded to each other. 'Adjudant-chef Paradis, this is Navarre, there are to be no prisoners. Acknowledge what I have just said. It is a direct order.'

They heard the click and whine of the open microphone in the field being switched off.

Dax hurried back to his radios next door, returning a minute or so later. 'It's too late; they've called for medical help on the gendarmerie emergency radio frequency. It's a matter of public record. The casualty, apparently a young man in his twenties, has been hit three times, but is conscious. Aumonnier has sent a helicopter to take him to Chartres – Paradis reckons he is in with a good chance.'

Navarre and Nevinson excused themselves, moving next door into the Duff Cooper Library. A shouting match followed. Navarre roundly condemning Jacot in French, and Nevinson having her say about Paradis in English. Carolet de Liron turned pink at some of the exchanges and decided to speak to his wife on his mobile phone. Barkstead appeared tense, but amused. They passed the time checking emails and text messages on their phones.

Dax crossed the room, knocked on the door behind which Navarre and Nevinson were arguing, and opened it without waiting for an answer. 'There's a gendarme in the helicopter with the casualty. They're cleared to land at the Clinique Notre Dame de Bon Secours – not far from the cathedral. He could well make it, according to Aumonnier. He will be under guard in the operating room and no one will have access to him without your personal authorisation, Monsieur le Directeur.'

The group round the table concentrated on their phones, embarrassed at the overflowing tensions and the unravelling of the operation. Dax returned to his radios.

A few moments later Navarre's head came round the door, 'Gentlemen, let's have a drink while I work out what to do next. Colonel Carolet de Liron please let's have a little time before we alert the Elysée.'

'Of course, Monsieur le Directeur, five or ten minutes will be fine. I am not looking forward to it. Certainly time for a glass of something.'

Barkstead looked sharply at Carolet. And then at Navarre, who smiled wanly, beckoning him into the study and the generously supplied drinks table.

The fire was burning fiercely in the grate. A pair of candelabra, originally from Pauline Bonaparte's library, had been lit, casting their gentle shadow over the room. Lady Nevinson herself, assisted by Barkstead, dispensed the drinks – the Frenchmen, including Navarre, opting, to her surprise, for gin and tonics. Despite the elegance of the room and the strength of the gin and tonics, the atmosphere was uneasy. It was clear to everybody that Navarre and Nevinson were playing for time – trying to keep the other attendees at the meeting in the room for as long as possible, while they tried to come up with a plan.

But just as the guests were gently refusing a second drink, and Carolet began to insist loudly that he must telephone the Elysée, Dax burst in, 'He died in the helicopter. There was more damage than the first aiders thought.'

'Pass a message to Sergent-chef Paradis from me personally,' said Navarre, menacingly, 'I have no further use for his services. His acting rank has lapsed, and he should report back to Aubagne tomorrow.'

'And tell Jacot I expect him here first thing in the morning. After that he can pack his kit for a return to London,' said Lady Nevinson. She wasn't smiling. But on his way out of the room, Dax managed what looked like a smirk of pleasure.

As they descended the staircase Potter emerged into the corridor to watch them go down. *It worked. Thank God for that.*

LIV
Base aérienne 103, Cambrai, Pas de Calais

'Say again call sign.'

The air traffic controllers in the tower at Cambrai were taken off guard and were busily looking in a fat air force file to see what kind of aircraft had just requested an emergency landing.

'Romeo Alfa 005. We have a sudden, unexplained fuel shortage. We will be with you in ten minutes. Are we cleared to land?'

'Romeo Alfa 005, yes. Are you in trouble?

'No, just very short of fuel. Let me know wind speed and visibility.'

'It's an AWACS, in fact the command AWACS out of Avord. Very strange. Hang on – we now have a special operations helicopter coming to pick up a passenger. Check the radar picture and get both aircraft to authenticate. Better contact the base commander.'

'What on earth are these guys doing up here – we're a training and diversion airfield?'

'Don't ask me, I'm just the man in the tower. Message from the air ministry on the computer – the aircraft is to be refuelled, the crew fed, and then sent on their way as soon as possible.'

It was an evil night with a gale blowing off the Channel fifty miles away. The windscreen wipers on the aircraft were set to maximum. A single post-it note remained on the instrument column. Cambrai was the final diversion airfield. As the crosswind buffeted the fuselage the rosary swung crazily from the switch it was hanging on.

The colonel landed the plane himself. The young co-pilot was impressed – textbook stuff and in a high crosswind. From the cockpit they could see the special operations helicopter landing a hundred metres to their left. They had better say good-bye to their passenger.

A brace of colonels and a captain from the armée de l'air, and a group captain from the Royal Air Force watched Zaden walk down the passenger steps into the rain towards the waiting helicopter, its rotors still turning. At the bottom she turned to wave. They all waved back. The commander of the aircraft became a little embarrassed and said, 'Come on, gentlemen, it's not as if we haven't seen a pretty girl before.'

The group captain smiled, 'It's not just her looks. It was the way she handled herself. She said Colonel Jacot was a friend – didn't bat an eyelid when the shooting started. You could hear the rounds coming towards them and chewing the trees. It looked to me as if she was smiling at one point. And for a while it looked as though the whole operation had gone down the toilet. Ice cold, old boy, ice cold.'

Jacot was wearing khaki service dress with a silk shirt and tie of the same colour, dark brown shoes with toecaps – polished black; and, contrary to Brigade of Guards regulations, cashmere burgundy socks. His shoes and buttons shone – the Sam Browne belt glistened in the morning sunlight like very dark, just made, chocolate icing. He was feeling a little lopsided – his campaign medals hung just above the left breast alongside the scarlet and gold aiguillette signifying diplomatic attaché status at the embassy. On the left cuff he wore a single wound stripe – 'Gold Russia braid, No.1, two inches in length, sewn perpendicularly on the left sleeve of the jacket to mark each occasion on which wounded' – so British Army Regulations had stated for nearly half a century. This civilised custom had been stopped after the Second World War. Jacot had re-instated it for himself.

He was immaculate, freshly shaved, highly scented with the usual Extract of Limes, rather pleased with his new burgundy socks; and not quite sober, having drunk a bottle of Foreign Legion Calvados with Paradis late the night before, and poured a couple of shots of the same into his breakfast coffee. He was everything a Guards Officer on his way to a career-ending interview ought to be. As he walked past the embassy, he stuck out his chest and began to flip his swagger stick through the gloved fingers of his right hand in a show of defiance – in case Barkstead or any one else was watching.

Lady Nevinson kept him waiting outside her study for more than half an hour. Eventually, she called him in. He saluted smartly.

'I suppose you think, Colonel Jacot, that calling the head of France's domestic intelligence service, my close personal friend of more than forty years, and the man who, as you well know, rescued me from the Fall of Saigon, a useless lounge lizard on a radio being listened to by the great and the good of France's intelligence world – men under considerable stress at this time – not to mention the president of the republic's personal intelligence staff officer, was somehow clever…'

Jacot stood absolutely still trying to pretend he wasn't hung-over.

'Actually, it was the high point of the evening for me. The look on

Gilles' face was priceless. He is a bit of a lounge lizard. But you might apologise when you next see him. Say you were carried away by the pressure of events.' She laughed, rose from her desk, and stood in front of him. 'Anyway, well done and thank you.' Standing almost on tiptoe, she kissed him lightly on both cheeks. He had to lean forward slightly, hurriedly removing his forage cap and blushing. 'If you would kindly pour a couple of glasses of champagne – it's that time of day.'

'Did we get what we needed? Names and addresses of those who were part of it, or knew,' he asked while uncorking a bottle of Bollinger set in an ice-bucket on a table by the window.'

'Yes, come and sit down. Sorry to keep you waiting. Yes, all of it. Barkstead fell for the scheme hook, line and sinker. Thank God. He was so outraged by your attitude that for a few minutes he couldn't think straight. The possibility that it was all a set-up didn't occur to him. There was a bit of an electronic wobble at one point – he sent only a single text message to warn someone in Paris about the possibility of survivors, and then the whole thing went dead for a few minutes. They were getting tense in that AWACS, apparently. Vince under stress is less mature than I had thought. But then the dam broke. The network was using a cascade system and the single contact in Paris pushed the message out widely.'

'Who are they, Lady N?'

'Politicians, civil servants, intelligence people and various others. London, Paris, Brussels, and Berlin. All well paid, all in senior positions, all angry about the way things are going, all confused about where their loyalties lie. Superior creatures who have evolved beyond patriotism. Vince is still working on the list.'

'Berlin? I didn't think the AWACS could pick up signals that far away.'

'You are right, Colonel, it couldn't. But the government quarter of Berlin is a surprisingly compact place. The *Auswärtiges Amt* was having a big, swanky cocktail party at the Adlon. We had some Magenta people there – our German group is expanding rapidly. No electronics – just observing who was checking their texts and looking worried. Same thing the Gestapo did on 20th July 1944. Classic basic intelligence work.'

'What now?'

'Nothing, now, I'm afraid.'

'What about Norton and Brookwood? That wasn't some sophisticated white-collar treason, but plain, old-fashioned murder. And the Frenchman pushed to his death at Napoleon's tomb? I thought if we got the terrorists we got the people who ordered the murders.'

Lady Nevinson looked away, then, leaning back in her armchair, up at the ceiling. 'We're sure that all three were killed by the same criminal gang that furnished the bombers to order. Almost certainly because one of them had stumbled on something. Most probably, Norton, we think, who had served extensively in Bosnia and Kosovo, and was at one time our military attaché in Belgrade. He had an in-depth knowledge of who was who in the great Balkan underworld. Most likely, he saw Barkstead with someone he shouldn't have been with in Strasbourg and then started to put two and two together. There's no trace though of him telling anyone anything or raising the alarm.' She seemed infinitely weary.

'He was going to tell me when he got to Paris, is my guess, assuming I would pass it on to you. Remember, we were going to meet for a beer. It's possible he was thinking of ringing or texting me the night before he died – when the DGSI checked his mobile my contact details were the last thing he had accessed.'

'I know, I'm sorry. And I am sorry to say there's no proof that Barkstead put anyone up to murder. The Balkan gang may, may, we are not sure, have been minding their own security in the traditional way. Our three messengers having a slap up meal in Strasbourg may just have been unlucky. You can see how they might have panicked.'

'But the bombs were real Lady N. I watched them, felt them go up. That would have been murder.'

'Possibly. Nasty bombs they were too. Even if a single one of them had gone off it would have caused mayhem. But I can't offer you or anyone else certainty. Maybe, they were fully functioning bombs that would have been discovered at the last minute, just as Mitterrand escaped a hail of real bullets, at the last minute. Maybe, some other complex variation that we haven't thought about.'

'So Paradis and I blew up eight criminals who may or may not have been planning a serious bombing campaign.'

'That's about it. Barkstead and his chums might have thought they could play clever with these people. But, on balance, I doubt it. Tell them to set off a bomb and they would have done it, regardless of the consequences.' She sipped her champagne. 'It's early days yet – matching the mobile numbers to individuals is proving difficult. Although, not in the UK,' she smiled, 'I've already got most of those: Foreign Office, Downing Street. I won't tell you how many in the other place – it might put you off your champagne. I'll certainly never go there again. No great loss. The only time I have been there it would have been unspeakable – except that I was gallantly rescued by a group of charming and flirtatious field marshals. But I am afraid the tentacles of the conspiracy seem to be everywhere…except, if our information is right, Albert Embankment.'

Jacot laughed, 'Well, I certainly wouldn't plan on doing a rubbish on my country with Ingoldsby prowling the corridors. He would have made a good assistant to Francis Walsingham. In the old days his speciality was catching out IRA men through interrogation.'

'The trouble is, Jacot, most of these people seem to have lost any idea about what a country is.' Lady Nevinson sighed. 'All ties in, I'm afraid. Ingoldsby has long been unhappy about developments in certain parts of our establishment and their connections to Brussels. He has some contacts that have been trying to warn him for a while. Give people a parliament, a budget, a diplomatic service, a flag, an orchestra and even an intelligence service, and guess what – they start to behave like a country, and the people in their employment start to believe they are working for a country, not just on loan. And once they do that, it's not just loyalty that gets transferred – but the techniques we sometimes use to support it – even the more ruthless ones.' She continued, her voice shaking slightly, 'I've tolerated or even organised some ghastly things on behalf of my country. I don't lose any sleep over it at night. It's not a matter of morality but who you do it for.'

'Of course, Lady N. Armies couldn't function without that overriding loyalty and sense of purpose. We'd just be armed thugs, otherwise. Paradis wouldn't, couldn't have set off those bombs unless he felt he was acting in the interests of France. I wouldn't have been prepared to go along with him unless I thought we were acting against Her Majesty's enemies.'

'It's easy to lose your bearings in this world, Colonel. I lie every day. There are some people I never tell the truth to, because they don't need to know. There are some people, the prime minister most importantly, who want me to tell them the truth all the time – except when she expects me to lie. One morning a few weeks back I spoke the absolute truth to a Mossad illegal who Ingoldsby introduced into my changing room at the Berkeley Hotel Swimming Pool. You must meet him. An hour later I lied through my teeth to the PM about this operation. Sometimes, like President Nixon, I lie when I don't have to. But I like to think I do it for my country. Shakespeare, I know, has many wonderful things to say about it, but I prefer the South African formulation – *Beloved country*. I do it for my beloved country.'

'Queen and country, surely Lady N?'

'I am not a monarchist, but then I'm not a Guardsman. No, not Queen and country – just country. Unlike you, I don't believe in God. This is all there is – it makes it more precious. Our Beloved country – that's enough for me.' She smiled and took his hand gently. 'I know you believe that too – which is why I keep you around.'

She went back to her desk, sat down and started examining a file intently. Jacot looked out of the window, the burn scars on the left cheek glowing again. They were silent, both trying to calculate the implications of what they had discovered.

After a few minutes, she began to talk again, almost as if she was rehearsing a speech to herself. 'I don't believe much in hunches, just observation and analysis – not of events that ebb and flow, but of human nature which is more constant. What we are seeing has been identified before. Paraphrase a couple of observations that every schoolboy knows and you can get yourself in the mood or mind-set for what has been going on. Lord Acton, first. Insert secrecy for power. Secrecy tends to corrupt and absolute secrecy corrupts absolutely. What if Mitterrand had been able to keep his false-flag assassination attempt secret? A lot of the numbers we picked up on the AWACS belong to people who never have to publicly answer for what they get up to.'

She seemed briefly distracted but then got back into her stride. 'Talleyrand, second. He famously said that treason was largely a matter of dates. Well, isn't it? Is a Security Service officer of Scottish descent working on one of our disinformation campaigns north of the border a traitor or a patriot? Is it really treason to be prepared to kill for a dream – in this case the powerful, intoxicating dream of European unity? We kill, you and I – well you have on my behalf. Their dream is dying and one of the things killing it is terrorism, made worse by their straight-from-the-padded-cell attitude to borders. What better way to rescue the dream than to turn it into a victim and its supporters into victims of terror?' She was silent. After a few moments she rallied and went on, 'You remember the garbled report on a threat to the prime minster? Well, it was deliberately garbled. It was really a plot to change her mind and everyone else's by a series of Islamist attacks across the UK that would show clearly that leaving was reckless, insane almost, from a security co-operation point of view.'

'Come to think of it, I never asked you which side of the great divide you were on?'

'One of the advantages of a secret ballot, Lady N, is that I never have to say.'

Lady Nevinson smiled. 'Quite. Anyway, after the electoral developments in France and the unexpected result at home the plan was hatched.'

'The essence of cynicism, Lady N.'

'No, not entirely, Colonel. Cynicism and self-interest I can deal with. It's the dream part that's made these awful people so dangerous.'

Restaurant Kerellec, Place Saint Sulpice, Paris, 6ème

The Welsh Colonel had rung early in the morning to book a table for dinner – for two.

'Monsieur le patron, I'll be having dinner with a lady. So, your best table please. She'll be coming by car, but I will walk down the rue Bonaparte as usual from my flat.'

He sounded better, more alive. He seemed to be in trouble last time, deathly pale. Good, thought le patron. He wondered what kind of lady he would be bringing. Anyway, tonight was a special night devoted to food from Brittany – the land of his birth and where his heart migrated when he was tired of the bright lights of Paris. He had spent much of the morning haranguing various suppliers to ensure that he would receive the freshest seafood and vegetables. He would put a couple of special bottles aside to offer his special guests. Extra flowers too. The restaurant was already decorated with flowers, but he would order some more – an extra effort for the Welsh Colonel's lady friend.

'You took me through it before, briefly, but I'm still intrigued about what made you smell a rat about Barkstead?'

'TNF', as we used to say in the Celtic Guards. Trust no one.'

Lady Nevinson looked puzzled, 'TNO, surely – or is it something in Welsh?' She sipped her champagne, and waved him on with, 'Yes, yes, I see. Sorry.'

Jacot laughed, 'It was a useful motto for the army, even more useful in intelligence. But actually, in this case, we have both the Argentinians and the Americans to thank.'

Lady Nevinson looked puzzled and motioned for Jacot to refill her glass. 'Dear, oh my, are you wearing an apple scented after-shave? It seems to have overpowered your usual limes that I have got used to. But do go on.'

Jacot re-filled their glasses. 'It was all about hands. Let me explain. Most men do not notice other men's hands. Women do, but not men. I do. I also worry about my own hands and am very careful how I use and protect them. Not a problem in most activities. Never a problem with women – if they have to or want to touch my hands, invariably, it's a gentle touch. Women are just like that. It's not a problem with men that I know either – Ingoldsby, for instance, gently pats me on the back. Norton knew me of old and did the same the one time I met him in Aix. All courtesy of an Argentine missile.'

'I am still a bit puzzled, and you haven't explained your peculiar new after shave.' She laughed. Clearly in a good mood, thought Jacot – he could risk the truth about the distinct appley smell.

'The apple after shave I'm afraid isn't after shave at all, Lady N, it's the smell given off the day after by the Foreign Legion's own brand Calvados. But back to the matter in hand, so to speak.'

Lady Nevinson rolled her eyes.

'The American contribution next: I always rather dreaded shaking hands with American intelligence people or military I didn't know well. Most of them affect a crushing handshake, trying to outdo their president. I don't know why, possibly something to do with the Wild West, I should think. Some British soldiers seem to have acquired this habit, and so I am always on the lookout. I get particularly nervous about Americans because they often wear large and showy rings, particularly if they have been to a military academy or upmarket college.'

'But surely only on the left hand.' Lady Nevinson was looking at her own hands.

'Quite, Lady N, but even big chunky West Point or Notre Dame rings on the left hand can pose a threat to a sensitive soul like me. Too many Americans enjoy a kind of cupping handshake with two hands. American politicians do it a lot. The skin on the back of my hands is especially thin.'

The Bollinger was improving his hangover, but his cashmere socks were feeling rather warm, and he had fitted the Sam Browne belt a notch too tight.

'I made a couple of big mistakes from the start when I first down-loaded the photograph of Norton and Brookwood having lunch in Strasbourg – you've seen it. First, I assumed they were waiting for their food to arrive. In fact, as I realised too late, they were waiting for a third person, their French friend. Second, I assumed that the hand of a third person, shown in the picture resting on Norton's shoulder, belonged to the headwaiter or owner of the establishment. The hand looked like that of an old man, well, a man in advanced middle age – mid sixties, the skin slightly mottled. I only realised later that cold weather can change the appearance of hands significantly – the man could well have been younger. Also there was a ring on the little finger of the right hand with some sort of dubious design on it – what looked like an initial or logo of some sort. Only a foreigner would wear such a thing and in that way. I immediately conjured up various Gallic stereotypes reinforcing the mistake with my own prejudices.'

'Yes, Jerome Dax does wear more rings than you might reasonably expect, and not all on his left hand.'

Jacot turned bright red with embarrassment and turned away. He refilled their glasses. Lady Nevinson immediately regretted what she had said, but felt an apology would compound the offence. He went to stand by the window, nursing his drink as if in deep contemplation.

She looked at him. He was tall. Six foot three, at least. His Celtic Guards Service Dress was designed to flatter the male figure – neverthe-less, it accentuated the long legs and broad shoulders – always there but more noticeable now after his Foreign Legion training.

In uniform, he looked normal. Brown leather gloves were what you expected to see on his hands, although some might find it odd that he never removed them. In plain clothes, the black silk gloves that he wore were attractive but somehow strange. It was odd – she knew this man well but had never seen his hands in the flesh or touched them. He seemed completely lost in thought, uncannily motionless. The blush had mainly dissipated, but the flash burn scars on the left side of his face, usually nearly invisible, were still playing catch up.

As he stood there he seemed to her unremarkable – highly polished, nicely scented – even with the apples, but just another general issue army officer of his class and type.

He turned back towards her, and she was reminded forcefully once again why she had him on her staff. His blue-green eyes lit up, looking directly at her. In the same way that he sometimes stood motionless, his eyes were still but filled with energy and purpose. They held hers. She couldn't look away. The most important thing wasn't that he was attractive or amusing – though he was both. The key to him was that, above all, he was re-assuring – communicating a sense that life was manageable, just about, and the bits that weren't could be tamed by a well-mixed cocktail or a well-timed one-liner. He believed in God – she envied that. To him the Universe might be tragic but ultimately there was order…and justice. She took an altogether bleaker view, but it was nice to know someone who didn't.

He smiled and nodded. 'It was the ring. Lots of Englishmen wear signet rings, nearly always plain gold with some kind of crest deeply engraved on the flat surface. There is a ring in the photograph – a hand resting on Norton's shoulder. All you can see is the hand and the ring. The ring is clearly gold, but appears to have a giant *M* engraved on it. It looked rather naff, more like a logo than the sort of thing you see on a ring. No Englishman would ever wear such a thing, so I assumed, as I have said, they were talking to a foreigner.'

Jacot grabbed the bottle and poured the rest of the Bollinger into their glasses. 'I forgot all about it, but it must have been swirling around in my subconscious that Barkstead was left-handed. I first noticed when we did our shooting together. He is the only qualified British instructor in Paris on the Glock that you have me carry around. He presided over my Annual Personal Weapons Test at the DGSE range underneath the Boulevard Mortier, with a little shooting match between us at the end – for fun. It's not that unusual. But my mind did register the fact that as he went for his gun he drew it from underneath his right shoulder.' He mimicked the movement.

Lady Nevinson asked him to do it again, slowly and then remarked, 'You'd hardly notice. Particularly in a shooting competition.'

'Then I remembered when Barkstead had come to see me in my office one day. He's one of those Englishmen I have been complaining about with an over-firm handshake, not something one notices much, just an annoying part of life for me. His over firm handshake hurt to put it mildly; not that I let on at the time. But as I was massaging my hand after he left I noticed an indentation in my glove from his ring. I hadn't noticed it before.

'As you pointed out rings on men are usually worn on the left hand. Even some left-handed people keep to the rule. But rings and pistol shooting don't mix – the position and padding of the little finger can be crucial to accuracy: a *southpaw* who regularly used or trained on a pistol would have the ring on his right hand.

'One day when I bumped into him in the corridor of the embassy I lured him back to my office for a glass of sherry – not difficult, it's a rather fine Manzanilla that I keep ice cold in a fridge under my desk, and I had plied him with it when he came to introduce himself after I arrived.'

'Yes, yes. I'm aware of your peculiar personal routines.'

'He picked the glass up with his left hand, but I managed to get a good look at the ring on his right. Didn't look much like the ring in the photograph and his hands didn't look old – so I sort of filed it away as a false alarm until I noticed your coat of arms. That set me thinking again, so I popped along to see Peregrine.'

She glared at him. 'I wondered why you suddenly took an interest in my heraldry. I assumed it was just good manners. Go on.'

'Do you know what *transposed* means? Not in its normal sense, Lady N, but in the heraldic sense. Courtesy of our friend Beaumaris King of Arms?'

'A bit, I've heard him use it in our discussions on his ideas for me.'

'It means charges or bearings, the figures and emblems you find on a coat of arms, that have been placed contrary to their usual situation. Lots of coats of arms use things called *piles*, heraldic wedges, usually in a different colour from the background shield. Very popular, Lady N. Distinctive. Would have looked good at Agincourt. Some families seem to have gone in for multiple wedges.'

He drew something on a piece of paper and put it on her desk. 'I pushed the photograph over to him, the right way up for him to look at. He pushed it back after a few seconds inspection without turning it round.'

'You had been looking at it the wrong way. I see. It's all perception isn't it?'

'Exactly, Lady N. The ring looks slightly different in real life from the photograph. In the photograph the engraving looked like a capital M. When Peregrine made me look at it from a different angle the naff head-waiter's *M* was much closer to the heraldic description three wedges. The *M* turned out not to be so naff and Continental after all. *Argent, a pile azure, issuing from the chief between two others, transposed.* Roughly translated it means a silver shield, with a blue pizza-slice wedge hanging from the top of the shield, between two more blue pizza-slice wedges either side of it, coming up from the bottom. It looks like a slightly stylised capital letter *M*. I was still tempted to see the whole thing as a coincidence, because as I said, Norton's hands don't look worn or aged in any way.'

'What made you change your mind in the end?'

'Hands again. It's been a mild winter here in Paris but with a couple of extremely cold snaps. I go often to my restaurant du quartier. While sitting there in the warmth on a freezing day, I noticed a number of middle-aged customers coming in with mottled and old looking hands. The effects of the cold, especially if you have forgotten your gloves. Simple as that. A few minutes inside and everything is back to normal. I checked up – Strasbourg on the day in question was icy. It was clear anyway from Norton's photos.'

'Yes, good work. He was the man in the restaurant at Strasbourg.'

'Men in the restaurant, probably. I'm assuming there were others in the party. The usual gang of Euro hangers on, but also someone Norton recognised. Norton's face in one of the photographs sent to us by his daughter had a peculiar look on it – surprise, distaste, shock even. He put it on for laughs when I had lunch with him in Aix – he thought drinking Calvados rather than whisky a poor show.'

'He seems to have had a point. It smells like an autumn orchard in here.'

'Well, he had it on his face for real in the photograph. Why? What's the problem with bumping into *H* Paris in a Strasbourg restaurant? It's not as if Norton was up to no good – caught with a young mistress or boyfriend. He was a widower anyway and having lunch with another Queen's Messenger and a man who was the French equivalent. The restaurant was hardly an opium den. That's what put me onto him, plus the intelligence from your Israeli friend – we may never know the precise details and connexions. Without that I would have thought the idea of a conspiracy on those lines laughable.'

'Thank God for Mossad. With everyone obsessing about our bearded chums, Ingoldsby, as I suggested earlier, felt we had taken our eye off another more subtle form of treason. He had his suspicions but no hard facts. I don't know the details, but for some reason Mossad are in

Ingoldsby's debt. Their man said he would only speak to me. The first meeting was the usual stuff about what's going on in some European countries. It was a fishing expedition. Mossad have been surprised by the extensive involvement of various European intelligence services in suppressing dissent among their own populations over one or two current developments, rather than concentrating on more high priority but less politically congenial tasks. I think it was a kind of probing visit. It disturbed my swim at the Berkeley.'

'Well, that's pretty outrageous, I mean the intelligence stuff.' Jacot became animated.

'Oh, do grow up, Colonel. It's none of our business. But I promised them something if they could give me chapter and verse. At the second meeting, I think you were crawling around your forest at the time. Mossad gave me a list. I'm not sure I'll ever get over the shock – and seven o'clock in the morning was too early for a drink, even for us.' She smiled thinly. 'Some of the names matched what we got from the AWACS. But please don't argue about how to deal with these people. If I could, I would do what we have done for a thousand years – place them on trial… for their lives. But it's not as easy as that. I know you respond to military history. Trust me, and think of it this way: for now, we are like that rather marvellous general in the Indian Mutiny you once told me about who managed to fight his way into some besieged town filled with exhausted British soldiers, women and children, but couldn't get out.'

'Havelock, the First Relief of Lucknow.'

'That's the one. A moving story, I remember. It meant that everyone was saved, they couldn't be over-run anymore, but they weren't strong enough to break out until later. We will have to wait for our "until later", but I promise you it will come. The world is moving our way – that's why the awful people are so angry so much of the time.' Lady Nevinson was pleased to have remembered one of Jacot's lecturettes and relieved that he seemed to understand.

Jacot was pleased as well. She did listen to him sometimes.

Rue Bonaparte, Paris, 6ème

He set off again with a light, almost feminine walking style. It was his third slow promenade up and down the rue Bonaparte.

He didn't mind urgency, but he hated sloppiness and despised fuss. 'Now,' they said. 'It must be done now.' Followed by a cringing instruction to get to Paris by a round about route in case they had been compromised. And when he had asked for details they got more nervous and shirty and started communicating by text. They were in trouble for sure. No address even. Just the name of the street with the instruction: *closer to the Seine than St Sulpice*. It must be one of the longest streets in Paris. Plus a Mickey Mouse description of this Colonel Jacot person – useless for identification except that *he always wears gloves* which was something to go on. Or so he thought. It was a cold spring and most men seemed to be wearing gloves.

The final text had nearly sent him over the edge: *Target has recently undergone counter-surveillance training and carries a Glock 17 on which he is expert.* They had lost the plot, clearly. He was a professional hit man who specialised in lone wolf killings designed to slip under the forensic radar. Pushing, tripping, running over, occasionally a little strangling, household electric shocks, falling from buildings or down stairs, a couple of times clever poisons of one sort or another – those were his methods; and his victims were always unsuspecting and unarmed. He was proud of the service he provided – at a competitive price too. How on earth did they expect him to remove someone trained in counter-surveillance?

He had demanded payment up front in his Panama bank account before leaving home, making it clear that given the circumstances there was no guarantee of success, not immediately anyway. It might have to be a longer-term task.

Usually, he liked coming to Paris. The girls and the shopping were always good for morale; and the food – Paris still had the edge on food. But he wasn't happy this time. There were armed policemen everywhere, and the major monuments and thoroughfares were patrolled by alert and aggressive looking French soldiers – armed to the teeth. How could an assassin ply his trade with all these Islamist lunatics running amok!

Nor was he confident in his instructions. There was a brittleness, almost a panic in the verbal and text exchanges. And it was clear that they were angry with this man. Most unprofessional, in his view, most unprofessional, allowing emotion to cloud your judgement.

He would give it one more try and then call it a day, for now. From behind, in the gathering Parisian gloom, he could easily be mistaken for a woman.

'Monsieur le patron, I would like to thank you very much for your kindness last week.'

'It was nothing, do not worry. I hope you are better, mon colonel. Would you like a drink as you wait for your guest?'

'Yes, please. Let me buy you one, I think. My lady guest will be arriving just after eight.'

'Absolument,' said Kerellec knowingly. 'Tonight we have a special Breton menu.' He showed Jacot to the best table in the restaurant, private, cosy, set to one side but with a commanding view of the floodlit square – just the place for a lady guest. Kerellec brought him a gin and tonic with a barely suppressed grin.

He was astonished, therefore, when he saw Jacot's guest arrive a few minutes later. The woman was distinguished, attractive and wearing a dark blue satin dress that accentuated her figure and showed off her legs. She was clearly prosperous, with a large diamond and amethyst necklace round her neck, and a small gold Cartier watch twinned with another diamond bracelet on her wrist. Restaurateurs have a knack of quickly summing up their customers' position in the economic rat race, not in Kerellec's case through coarseness or unkindness, but because of a deep atavistic fear common to all innkeepers throughout history – that a client may turn out unable to honour the bill. But the lady was at least ten years older than Jacot.

Kerellec noticed that as one of his waiters led her towards Jacot's table he leapt to his feet – fast; and except for the fact that his arms were not rigidly by his sides, stood in the position of attention. They didn't kiss, but the lady guest took Jacot's hand gently and held it lightly for some seconds before sitting down. Restaurateurs are also seasoned observers of status, the human pecking order. Sometimes, nearby businesses would hold their summer or Christmas parties in the restaurant, and it was always clear to Kerellec, behind his zinc-topped bar, who was who in the group. And it was clear to him tonight that the lady guest, sitting with the Welsh colonel on the best table in the establishment, was his boss. Not a good idea then to put the cocaine on tonight's bill. He chuckled to himself.

Who was sleeping with who was something restaurateurs were also able to spot easily enough. They weren't lovers, for sure, but there was some connection, even attraction between them.

A few flicks of the fingers and two glasses of champagne were on their way to the table, followed by Kerellec himself, armed with two menus.

'Monsieur le patron – a pleasure to be here once again and thank you so much for the champagne.'

'Mon colonel.'

'Lady Nevinson, may I introduce Monsieur Kerellec the proprietor of my favourite restaurant in Paris and a good friend.'

Kerellec beamed with pleasure – a real English milady. He personally organised their dinner, both Jacot and Nevinson agreeing to his suggestions for food and wine. He then retreated behind his bar.

He tasted the *crêpes salées*, before taking it over himself. 'Both the sea bass and the sorrel arrived from home earlier this evening. To go with it a bottle of strong Breton cider, ice cold.'

For their main course he had suggested the quintessential Breton dish *homard a l'armoricaine* – 'Sadly even we Bretons call this miracle by its French name.' The chef had combined the garlic, tomato, and herb sauce in just the right proportions – no single flavour overwhelmed the others. And finished it with a splash of Armagnac – not Cognac as the recipe demanded. Kerellec was fond of describing Cognac as something fit only for Third World millionaires. Accompanied by a bottle of Muscadet.

He kept a quiet eye on his distinguished guests.

'Jacot, I don't know quite how to put this, but I'd like you in a proper uniform on Thursday night, not one of your louche, night club dinner jacket versions. We will have a lot of important people there. It's not just a party, more of a display of defiance and growing strength. Nearly all the people invited believe that we ran a successful operation against an imminent Jihadist attack – so on one level public relief and congratulations are completely appropriate. But I also want to put on a peacock display to rub certain noses in it, to show that we have the confidence, and that we're coming after them. I want word to get around.'

'Yes, I see. One of the reasons we improvise, Lady N, is that our mess kit is so unattractive.'

'No, no. I don't want mess kit, I want the full thing, what do you call it?'

'Tunic order. Not quite correct for that sort of occasion.' She looked at him through narrowed eyes, always a warning sign – if she had been a rattlesnake she would have rattled. 'But yes, Lady N I will be in tunic order, tight trousers, boots, spurs – all the trimmings, if you would like.'

'And your lovely bearskin hat, please. You can always offload it onto a waiter once the party gets under way.'

'And my lovely bearskin *cap*. Tell me, one thing I haven't worked out – how did you square all this with the PM and how did Navarre manage it with the Elysée?'

She smiled, 'Why do you need to know? You played your part – that's the end of it. Your French colonel chum was standing to attention apparently talking to the president – what more do you want? I can rely on your discretion and that of Paradis?'

'Absolutely, Lady N.'

'There's something else, something personal and worrying I need to talk to you about. Not as your line manager, but as someone who knows you well. While I am talking I want you to listen.'

'Of course, Lady N.'

'Navarre, at my request has been keeping a gentle eye on you since you arrived in Paris. Nothing fancy, the local police instructed to make the odd drive by your flat late at night. These are difficult times for the French but they helped – the increased police patrols often had your flat on their list. Early Sunday morning before last, one of his people became worried – all the windows in your flat were open and you wouldn't pick up on your entryphone. Your doors weren't properly locked, so this person slipped in to check things out.' Jacot went bright red with embarrassment. 'You were unresponsive, semi-unconscious through drink, and if your pulse had not been so strong they would have called an ambulance. Your flat appeared to have been doused in that after shave you wear.'

Jacot held her gaze but said nothing. He was trying desperately to remember if he had concealed his leftover cocaine.

'I suppose I should ask you what was going on, but I think I know exactly what was going on. All I want to say is…'

'…You should get help.' Jacot rolled his eyes.

'Yes, Colonel – that's exactly what I am suggesting. Not that you should go through the army system and end up in a jolly therapy group on Salisbury Plain; but I know someone who understands these things. He's expensive and it will take time, but I'll pay.'

'Lady N, you are too kind but I can't imagine the taxpayer wanting to fork out for some exotic psychotherapy.'

She took a long sip of her Muscadet and fixed him with her steeliest glare, 'Let me make it absolutely clear, Colonel Jacot, when I said "I'll pay", I did not mean sticking the bill on one of my secret budgets like the upcoming party at the embassy, or those nice first class Eurostar tickets for the string quartet from your regiment, who are going to play at our little bash next week. I have a rich husband, as you know, so my considerable salary is mine to spend, and I meant I will personally pay to have whatever it is that is wrong – fixed.'

'I'm sorry Lady N. I am hugely grateful for the offer. You don't understand. I am sentimental about music, poetry, children, dogs, and beautiful women – especially my line manager. But I am not sentimental about war or not the small war I was in. I can't say we were all grown-ups – young men are younger than you think in many ways. But we were all volunteers, and the cause was about as good as it gets. If I'd been in Bomber Command or a prisoner of war of the Japs, I might have a different view. Equally, if I had been very seriously wounded rather than annoyingly so…'

'I am trying to help, for Heaven's sake. Next time it could be even more serious.'

'Do you like the food, Lady N? Always good but I think Monsieur le patron is pushing the boat out for you. Like all restaurateurs he is something of a snob – a real English baroness accompanying one of his most loyal customers is quite an event. How's the heraldry?'

'Don't try to change the subject. So what are you going to do about these episodes?'

'I am touched by your concern, I really am. In a way, you are right. The problem when we were young was that no one talked about it. These things definitely need to be talked through. Anyway, I have had some help recently. Paradis has become a good friend and during our long hours in the forest, we went through our experiences, in detail, and how to deal with them. He is full of tiny bits of shrapnel.'

'Yes, Gilles told me about what happened to him. Sorry, go on.' A waitress appeared to refill their glasses and slide another bottle of Muscadet into the ice bucket. It was going down fast.

'I am impressed by his attitude. Every time he is tempted to feel sorry for himself or for the young Legionnaires killed on the patrol he was leading, including a very young man he felt personally responsible for – he imagines himself in front of the commanding general of the Foreign Legion at their depot in Siddi-Bel-Abbès on the evening of 7 May 1954. Ring any bells Lady N?'

'Yes, yes, how could I not know the date? Dien Bien Phu.'

'Well done, go to the top of the class.' He smiled, but underneath it they were both tense. He had decided to tell her the full story in dramatic terms, just as Paradis had told it to him – so that she would understand.

'The story is still engraved on the heart of every Legionnaire. The previous evening Paris time, there's a seven hour time difference, the high command in Hanoi warned the ministry of defence in the rue St Dominique that they were no longer in radio contact with GONO, *Groupe Operationelle du Nord-Ouest*, the official name of the garrison.'

'It sounds like an acronym for something very nasty.' She laughed.

'Now you are trying to change the subject. This is my reply to you, so please listen, Lady N. I took your point about Lucknow, and where we are and the limits to your freedom of action. Another siege, different lesson this time.'

'Do go on. I'm sorry.'

'Sometime mid-morning on May 7th French reconnaissance aircraft confirmed that Dien Bien Phu had fallen, although in reality some of the Foreign Legion and others were still fighting. That afternoon, the French prime minister announced the news to the chamber of deputies, in tears. The Cardinal Archbishop of Paris said a solemn mass for the dead, and those taken prisoner, in Notre Dame. All radio programmes were cancelled, except for one official channel remaining on air playing French classical music, with Berlioz' Requiem played every hour on the hour.'

She was silent and still. She looked away from Jacot out of the window.

He went on. 'That evening every Legionnaire in Siddi-Bel-Abbès was ordered to parade in full dress uniform, carrying arms, in front of Legion Headquarters. The news had gone round the military quarter like wildfire. The general came out and stood on the steps. He said simply that Dien Bien Phu had been overrun early that morning, and that the following units of the Foreign Legion had been wiped out – he read out their full official designations. I can only remember a few on the long list: *Treizième demi-brigade, Légion étrangère, Deuxième regiment parachutiste, Légion étrangère.* Some of the units had unglamorous enough titles – composite mortar platoons, transport companies, vehicle maintenance groups, but each ending in the words, *Légion étrangère* – always said in full, after a pause. Hearing Paradis recite them is like listening to someone recite their most holy prayer. The effect piles up. Just Foreign Legion units that had completely gone. No individual names, no sentimentality. The general then said he was going to read out the text of the final radio message from GONO, sent as the Vietnamese were fighting their way into the command post at the centre of the position: "Adieu. Vive La France." The troops then presented arms. The general went back inside, and they marched away singing their most famous and mournful song, *Boudin*.'

She looked unimpressed.

'Sorry, Lady N, I don't mean to browbeat you with military history. In any case, in these gentler times, a trial run in your twenties for something that we all have to face up to sooner rather than later may have been no bad thing. Train hard, die easy.'

'You normally pick up the signs when I am angry, but you haven't tonight. So I will have to spell it out.' Jacot tried to speak. 'If you interrupt me, I will make a scene and leave. You were off-duty, yes, not that there is such a thing when you work for me, when you drank yourself into oblivion, or worse. Our whole operation could have been compromised. It was just lucky that a grown up, if I can put it like that, happened to be passing by. Gilles told me. I only know unofficially so my options are limited. At first, I was tempted to ring the nearest military police post and have you placed under arrest. It's in Mons – two hours drive from here. Be interesting to see what a blood test on you would show up. Gilles calmed me down. OK, but then during the operation it occurred to me that one of the reasons Barkstead fell for the trap was that he was convinced you had been drinking. You slurred your words beautifully for effect, but it worked because he is obviously convinced you're an alcoholic or nearly so. Which means you probably are. I feel a little guilty because I drink a little too much myself and have encouraged you.'

Jacot was silent.

She continued. 'You won't listen, so instead of motherly advice or the military police, I'm going to play another much more powerful card that I hope will bring you to your senses. The person who discovered you drunkenly sprawled in your flat works for Gilles Navarre. This person sought advice, in the strictest confidence, from a DGSI doctor – who passed it on to Navarre in the strictest confidence. Which is why I said I only know unofficially. Do you know who this person was? Monica Zaden. She was taking a walk in civilised Paris after a tough day in uncivilised Paris and it brought her past your door. Perhaps, she was going to drop in anyway. You need to work out, Colonel, whether she would have been impressed – or unimpressed. You could have blown our operation through your reckless behavior. Let's hope you haven't blown your chances with her.'

'I received a charming note from your Colonel Jacot yesterday,' said Navarre.

'Oh, what did it say Gilles?' Said Lady Nevinson, casually looking at her menu.

'This and that, mainly things between men. But written in French. Formal, perfect French, and on the thickest writing paper I have ever seen.'

'I'm surprised he didn't spray it with that scent of his. What did your people say his flat smelt of?'

'It was only one person, Zaden. Limes, limes everywhere, she told the doctor. Remember, I am not meant to know. No, there was no smell of limes on his letter.'

'Of course not, Gilles, I was joking.'

'Ah, the famous English sense of humour. So difficult for us mere Frenchmen to understand.'

'And what about Miss Zaden?'

'Cherie, private lives are private lives, even in the DGSI.'

'I think I'll have the Couscous de la Mer and a green salad. Come on Gilles, you are the chief of France's formidable internal intelligence service – responsible for the safety and security of Metropolitan France. You have just led an immensely professional and daring operation that uncovered treason at the highest levels of four countries, and managed to begin the process of avenging the murders of three deeply loyal and patriotic public servants.'

'Actually, it was a professional and daring operation to interdict and destroy a group of Islamist terrorists, if you remember.' He smiled and gave a Gallic shrug of the shoulders.

'I know, I know. Just between ourselves. The real brilliance of it is that no one can do a thing about it. For our enemies to question or complain about what we have done would be to admit treason. It's only us, and the people who were organising the false-flag stuff who really know what the point of the operation was. After all this elegant brilliance, are you really saying you have no inkling about Zaden?'

'Naturellement, one notices details. But really, one cannot snoop on one's subordinates.' Lady Nevinson gave him her filthiest look. 'OK, OK. Dax has just bought a dinner jacket from an expensive tailor in the Place Vendome. It's hanging in his office in a very smart cover. He has some medals from his military service and an award for his recent undercover work in a box on his desk.'

She was onto him, quick as a flash. 'If it's in a cover, how do you know it's a dinner jacket rather than a suit?'

'I unzipped the cover and looked inside. C'est *un smoking,* as we call it. Trust me.' Navarre took a long sip of his red wine to cover up his increasing discomfort under Lady Nevinson's interrogation.

'Hardly worth snooping for. So what? Dax was an essential part of our team and of course has been invited to the party,' she almost snorted in reply.

Navarre sipped again. 'There is a "so-what", I am afraid. The tailor was Charvet, not somewhere French civil servants would normally buy *un smoking.* Yes, yes, a belt, a tie; my wife sometimes buys me Turk's Head cufflinks. They come in lovely colours and they put them in pretty little envelopes. But a silk *smoking*…it seems a bit much even for a special occasion. Unless, he has something else to celebrate.'

Lady Nevinson's irritation increased. 'What about the cars? Your office is organising the cars isn't it?'

'Separate cars for Dax and Zaden. But it doesn't mean anything as they live on opposite sides of Paris. Please, Celia, I can't discover any more. It was difficult enough asking questions as it was. Anyway, Jacot works for you. You must have some idea about his private life.'

'There is a divorcee with whom the good colonel has been connected over the years. Before you ask – no I wasn't prying – someone like Jacot goes through a vetting process periodically, and it is part of my job to keep tabs on his private life.'

'Do we know if she is coming to Paris?'

'I don't think so.'

Navarre smiled, 'What does that mean?'

Lady Nevinson was clearly embarrassed. 'Well you know that peculiar little chap from GCHQ who came up with the AWACS idea.'

'Naturellement. If you don't give him a medal, we will.'

'I got him to do a little freelancing for me. The reason I don't think Jacot's long standing lady friend is coming to Paris for our jamboree… is that no one of her name is due to travel to Paris in the next few days on the Eurostar…'

'I'm going to have to vacate that lovely study upstairs and hand it back to the ambassador tomorrow. Sadly, Gilles, my little French adventure is over.' Lady Nevinson looked out into the courtyard through the glass double entrance doors. The magnificent port cochère, with its stout oak and steel gate and pair of flanking gatehouses, cut the house off from the rue du Faubourg Saint-Honoré. It was odd, she thought, how different grand houses were in Paris and London. In London, they were generally visible from the street; here in Paris they were barricaded against the public thoroughfares. The French aristocracy always half suspected the revolution was on its way.

'Only a British Embassy could have a throne room,' he said smiling. 'We could be in Buckingham Palace. It's all crimson and gold leaf and Queen Victoria. She is everywhere – look a huge portrait, a marble bust, her initials on the mirrors and furniture. Even the French-made carpet,' he inspected it, cocking his head 'Aubusson, I think. Even that has Queen Victoria's royal arms incorporated into it. And you, Madame la Baronnesse, tease me that Napoleon had poor taste.' He flashed his teeth in cheeky pleasure.

'I think it was designed to make a point to our greatest rivals on the world stage – a dramatic room filled with the memorabilia and symbols of Empire in a house bought at best price by the Duke of Wellington from Napoleon's favourite sister. I'm not sure we English are as subtle as we like to make out.'

She looked at him, her one-time lover, and now friend of over forty years standing. Dear, oh dear, he had been handsome in Saigon all those years ago. As a young diplomat, she had been up-country when the British Embassy had been evacuated. She could have gone to the Americans for help. They would have got her out – which was why Jacot's snide, almost casual anti-Americanism sometimes grated on her. Instead, she had bumped into Navarre and felt safe. Escape and a whirlwind affair followed. Then a parting of the ways, their paths crossing from time to time as they both forged distinguished careers.

Forty years on, she still felt safe when she was with him – not that she was completely – he still made passes at her from time to time. Even in his sixties, he remained handsome; and, as ever, dapper in a midnight blue dinner jacket, silk shirt and patent leather, black Gucci loafers.

'Our guests will be arriving soon, but I think there is just time for us to have a glass,' said Navarre. A footman in a black evening tailcoat appeared with a tray of champagne, and they helped themselves. 'It's like a stage set, don't you think? You and me the two characters in the play waiting for the curtain to go up.' He turned to watch the footman go back into the pantry. 'Come, Madame la Baronesse.' Taking her hand, he led her firmly up the two steps to the overstuffed gilt and crimson throne. They turned round to look along the length of the ballroom where the reception was about to take place. It was a riot of mid-Victorian kitsch, the walls broken up by gilt pilasters enclosing mirrors in front of which burned candles in silver candelabras. The room was a blaze of flickering candlelight. 'Look at those chandeliers. Magnifique.'

'The ambassador told me they were made by the same firm who supplied all the Indian maharajahs' palaces,' said Lady Nevinson, absorbing the atmosphere.

The Throne Room, a little ridiculous to modern eyes, thought Lady Nevinson, flowed smoothly into a much more impressive and useful room – the Ball Room that she liked very much. In the absence of the ambassador, one of the footmen had explained its history to her. Built by a Nineteenth Century ambassador in opulent Napoleon III style in an effort to suck up to the then Emperor of France. Sadly, Napoleon III had inherited neither his uncle's military prowess nor his talent for administration. But he knew how to have a good time and understood ballrooms. It stretched in waves of white and gold stucco and highly polished mirrors for a hundred yards towards the garden. *A good place for a wet weather girls' school sports day.*

She checked herself. *Mustn't drink too much champagne before the guests arrive.* But she couldn't help it. It was a magnificent setting in which to celebrate the first offensive action, the promising start to a full-blown campaign. She felt a little guilty at her penchant for Jacot's RAF jokes. They were extraordinary people and their predecessors must have felt like this years before, when amidst setback after setback and defeat after defeat, they were finally able to take the fight to the enemy.

At the far end of the room, set against a huge picture window overlooking the floodlit gardens, she could see music stands where a string quartet from the Celtic Guards, Jacot's regiment, would play light music – to make the party swing. There seemed to be more than four music stands, many more, nearly a full orchestra. It was meant to be a string quartet, but a large chunk of the Celtic Guards' Band seemed to have accepted Jacot's invitation. Everything looked glorious.

'Come cherie, sit with me.' In one fluid, elegant, fast movement, Navarre sat down on the throne and pulled Lady Nevinson onto his lap. She squealed with a mixture of mock outrage and pleasure, but made no attempt to move. 'We have risen in the world have we not? Me, an ambitious boy from a not so smart suburb of Paris via Sciences Po, and you the lovely girl just out of a Cambridge quad...'

'*Down* from Cambridge. It's not *out* of Cambridge. It's *up to* and *down from* Cambridge.'

'Up, down – who cares?'

'And, Monsieur le Directeur, it's a *court* not a *quad*. "Lovely" though, I accept with good grace.' She gently removed his hand from her thigh but remained sitting on his lap. 'Just one professional question before the party begins.'

'Please.' His hand went back on her thigh, slightly lower down, nearer the knee. She didn't object.

'Did you tell the president?'

'Cherie, you saw Colonel Carolet de Liron, the president's personal staff officer for intelligence, speak into the blue scrambler phone, standing rigidly to attention.'

'It's not the same thing.'

'Did you tell the prime minister?'

'Do you need to know?'

Clasping her waist he turned her towards him, 'I want you to know, Celia, I would trade it all in, all of it, everything, just for a few days in Saigon forty years ago.'

'Come off it, Gilles, Saigon was in chaos and about to fall.'

'No, no, that's not what I meant. I meant...to be young again...with you.'

At the sound of footsteps, she leapt up, straightening her dress just in time to greet the Director of Music of the Celtic Guards and his musicians. They were immaculate in their scarlet, blue, and gold uniforms. She welcomed them all enthusiastically, successfully concealing her surprise that some of the bandsmen weren't men at all. She felt both old-fashioned and old as she watched them moving towards the music stands at the far end of the ballroom. The Director of Music lingered and introduced both Nevinson and Navarre to a young woman in her mid-twenties in a Guardsman's uniform. She was carrying a trumpet but was also going to sing:

'Traditional Welsh songs, Lady Nevinson, and some arias. Colonel Jacot's orders.' Smiling, he tapped his conductor's baton against his trousers enthusiastically. 'She sings like an angel.'

The Director of Music and his protégée marched away in step towards the others. Lady Nevinson passed her arm through Navarre's and repeated back to him, 'To be young again, with you,' kissing him lightly on the forehead. 'Come, let's not get sentimental, we have nearly a hundred guests to greet.'

Two by two, the guests came in. Each pair carrying their invitations as instructed. A footman in a tailcoat took the invitation and then announced the guests to Nevinson and Navarre – who expressed their thanks for the help provided during the recent triumphant intelligence operation and exchanged general small talk. After a lifetime of being trapped in long, wearying reception lines, often without a drink to hand, Lady Nevinson had made sure that plenty of champagne was available to those waiting to be introduced.

The Foreign Legion contingent arrived together as a group: the commanding general of the Foreign Legion and the colonels from Aubagne and Castelnaudary. All fit looking men, their uniforms sprinkled with medal ribbons and their wives smartly turned out in cocktail dresses. She had never quite understood the military, but Lady Nevinson noted approvingly that they all seemed to have attractive and cheerful wives.

At the end came Adjudant-chef Paradis accompanied by a young woman also in uniform. The footman announced them in English:

'Warrant Officer Thomas Paradis, French Foreign Legion, and Sergeant Christine Reymer, Gendarmerie Nationale.'

After they had moved through to the ballroom Lady Nevinson turned to Navarre commenting, 'What a lovely girl.'

'She works at the station in Chartres. I have my sources.' Navarre winked at her. 'What do you think of Paradis?'

'Tall and good-looking. Most impressive in his Foreign Legion uniform. I love the way they all have their képis under their arms.'

The small orchestra, or giant string quartet, initially played gentle waltzes. They made an impressive noise as the footmen circulated with canapés and champagne. The Celtic Guards soprano stood up to sing. Lady Nevinson still couldn't quite get used to the idea of a woman in a Guardsman's uniform, but she had a beautiful voice, and the uniform gave her an almost fairytale appearance.

'What language is that, Breton?' asked Navarre.

The melancholy, haunting words and music of *Myfanwy* filled the ballroom. The voice was strong and passionate and seemed to roll along the parquet floor and bounce off the walls.

'Welsh, Gilles, you should know that, or at least have worked it out given Jacot's regiment.' She laughed. 'It's their most famous love song and rather sad, I forget how, exactly. Jacot told me that it is always sung at Celtic Guards' weddings – usually by a single Guardsman, unaccompanied.'

'Or Guardswoman, it would seem. By the way, did you invite Barkstead?' Navarre asked with a twinkle in his eye.

'Of course, he was on the winning team. Seems a shame to leave him off the list. The penny has probably dropped by now. He knows Jacot has not been posted away in disgrace. Gilles, have you decided about your people, what to do with them?'

'Sadly, we stopped using the guillotine in 1974.' He flashed his teeth menacingly. 'No, we haven't decided. The question is how do we turn these events, these disloyalties, to the advantage of France. The time may not be right. Let history take its course and we can discredit them afterwards.'

'Sounds a little sophisticated for me.'

'It has always been more complicated here. We have done it that way in the past.' Navarre drained off a glass of Pol Roger, grabbed another from a passing footman, and squeezed Lady Nevinson's arm playfully.

She wondered where Jacot had got to. From the corner of her eye she glimpsed the Foreign Legion group half way down the ballroom. One of the colonels seemed to have his arm around Paradis. The party was going well. There was no sign of Dax either.

Choosing the champagne had been the easy bit – Pol Roger, Churchill's favourite. The footman who had guided Lady Nevinson round the house was particularly pleased with this connection. Apparently, Madame Pol Roger sat next to Churchill at a grand lunch in the house just after the Liberation. To celebrate, she had brought with her a case of possibly the greatest champagne vintage of all time, 1928, hidden for nearly four years from marauding and thirsty German soldiers. She was charmed by Mr Churchill, and is said to have kept him supplied with as much champagne as he needed for the rest of his life. He acknowledged the kindness and generosity by calling one of his race-horses *Pol Roger*. After his death, Madame Pol Roger redesigned the label to include a small black edge as a sign of mourning for the great man.

Lady Nevinson sighed. The food had been a different matter. Jacot became quite argumentative over it. *Funny how men could be sometimes.* His idea of cocktail party food was completely different from hers. Little bits and pieces that looked good on a tray but provided little sustenance. Odd and unexpected from a soldier. She preferred something simpler, something that a normal person could regard as a substitute for a proper meal. She was paying, rather a lot for the biggest string quartet she had ever seen as it turned out, and so her will had prevailed.

As a result, circulating around the ballroom were two old-fashioned carving trollies, the kind of contraption still found in the more traditional French restaurants. One dispensed slices of smoked salmon on brown bread, and the other slices of beef fillet onto French bread. The waiters carved as they went. Jacot had snorted his disapproval with a comment about 'mobile hot dog stands', but she noted with relief that her guests saw it her way. Colonel Aumonnier seemed to have taken up a permanent position near one of the trollies and was gallantly squeezing slices of lemon onto the smoked salmon of a group of wives and girlfriends who were giggling like schoolgirls.

Alongside an air of enjoyment, there was an air of expectation. The guests knew that their partners had been involved in a successful enterprise – good for careers and good for France. Perhaps they also suspected that some decorations would be announced. The British had a long drawn out, bureaucratic process for awarding medals that Lady Nevinson had set in train already. It would be nice to get something for Zaden and Paradis. The French did these things differently, presenting the various grades of the Légion d'honneur immediately, as Napoleon the order's founder had done – the verbal agreement of the president of the republic, even a nod, was sufficient authority.

'Look, look, it's Zaden.'

She was standing still at the door into the Throne Room, half in, half out, plainly dressed in a midnight blue, silk cocktail dress, decorated with horizontal stripes of an even darker blue satin – short, not mini-skirt short, but shorter than the military wives in attendance. Her long legs were encased in sheer, flesh-coloured silk stockings worn with patent leather court shoes.

Chanel, to Lady Nevinson's practiced eye, or a very good copy. No rings, no earrings, just a small gold cross on a gold chain round the neck. Navarre was still staring. She seemed suddenly younger than her age, and curiously hesitant for a girl who had operated independently under cover in the most unpleasant and dangerous circumstances. The Guardswoman began another song, rich in tone, lyrical. The room went quiet.

'Gilles, I'm having a blank. What a lovely song. I should know it. And the language?'

He laughed, 'Czech, and you a Cold War Boadicea. Dvorak. It's Rusalka – she's a water nymph or something like that, who has fallen in love with a human, hopelessly. She's asking the moon to intervene on her behalf.' He took her arm and they listened together.

The only noise in the huge ballroom was the music. Conversation had stopped. Zaden was still waiting by the door. Nevinson and Navarre were now holding hands, enchanted by the music. Everyone was enchanted by the music – hard-bitten Foreign Legion colonels looked dewy eyed at their wives of many years who had shared their lives in garrison towns and waited on their return from many campaigns. Carolet de Liron kissed his wife – doting mother of his Catholic brood. Paradis stood behind his girlfriend, both arms round her as if they were listening to a favourite song at a pop concert – his képi discarded.

The song came to a triumphant end, and the musicians paused for a few moments rest. There was silence. The Celtic Guards Band had cast a spell on the party.

A curious, metallic, clinking sound came from the hallway. A sound the 17th and 18th Century stones of hôtel de Charost knew well and had known for longer than the sound of traffic in the street. A strange sound to modern ears – it was the sound the great Emperor himself would have made on entering the house when it belonged to his beloved sister.

Zaden turned fully towards the doorway, smiling, holding out her hands, her head turned upwards as if waiting for a kiss. Lady Nevinson squeezed Navarre's hand and beamed with pleasure, 'Listen Gilles.'

He could hear the clinking sound as well but didn't understand. 'Why? The lovely song is over.'

'Spurs – it's the sound of spurs.'

'Quoi?'

'Spurs, Gilles, and you the head of French intelligence!' She made a face. 'Guards colonels wear spurs.'